DRINKING WITH BUKOWSKI

DRINKING WITH BUKOWSKI

RECOLLECTIONS OF THE POET LAUREATE OF SKID ROW

EDITED BY DANIEL WEIZMANN

Thunder's Mouth Press
New York

Published by
Thunder's Mouth Press
841 Broadway, Fourth Floor
New York, NY 10003

First edition

Library of Congress Cataloguing-in-Publication Data

Drinking with Bukowski; recollections of the poet laureate of Skid Row / edited by Daniel Weizmann.

p. cm.

ISBN 1-56025-262-6

1. Bukowski, Charles. 2. Bukowski, Charles—Friends and associates. 3. Authors, American—20th century—Biography. 4. Beat generation—Biography. I. Weizmann, Daniel, 1967.

PS3552.U4 Z627 2000
811'.54—dc21
[B] 00-022227

Manufactured in the United States of America

CONTENTS

INTRODUCTION

If Harold Bloom is right, and the anxiety of influence determines the shape of the canon of literature, then you better make way for Charles Bukowski because he has spawned more imitators, more bad imitators, more misunderstanding re-readings than all the would-be Whitmans in Bohemia. How did this voice without a category rise from the morass of twentieth-century poetry and literature to become a real-life legendary hero?

Henry Charles Bukowski, Jr. was born in Andernach, Germany in 1920, the son of a U.S. Army sergeant and his wife who was a local seamstress. By the age of three, Bukowski's parents took him and set sail for the States, landing first in Pasadena, then in Los Angeles. Dyslexic and with a severe case of acne vulgaris, Charles Bukowski dragged himself through the LA public school system while suffering brutal, sadistic, and ritual beatings from his father.

By the time he graduated high school, Bukowski was a marginal figure in the already depressing, Depression–era Los Angeles, roaming the public library searching for something, anything that would echo the harshness of his reality. He found it in the taut, passionate writing of John Fante's *Ask the Dust*, the first work of literature to capture the darkness of downtown Los Angeles, the seed of Bukowski's work.

Bukowski wandered the states, taking and losing job after menial job, and finally got a piece of fiction (*Aftermath of a Lengthy Rejection Slip*) published in *Story* in 1946. It was an early half-triumph, and the beginning of ten years of severe drinking and struggle for Bukowski. Back in Los Angeles he met Jane Cooney and began an on-again off-again affair, the tragic alcoholic love affair immortalized in *Barfly*.

In the early '50s, Bukowski started a correspondence with Barbara Frye, a *Harlequin* magazine editor, and talked her into marrying him through the mail. His marriage to the Texas heiress was short and brutish, but it would prove to be an omen of Buk's cosmic connection with the U.S. postal system.

At thirty-five, after his decade-long bender concluded with severe internal hemorrhaging at Los Angeles County Hospital Charity Ward, he began to write poetry.

For fifteen years he worked at the post office, but it was more than just grueling menial labor. He submitted his poetry and prose to every mag large and small, getting published in *Nomad, Coastlines, Quicksilver, Targets, The Outsider*, and others. For someone with his reputation as a drunk and a wanderer, he was intensely prolific, driven, and focused.

He began to see Jane Cooney again in the early '60s, and was devastated by her death from hemorrhaging, cancer, and alcohol poisoning. About a year later, he hooked up with another pen pal, Frances "FrancEye" Dean, and in 1964, FrancEye gave birth to Marina Louise, Bukowski's only child.

By the mid-sixties, Bukowski began his "Notes of a Dirty Old Man" column for John Bryan's radical newspaper *Open City*. Bukowski's column was the most revolutionary thing about the paper. Free, humorous, moving, raw, with a voice that is unique—like a diary or an interior monologue.

Reader by reader, he was becoming a Los Angeles cult celeb. For one thing, Charles Bukowski was the first Los Angeles writer to capture the city from the inside. His native eye took on the depravity and the inner majesty of the new landscape in a way that visitors like Raymond Chandler, Joan Didion, Reyner Banham, and so many others could only sense and write around.

He was also accessible. Cops and criminals, teachers and students, old codgers and fair maidens, all can dig Bukowski. Literati and people who don't read can dig Bukowski. Even as his Beat contemporaries clung to very traditional Western notions of capital A Art and its power to transcend, Hank delivered *actual* telegrams from the soul that gain a reader's trust with their frankness. The writing can be angry, desperate, utterly hopeless, at times inane and self-congratulatory, but it is never cold, and we always believe him.

Forced to quit the post office in '69 for absenteeism, he cut a deal with an office supply company manager named John Martin who recognized Bukowski's serious potential and decided to become his publisher. Through the '70s, Martin published a series of Bukowski novels—including *Post Office, Factotum, Women, Ham on Rye*—and poetry—*Mockingbird Wish Me Luck, Burning in Water Drowning in Flame, Love Is a Dog From Hell, Play the Piano Drunk Like a Percussion Instrument Until the Fingers Begin to Bleed a Bit*—which expanded Bukowski's rep as a serious writer once and for all. Documentaries by Taylor Hackford and Barbet Schroeder, films like *Tales of Ordinary Madness* starring Ben Gazzara as well as readings and recordings finally made him a star.

His other most important relationship in that decade was to Linda King. Their tumultuous relationship, the subject of so much of his work, is covered in this book by her for the first time.

In the 1980s, he bought a house and a BMW, married Linda Lee Beighle, and became the toast of Hollywood, following the release of *Barfly*. The post office across the street from Chatterton's had been refurbished, Chatterton's itself was sold to new owners, and Vermont Avenue in East Hollywood became a hipster mecca; the bridge to Silverlake. In his way, Bukowski had evolved into a kind of institution.

He died at seventy-three on March 9, 1994, a literary lion, a star, a long-distance survivor.

This book is a testament from the people who actually inhabited Bukowski's world: the poets, the indie publishers, the scoundrels, groupies, drunks, book collectors, schemers, shleppers, dreamers, enemies, friends, and lovers who saw the man and the myth explode.

In assembling this book we reached out to everyone who played a notable role in Charles Bukowski's life. His widow, Linda Lee Bukowski, respectfully declined participation, as did the publisher for the greater part of his career, John Martin.

Special thanks go out to Harvey Robert Kubernik, Jeffrey Weinburg, and Laura Nolan for their extensive support of this project. Also, special thanks to A. D. Winans and Joan Jobe Smith for their thoughts and contacts. Thanks also go out to Doug Blazek for searching the attic.

HOW TO GET ALONG WITH CHARLES BUKOWSKI

by Gerald Locklin

1. Never call him on the phone. (I never have.)
2. Never drop in uninvited. (I never have, and I don't like ANYONE to drop in uninvited on me. I'm not crazy about phone calls either.)
3. If you must visit with him, make it early in the day. (Bukowski, like the rest of us, is a little closer to docile when still hungover than when working on his next hangover.)
4. When Bukowski says, "So here we are—back to the old literary chitchat," it is an excellent time to leave.
5. Don't hesitate to correspond with him. He is one of the great letter writers since Keats, and prompt to boot.
6. Don't dance with his woman. (Don't dance with mine either.)
7. It helps to believe he is a great writer. (I do.)
8. But do not kiss his ass or accept abuse from him without appropriate response or he will have no use for you.
9. Keep your mouth shut when you don't have anything to say. (Come to think of it, these are not bad rules for life in general.)
10. Bring your kids along. (When I brought my teenage daughters to his sixtieth birthday party he was the perfect gentleman the entire evening.)

11. If you allow yourself to be put in a position of taking responsibility for him, you are asking for trouble. (I did, twice.)
12. Do not betray his trust.
13. And most importantly, NEVER NEVER NEVER NEVER NEVER push your luck by writing HOW TO GET ALONG WITH CHARLES BUKOWSKI.

AN EVENING AT BUK'S PLACE (FEBRUARY 17, 1986)

Jean-François Duval

The meeting took place on a Monday evening. Several weeks earlier, on the other side of the Atlantic, I had received a card from Buk with the simple typewritten message: *Interview o.k. Skim over Hades.* The card was accompanied by a small funny drawing, as was Buk's custom. On the Sunday evening, I called from my hotel—the post-modern Westin Bonaventure, which Jean Baudrillard describes so well in *Amerique*—to make sure our meeting was still on for the next day at 2 P.M. Linda, his wife, answered the phone. Hank thought it would be better for me to come at 8 P.M. Okay. The next evening outside the hotel night was already falling—it was in February—and an inactive limousine chauffeur offered me his vehicle, which was as long as three Cadillacs and had the full works—bar, saloon, and TV—for the price of a normal cab. So I arrived in style in San Pedro at the house hidden by greenery where Charles Bukowski and Linda had lived for several years. A path lined with pantagruelian rosebushes with worrying thorns led to the front door that I knocked on.

How long did we spend in the candlelit living room? Buk and me on the sofa; Linda, young, slim, and beautiful, sitting on the floor; the coffee table in front of us bearing the red bottle and large glasses. Was it three, four hours? Everything else around was quiet, only the occasional sound of a cat knocking into something. We saw the large trees outside rustle. The evening remains unforgettable.

Jean-François Duval: Hey, there is just this tiny candle light on the table. . . . You prefer the dark?

Linda Bukowski: Oh! You don't like it?

J.-F. D: Well, I really don't mind.

Linda: You see, Hank ordinarily prefers the light out, or less light . . .

Charles Bukowski: That's just when I'm drinking.

J.-F. D: Yesterday, on the phone, you told me you preferred me to come at 8 P.M. rather than at 2 P.M. as we first arranged. Is there any meaning in this?

C.B: Oh yes, there is. I'm not at all alive in the daytime. I just walk around like a dead thing. I was always like that. As a child, till the sun went down, I got dark, I didn't lighten up. My mother always used to say: what is it with you . . . nothing happens till it gets dark and then you start doing things. . . . So I relate to night. Night to me is more lively, more romantic, more real than the day. Daytime makes me dizzy. So it's better you come at night. If you were here in the daytime, I would just sit here and say: yeah . . . okay. . . . Maybe I'm doing it now . . . (*laughs*)

J.-F. D: And no night without wine? You prefer it to beer now?

C.B: The blood of the gods. You can drink a lot of it and stay relatively sane. I used to drink an awful lot of beers. But wine is the best for creation. You can write three or four hours . . . You drink whisky, there is trouble . . . so I don't want to drink any whisky around you. Because then I think I'm tough. Then I got to prove it.

J.-F. D: (*laughs*) Do you still have to prove it, sometimes?

C.B: (*roars*) Oh, only when necessary. But it was always like that.

J.-F. D: (*laughs, a little uneasily*) Huuh! But what do you mean by only when necessary?

C.B: When I feel like it, it's necessary. It may not be just . . . but it's needed. Hey man, don't take us too seriously, Linda and me.

J.-F. D: Is life a fight, from the beginning to the end?

C.B: It appears that way. However I think the secret is pace. Fight a little, rest a little. Fight again, rest. Pace is the secret. That means stopping, starting, going at a certain rate . . . a rhythm of doing things.

J.-F. D: But we do need to fight?

C.B: That's what they tell us. They also tell us we need pain. Who are these people who tell us these things? All I want is happiness. I'll take it twenty-four hours a day if I get it. But I can't seem to get it. Any other questions? This is it?

J.-F. D: (*laughs*) Of course not, it's just the beginning of it! So you're not happy now?

C.B: Oh, I'm just like you. I'm happy some time, other times I'm very depressed. And most of the time I'm just in the middle—a little happy, a little unhappy, a little content . . . I'm generally contented.

J.-F. D: Did you write today?

C.B: No, I was at the track. Race track. I probably would have written tonight. But see, you're here, so . . .

J.-F. D: Sorry.

C.B: (*laughs*) So you spoiled my night.

J.-F. D: But did you write last night?

C.B: No. Just the night before.

J.-F. D: And what are you writing now?

C.B: Just poems. I'm on a poem kick, and I hope it will end soon, and I'll get to short stories. But right now, it's all poetry. It just keeps coming out, poetry. I don't know why, and I don't question it, I go with it. So I never plan anything. Whatever comes out comes out. So . . . right now, it's all poetry. Perhaps because my next book is going to be all poetry, and I'm giving him—my editor—this so we have a good choice, I hope.

J.-F.D: I think you are best known in the U.S. as a poet, whereas in Europe, we don't know much about your poetry. We read mainly your short stories or novels.

C.B: Yeah, I think you're right. I don't know why. But here in the United States, poets seem a romantic kind of people. A man as a poet, he is supposed to be more exceptional, have more soul, or something . . . I don't agree with this. But they tend, here in America, to make a poet out of a man if they possibly can, because it's more romantic in their eyes for a man to be a poet than a novelist. What the hell is a novelist? He takes two or three years to write something! A poet is always on fire! Shit, he is typing every other night. So if I'm known as a poet, that probably has something to do with a more romantic aspect of looking at a person. That's all I know . . . Is it over now?

J.-F. D: (*laughs*) No!

C.B: No?

J.-F. D: Well, that's just the beginning of it, I told you.

C.B: All right.

J.-F. D: I've plenty of questions as you see.

C.B: (*as if apologizing*) Oh, I was just worried: when I run out of wine, I stop talking. You see, we have two bottles . . .

LINDA: No, we have three!

C.B: Three? Well, that should do. One for him, two for me, okay. Or two for him, and one for me.

J.-F. D: (*laughs*) A drinking contest? You used to do drinking contests, I think.

C.B: Yeah, I remember that. (*filling the glasses*) The drinking contests? Yeah, I often won them.

J.-F. D: Did you ever lose?

C.B: Not that many. But at the time I was very good. I could drink a lot, and I could outdrink about everybody. I think I've always had a taste for it, you know. It's pleasant. It feels good. And during these contests, all the drinks were free, you know. It was very nice. And to get paid for drinking.

J.-F. D: Alcohol, wine, are they a kind of veil of illusion you throw upon reality? Or is it a way to see things more clearly?

C.B: Well, to me, it gets me out of the normal person that I am. Like I don't have to face this person day after day, year after year . . . The guy that brushes his teeth, he goes to the bathroom, he drives on the freeway, he stays sober for ever. He only has one life, you see. Drinking is a form of suicide where you're allowed to return to life and begin all over the next day. It's like killing yourself, and then you're reborn. I guess I've lived about ten or fifteen thousand lives now. But a man who drinks, he can become this other person. He has a whole new life. He is different when he is drinking. I'm not saying that he is better or worse. But he is different. And this gives a man two lives. And that's usually in my other life, my drinking life, that I do my writing. So, since I've been lucky with the writing. I've decided drink is very good for me. Does that answer your question whatever?

J.-F. D: So you drink to write?

C.B: Yes, it helps my writing.

J.-F. D: Preferably wine, as you said.

C.B: Wine helps keep things normal. I used to drink beer and scotch together. And write. But you can only write for an hour, or maybe an hour and a half that way. Then, it's too much. But with wine, as I said, you can write three or four hours.

J.-F. D: And with beer?

C.B: Beer, well . . . you have to go to the bathroom every ten minutes. It breaks your concentration. So the wine is the best for creation. The blood of the gods.

J.-F. D: Does all that make you feel near to such poets as Verlaine or Rimbaud, all this tradition? Though, I think, you don't seem to like Rimbaud . . .

C.B: Their lives are sometimes interesting, but their work isn't. I always had problems with the poets. Frankly, they just bore me. They don't do anything for me. And also the prose writers. All my life I've had problems finding something to read. And I guess this is why I write the way I do. In a fashion that I think can be read by somebody else. It's very difficult for me to enjoy a book. Like *War and Peace* . . . Tolstoy, Shakespeare . . . I can see why the children in literature class are as bored. The stuff is bad.

J.-F. D: (*laughs*) Diogenes was looking for a man. So, you're looking for a book?

C.B: Oh, I see. He didn't find his man, did he? I haven't found my book . . . Oh, there are maybe six or eight books I've enjoyed. But nothing that makes me say: this is so exceptional. So I'm just not built to read literature. I'm not made right to appreciate literature. What I enjoy reading, I think, are the daily newspapers. I can start at the beginning, and find little things here and there. It's much more interesting than a great novel, the daily newspaper. And sometimes, you know, I get a short story out of it, a short story idea of something I read in there, what people do . . . And what does a newspaper cost? Twenty-five cents . . . A book costs money.

J.-F. D: And which are those six or eight books you like?

C.B: Well, I have to think about that . . . Dostoyevsky. All of him. All his books. And there is Celine's one book. I never get the title . . . *Journey to the End of Night? Journey to the End of Time* . . . or *of Night*? I never get it right! okay. Anyway I really enjoyed that. When I went to bed, I read it cover to cover. Shaking with laughter in bed. It was so good, it made me laugh aloud. Strange what it did. And I said: Here is a man that can write better than I can. There was no jealousy. I loved the fact, that somebody could write better than I could . . . Then, let me think . . .

J.-F. D: But Celine wrote out of hate, of a horrible hate . . . Is this also the case with you?

C.B: No, I don't write out of hatred. If I write from anything, it's from two things: one is disgust, and the other is joy. If we have to name something. It's very difficult to name what makes you write. Then I would say those two things. Disgust and joy. I don't have them at the same time. But that's my rocket field.

J.-F. D: Where does your disgust come from? And your joy?

C.B: You see, if I analyze that, it might go away. If I found out where joy came from, maybe I would never have joy again. I don't play with things like that. I let them be. That's for the philosophers to play with. Whoever wants to.

J.-F. D: And style? What is style to you?

C.B: Style is just doing the best you can under any given conditions. That's all it is. And when people don't do the best they can, under any given conditions, they don't have style.

J.-F. D: I meant style in writing.

C.B: Oh, I thought you meant in living.

J.-F. D: Maybe it's the same.

C.B: Well, again, writing . . . I can't tell you about my own writing. Because that's a gangue, you break the egg to see what's inside, you don't get the chicken. So that question I don't quite understand it—what is style in writing.

J.-F. D: But the fact that you never found the book you wanted in libraries, is it not a question of style? Was it not the style that disappointed you in all those books?

C.B: Oh, yes. They took too long to say too little. And they said it in an uninteresting fashion. They wasted a lot of pages. That's all. It's disappointing.

J.-F. D: But who are "they"?

C.B: Name anybody!

J.-F. D: Norman Mailer . . . Shakespeare!

C.B: Shakespeare! You can put him at the bottom of the list.

LINDA: Oh!

J.-F. D: But wasn't he good in his time?

C.B: Yeah, I realize there is a change of language that make it difficult. But even with the language changes! He says things now and then. I can take a sentence or two, you know, a phrase that's very nice. But it's tied in with kings and ghosts and all that crap, you know . . . It's too fucking fancy for me. Even though at times you get awful good shots here and there, it's not worth it to me. I'd rather read the newspaper.

J.-F. D: You prefer what your friend Becker wrote, which you tell about in *South of No North* and *Ham on Rye* . . .

C.B: It wasn't his real name.

J.-F. D: He was just an unknown guy, whose talent was promising. You say, it was full of emotion and at the same time very contained. But he could have become a great writer . . .

C.B: I think in the book, I have him sitting in a bar and he is going to the war, and he says: suppose some stupid son of a bitch points a machine gun at me, and squeezes the trigger . . . That's what happened. He caught I don't know how many bullets, and he didn't make it. Who knows if he would have been a good writer or a bad writer . . . but he was good at the time.

J.-F. D: But what did you like about his writing? His ability to express emotions?

C.B: Yeah, he was a good writer, but he was careful. Too careful. He didn't gamble enough with his words. And if you don't gamble, you're not gonna go anywhere.

J.-F. D: Do you think that in their life also people are in general too careful? That they live too restrained a life?

C.B: Well, in our society, they are almost given no choice. Either do your eight hours job, or yzou starve to death. So the restraint is laid upon them by society and their fear keeps them that way. How many can break out of that? What can they do? Some people can't paint, some people can't put on boxing gloves, I mean you have to have some exceptional thing to get you out of this eight hours day, and the restraint is their choice: should I die in the street, or should I go to my job everyday, which I hate? It's not so much restraint. There is no choice for them.

J.-F. D: Did you feel that you had choice, yourself?

C.B: No, I always figured that I would be at the eight hours job for ever, and the only thing I could figure out was: the only way to save a little of yourself there, was to keep changing jobs all the time, no matter how bad the jobs were. And to travel, from city to city. At least you get some variety. It's not the same place everyday back and forth. So that's all I could see, my only way out was to change jobs, work as little as possible, and change cities, which I did for many many years. Then I got lucky, and now I just sit by the typewriter, I go to the race track, I give interviews . . .

J.-F. D: You felt rejected from society from the beginning. You mentioned your father just before. You dedicate *Ham On Rye* "to all the fathers," adding later on in the book that "fathers aren't much" That's hard.

C.B: Yeah. I'm hoping all the fathers read that. So maybe they will be better fathers to their sons. The fathers aren't much, so when I say "to all the fathers," it's kind of like a joke. Care of you, to all of you, who act this way . . . I didn't feel rejected. I just felt as if I were in the wrong place, being a child with those parents. Like when I went to sleep at night . . . I'm sure many children have this feeling. You lay in bed in the dark and you say: those aren't my parents in the other room, that's somebody else. That's the feeling you get. It's more lost, confusion, because you really don't want them, because they don't act right, you understand. You can't be rejected by somebody you don't care too much for. So, it's more confusion of being where you don't feel like you should be. And then you go to school: it's the same thing. The teachers are just like your parents. And then you get a job, and your boss is like your parents. And you get married and ha, ha, ha . . . No, no, that's a joke. (*To Linda*) We make little jokes, don't we?

LINDA: Mmm.

C.B: All right.

J.-F. D: You felt as if you had been adopted by your parents?

C.B: Yeah. I've read many other children have that feeling. That's a normal feeling. You probably had that, right? You just say, my parents wouldn't treat me like that.

J.-F. D: At that time, the air seemed to you completely white . . .

C.B: Milk white. You got it, the air was always white. It was not right. Everything was wrong: the air, the people and there was no smog either.

J.-F. D: You felt a kind of cruelty, especially from the other children at school.

C.B: Children certainly tend to get together and gang up on anybody who is a little bit different. Adults do too. But children are very good at it. And I was one of the victims of the schoolyard gang. When I was small, I was what they call the "sissy." Because my father never let me go outside to play with the other children. So I didn't know how to catch a ball, swing a baseball bat. I didn't get in the games. So suddenly I am at school! I'm put in a game, somebody throws a ball at me, and I didn't know, I couldn't care, I dropped it, 'cause I had no practice (*with a child-like mocking voice*) "Hou! Henry can't catch a ball! Hou! Henry can't catch . . ." They had been practicing for, you know, all their life. So this was my father . . . (*with the voice of his father, trying to make him feel ashamed*): Henry, you can't play with those children. See, all this helped make a writer out of me, my father was a good man . . . Anyhow, in school, this continued, but I did get some practice, you see, finally, and gradually, from being the sissy, I turned it all around, and I became the leader, the tough guy. They came to me. Well, this took six, eight, ten years . . . Till I was going to high school, or junior high . . . They started following me around, kind of a leader, in high school, and then in college, I was the guy, in class and out of class. So from being the sissy, I turned all around into, I don't mean the leader, but the mean and the vicious. And now I don't know even what I am . . . That's all.

J.-F. D: Was it so important to become the tough guy?

C.B: Well, it's wearing to be picked on, it is not nice to be followed home by eight or ten people threatening to beat you up. And for your own survival, you must do something about this or you keep taking the beating. So I started beating people up. And I found it wasn't bad. Better to beat than to be beaten. It feels better.

J.-F. D: It all happened in the school yard?

C.B: Not too often. Because they knew that I wasn't a true sissy. They knew there was something very dangerous about me. They used to follow two of us home, me and my friend Wencho. And they'd circle us, and they'd finally close in on Wencho, and start beating him on the ground, hitting him. And they would circle me, and I would just wait . . . but they never closed in on me. They felt there was something dangerous there. And I felt it too. I said if they come in on me, I'm gonna do something . . . (*To Linda*) You're taking notes now?

LINDA: (*laughs*) That might help.

J.-F. D: You say somewhere that you felt the other children always knew something you didn't know.

C.B: I said that? No, no, I always had the opposite feeling . . . Oh, you mean when I was very very young? . . . The school yards are very confusing . . . The most terrible places . . . They always knew what to do. They played little balls, ran around in circle. And I would stay watching them and saying: what are they doing? why do they do that? why do they run in a circle like that, back and turn this way? But in another sense I said: this is stupid. I said: they know something, at the same time they don't know.

J.-F. D: How did you feel about girls, at school?

C.B: Well, I feel about girls now just like I did then. That the calling part on the part of the male induces a lot of bullshit and falseness. That I had better not go through. Like dating and talking and making all the jeers and going through all these movements, making little jokes and cleaning yourself, studying in front of the mirror, all this bullshit, I didn't want to bother with that. I think that's why I went directly to the whore. I said, hey, have a drink, you know, and that was it. We just dispense with one other. Courtship? Nonsense! Because there is a lot of lying in that. A lot of untruth. A lot of game playing, what I don't come to do.

J.-F. D: People who don't suffer lack something? All that suffering helped you create?

C.B: I guess it did. But . . . you know, that's an old theory, an old formula, that you have to suffer in order to write. It might be true . . . but I dislike it. I'd rather be happy, and never write. Writing is not that important. It is to me now, because they have me all fucked up, and I have to do it.

J.-F. D: Who?

C.B: You, them (*laughs*) . . . You know, a long time ago, I used to fight against happiness, I'd say: anybody who is happy, there is something wrong with him, they are not thinking right . . . I don't do that anymore, and I say: I can be happy, and I'll take it, and if it's unsophisticated, I'll be unsophisticated. And I'll take all the happiness I can get. So you see, I have changed in a certain way . . . and I've often written what I think is my best stuff when I'm feeling very good. So no, I don't entirely agree with that theory. I think happiness can create great works of art. You take Bach's music, he is very joyful. He believed in God. I don't. But believing in God made him very elated. His music doesn't come from pain. And Haydn, his music is very joyful. Great poetry comes from happiness, from unhappiness, from disgust, joy, boredom, it comes from everywhere. So I guess that's an old formula. Everything creates poetry. And very little poetry is created. Does that answer some of it?

J.-F. D: But each time you are celebrated, invited to give some lecture, you destroy the party—as if you didn't want people to love you . . .

C.B: I gave readings for money. To get the rent. To eat. For a drink. But I didn't like the people at my readings. And I didn't like to read. I don't think writing has anything to do with getting up and reading your writings in front of a crowd. I think that's a form of vanity. That's acting. Nothing to do with creation. So I only read because I needed the money. And I disliked it, and I disliked the crowd, and I disliked the whole thing. So all I did was get drunk, read my poems and insult the audience, collect my money and leave. Because it was just another job.

J.-F. D: There is also this moment of grace in your childhood when you discover you can write. You had to write for the school something on the arrival of president Hoover in your town. And you had great sucess. It was read in front of the class. And you had great success—for the first time in your life.

C.B: Yes, this was the best piece. And I wasn't even there! She read it to everybody, and I sat and I said: say, that's pretty good (*laughs*) . . . Pretty good bullshit! I described everything, I wasn't even there: Secret Service men, and the crowd . . . I wasn't even there . . . So, everybody started looking at me, even the little girls (*imitating their little voices*): "Henry? Really?" That was so strange. That was probably the first indication that I was a writer. And another one was when I was in college. We had a class we were suppose to submit one article every two weeks, or as many as we wanted to do. So the teacher, at mid-term, she read, now these articles, Smith's: one, Daily: two, Mac Alvy: four, that's good, Bukowski: seventy two! The class went: OOOOH! And she said: and they are all good! So that gave me a strange feeling, you know, like you're loaded with something, loaded with something strange. So then I went out, and I was a laborer for forty, fifty years . . . (*laughs*) after that. So you can't tell . . .

J.-F. D: About that piece on Hoover's coming, you said: I had success, and I was celebrated, and I was recognized, but I lied . . . Did you lie, or was it a first step into fiction?

C.B: That was one of the few times that I lied, maybe the first time. In a sense, that could have been my way of writing fiction, of being a fiction writer. But I did lie. I wasn't there and I said I was there. You've got me. I have sinned . . . Good wine.

J.-F. D: Excellent. Where does it come from?

LINDA: It's domestic. In northern California, there is very good wine.

C.B: Hey baby, so do you do this very often, interviews?

J.-F. D: Well, from time to time.

C.B: You know, the strangest thing I find about meeting famous people—I met quite a few—I find that they are not very much. So, I hope you have some luck (*laughs*).

J.-F. D: (*laughs*) I'm sure. Though you write in a very crude way, there is much poetry emanating from this crudity, and despair . . .

C.B: I prefer the term simple. I always try to write clearly, so people know what I am saying. And so that I know what I'm saying. So I try not to use large words. I try to use the easiest, smallest word possible to say anything. I don't use the dictionnary, and I like it raw, easy and simple. That way, I don't lie to myself. Because what I've read, first, the classical literature is not raw, easy, and simple. It's confusing, contrived, cloudy, and devious. I want to get rid of these things.

J.-F. D: But why do we need simplicity so badly, just now?

C.B: Well, I need it anyhow. Maybe as we get closer to the end, we bullshit less. This could be our last night together as we are talking here now, you're aware of that?

J.-F. D: Well . . . I don't . . .

C.B: You think we're gonna make it then, for five or six hundred years?

J.-F. D: (*laughs*) I don't know. But this is surely not our last night . . .

C.B: But it is not a good time to bullshit, with the bomb hanging over your head, right? It's time to start saying things. So I try to keep it simple and clear. That's all I can do.

J.-F. D: You respond to the violence and decaying of society with the violence of your writing . . .

C.B: I only photograph society. If it's decaying, if it's violent, then my writing will be decaying and violent. I don't want it to be that way. But if it is, there is nothing else I can call it.

J.-F. D: Where is hope? And hope in your work?

C.B: The hope is a touch of graceful humor, no matter what's occuring. The ability to laugh, the ability to see the ridiculous, the ability not to tense up too much, when things become impossible, just to face them anyhow. A touch of humor. Let's say laughter through the flame. Or, guts. Courage . . . Humor, guts, and courage, no matter the odds. We can always face that . . .

J.-F. D: How did you meet, Linda and you?

C.B: Well, I think Linda will tell it better than I could.

Linda laughs

C.B: I shift the load.

LINDA: I knew about him before he knew about me. I had read all the books that had been printed, of his. And he would give poetry readings a lot, in those days—this is about twelve years ago. And I would go to the ones that were within a hundred miles or so. And so finally I went to one in Hollywood and—that was during an intermission—he came out to the bar and was sitting at the table, and he was very drunk, and there were about fifteen women around him . . .

C.B: Oh, it was glorious.

LINDA: All types of sighing, shaping forms, and so I said it's about time I introduce myself to this gentleman. And so I said something after everybody had left, and (*turning to Hank*) I gave you a note with my telephone number.

C.B: Oh Oh!

LINDA: And he gave me a note with HIS telephone number on it and a little picture of a little man with a bottle (*laughs*). And he called me two days later . . . And a few days after that he drove down to see me—I used to have a little natural food restaurant, called the Dew Drop Inn, at Redondo Beach, and he came there. And—that was in September 1976.

C.B: Oh, God!

LINDA: And that was it. Because he was doing research . . .

C.B: Hum . . . I ate a sandwich.

LINDA: He was doing research at the time on a novel called *Women*. And so he was stuffed with experience researching women. (*Hank laughs with some embarrassment*). And so I found that I was part of that in the beginning. And then finally, the women would sort of dwindle away, and then this one would be gone, and that one, and finally they are all gone. I am the only one to have the guts, the courage, and the humor to stay. Ha! ha! ha!

C.B: There, she took my words!

LINDA: And then we got married last August. (*Showing a photograph*). This is me, with my wedding gown.

C.B: Just like that . . . after eight or nine years, right?

LINDA: We believe in long courtship. It's good to wait a long time, as long as possible.

C.B: Yeah.

J.-F. D: So that the decision will be more meaningful?

LINDA: So you more or less know with what you're gonna put up both with one another.

C.B: For you never do know (*laughs*). But you can guess a little bit. You worked me out that much anyway, didn't you Linda?

J.-F. D: So you do believe in love, after all?

C.B: You're asking me? Love is a word . . . I really mistrust it, 'cause everybody uses it so much. I wish we had another word for love. It's a very abused word. It spoils the sound of the word. So when you say do you believe in love, I can't answer that at all, But if you ask me: do you believe that treating another person as nicely as possible and being around and continually, do you believe that makes you feel very good, do you think that's a valuable feeling, I would say yes.

J.-F. D: And friendship? Was it difficult for you to make friends?

C.B: With anybody. Man or woman. I had problems. I don't have the same interests. I guess I would call a friend someone who drank with me, ha! ha! ha!

J.-F. D: That's the illusion of friendship . . .

C.B: Nothing wrong with illusions as long as they work . . . Good wine, hey?

J.-F. D: What does money mean to you?

C.B: Money means nothing, except getting by without having people crashing your doors down, or wanting to take you away somewhere. To have enough money to live quietly without anybody bothering you, so you can do the few things that you wanna do before you die. But a lot of money is not needed. Enough money is needed so they don't fuck with you. So you can do your thing. That's all. You get a flat tire, you get a new tire on your car, instead of leave that one there and just buy a new car. I have an old saying: there are only two things wrong with money: too much, or too little . . . Go ahead!

J.-F. D: Is it true that during, the Great Depression, in the thirties, you seriously thought about holding up banks, like Dillinger?

C.B: It entered my mind. And you can never tell how true a thing is until you do it. Before anybody does anything, they first think about it a little bit. This is the beginning of it . . . I would make a good bank robber.

J.-F. D: Yeah? Why?

C.B: Because I have guts, humor and style (*laughs*). But I couldn't find anybody who could go with me. You know, two or three good guys. Or maybe just one.

J.-F. D: (*laughs*) Well you should have met me at that time . . .

C.B: Oh, you were probably in the cradle . . . Hey baby! you wan't hold up the bank? Take your milk! (*laughs*) . . . Well, that's just a joke. You don't have a cigarette, do you?

J.-F. D: Sorry, I don't smoke.

C.B: Well I don't either, I hoped that . . . (*Linda is trying to find some*)

J.-F. D: So during that whole period of your life, you preferred to stay alone, isolated, drinking your wine?

C.B: I seem to get more happiness among four walls than when I'm looking at people or listening to them. That's all.

J.-F. D: Does that mean that you came to appreciate loneliness more than mixing with people? First it's hard to be alone? And then you get so used to it that you can't do otherwise, you need it . . .

C.B: Well for me it was never hard to be alone. It always felt best . . . It's natural. Some animals, they dig a hole in the ground, they go underground, I'm kinda like a mole or one of these animals who goes underground. He feels good alone in a hole. It's my natural instinct. When I'm alone, I charge my batteries. I build. That's just that. I feel good. I've never been lonely. I've been depressed. I've been suicidal. But being lonely means another person will solve your problem. Loneliness means you need something or somebody, so I never had a loneliness in that sense. I never felt like another person would solve my problem. I always felt that I would solve my problem. So all I needed was myself.

J.-F. D: And suicide? . . .

C.B: Suicide?

J.-F. D: Yes, you just mentioned it, but that idea doesn't appear very often in your work.

C.B: Suicide is just discouragement with things on hand. You want to roll the dice ticket gamble and try something new. A new deck of cards. You understand, it's a gamble. The idea of suicide comes from there. Then you have got to cut your damned throat, that's messy, you know, it takes nerve. So there is a lot of things that make you want to suicide, and a lot of thoughts that say, hey, wait! maybe I won't make a clean cut and I'll go around all my life talking with the other side of my mouth. I always thought when I was thinking of suicide, I could get in a worst place than I am now. How do I know? So that always gave me strength. I finally decided against it. I think I have.

J.-F. D: The only people who approached you were losers, you attracted them?

C.B: Yeah. I attracted some bad numbers. I attracted some real imbeciles, (*Turning to Linda*) like Baldy, you know. Some took me a lifetime to get rid of.

J.-F. D: How do you explain that?

C.B: They found somebody who fed them with something. Some kind of strength. Something that made them feel better. And so they hung around me. Sometimes I'd say : go away! Listen, I'm tired of you, go away! And they would for a while, and they'd come back. So . . . The losers seem to like me. Maybe cause I symbolize losers. Or better, I symbolize a loser who hasn't jumped off the cliff yet . . . I get a lot of letters from people in prisons, New Zealand, Orient, various places. They love my books. One guy in New Zealand, he said, no it was the guy in Asia, he said: "You are the only writer the convicts read. They pass the book from cell to cell." To me this is a great honor. Because the hardest people to fool are those in hell. So I think there is a good gang there reading me. One guy, this is the guy in New Zealand, the guard said to him: "Can I read your book?" He said: "Nooo! Bukowski wouldn't want it!" He said he walked away and his ears were red, he was angry. So you see the guards and the prisoners in New Zealand are fighting over me . . . The losers tend to like me. There are even some winners starting to like me, now, I'm getting worried about that. But that's another story.

J.-F. D: Do you still feel a loser yourself?

C.B: I was never a loser. I was just losing. (*Snap of a cigarette lighter.*) Some days I'm a loser, and some days I'm not, I'm like you, depending what happens during that day, or that night. At the track, outside at the track, each day is different. And life is like that. Somedays I feel like a loser, somedays I feel like a winner, somedays I don't feel a damned thing at all! . . . Good wine.

J.-F. D: If you are getting fed up, or tired, tell me . . .

C.B: Oh hell! You're kidding. Tired? I can talk for eight or ten hours. If there is only enough wine, I can talk for days, like . . .

LINDA: But you must think of this poor man . . . (*laughs*). Maybe he is tired.

C.B: When he gets tired, we're done! . . . Like Barbet Schroeder. He shot a documentary on me, and I talked what? for fifty-five hours.

LINDA: No, fifteen hours.

C.B: I'm endless. As long as there is something to drink . . . Go ahead!

J.-F. D: In your young days, did you drink to prove your manhood?

C.B: Yeah, in the worst sense, yeah. We used to think that a man drank, you know. That drinking made a man. Of course, that's entirely untrue. And those ten years I spent just in the bars . . . An awful lot of people who drink aren't men at all, they are hardly anything. And they get on my ear, and they talked the most terrible dribble into my head you've ever heard . . . so drinking doesn't create anything. It's destructive to most people. Not to me, you understand, but to most people.

J.-F. D: To you it's not?

C.B: No, it's antidestructive.

J.-F. D: (*to Linda*) Do you agree, Linda?

LINDA: In some ways he is right. Not all the way.

C.B: I do all my writing when I'm drunk. All the time I type I'm drunk. How can I complain? Should I complain about the royalties? I'm paid for drinking. They're paying me to drink. That's lovely. (*He puts firmly his glass back on the table.*)

J.-F. D: Mmm, I can't remember what I just wanted to ask you.

C.B: You need a drink, you'll remember (*He fills the glasses*).

J.-F. D: Thanks.

C.B: I was a barfly . . .

J.-F. D: A what?

C.B: A barfly. In this one bar for about five years, I would run air for sandwiches, you know. I didn't do anything but stay in this bar night and day, and how I survived I have no idea. But one thing that helped, I said, at least I've not worked an eight hours job—it was a twenty-four-hour job (*laughs bitterly*). I wasn't pointing at the time clock or anything . . . Just running a little air, and fighting the bartender, and being the bar clown. I was the personality the guy laughed at. The bum. And I was waiting for something to happen. Somebody to say something . . . I was waiting for some magic to occur in this bar . . . It never did. So finally I just walked out. I waited a long time . . . So I wrote a play about it called *Barfly*, a movie script for Barbet Schroeder, and it might be produced, it's getting close, but we'll see.

J.-F. D: How did you discover alcohol?

C.B: Oh, I had a friend called Baldy. His father was a doctor who lost his licence for drinking too much. And one day he took me to his father's wine cellar. I don't know if we were eleven, twelve years old . . . So Hank, try some of this wine! I said oh! Come on, he said. No! Come on! Stick you head under there, turn that spigot. There was a big barrel. I tried a little, and I said, eeeeh it stinks like shit! He put his head there and got a little wine. And I said, let me try some more of that. So I took a big one . . . I grew, I expanded, I was twelve feet tall, I was a giant of a man. And my heart felt wonderful. And life was good. And I was powerful. And I said: Baldy, this is good stuff. And that was it. I've been hooked ever since.

J.-F. D: If you had to choose between wine and women?

C.B: (*laughs*) Linda, do you want to leave the room?

LINDA: I won't, no.

C.B: That's like a friend of mine. His wife said: either you have to give up playing the horses, or you give up me. And he said: goodbye, baby . . . Ha! ha! ha!

LINDA: True story (*laughs*).

C.B: Yeah, I see him every day sitting on the grand stair. Alone . . . But I would rather have the whole thing: wine and lady. Go ahead!

J.-F. D: What about the human heart? Is it good or bad?

C.B: The human heart, as we all know, is essentially good. But between government, God, striving for survival, the heart gets mixed up with the head and the feet and the elbows and the intestines. And peace and madness. And the heart gets strangled out a bit. It's a good organ and there is complete hope for humanity if it ever gets a little bit straight. It's all there, it's totally there, there is total hope of goodness for ever. But we got lost somewhere. How we can ever straighten that out, I don't know.

J.-F. D: Do you still have a feeling of wonder towards life?

C.B: Wonder? There are times . . . My God, when I'm looking into the eyes of my cat, ha ha—I didn't say my woman . . .

L. B. Oh!

C.B: . . . there are small things . . . I mean, you bet a horse, you got twenty dollars on it, it wins by six lengths . . . There are things that make you feel good. Hell, we wouldn't go on without these little pick-me-ups, now and then, that continually occur. You wouldn't go on. But I mean if you always wake up in the morning and say: oh, life is good, there gonna be another beautiful day, I don't think there are many people who are awaking that way. Or if they are awaking that way, by the time they're going to sleep, they think entirely a different thing. But what was the original question? (*laughs*)

J.-F. D: If you still had a feeling of wonder towards life.

C.B: I still like it. I still think it's fine. I'll buy it.

J.-F. D: What is your great dream, just now?
C.B: Oh, my dream has always been to be a great horse player.
J.-F. D: A great horse player!
C.B: Yeah, you make money playing the horses. I only pretend to be a writer. To all other people, I'm a writer. Well, truly, I'm a horse player, going to the track everyday, winning money, and just for the fun of it! Having all this money hidden away from the taxman . . .
J.-F. D: So you're a horse player more than a writer?
C.B: I'm not going to say. (*laughs*) You're gonna have your . . . in a minute . . . I am a lousy horse player . . . a terrible horse player.
LINDA: (*gently*) That's not true.
C.B: (*strongly*) Be quiet, Linda! . . .
LINDA: Okay, he is terrible.
C.B: No, it's just a hobby . . . No special dream.
J.-F. D: And no special despair?
C.B: Mmm, I have the same thing as you have and anybody else have, I have despair, nightmares. But generally, as I said, I accept almost all given situations. I try to do things about them, but I can't do too much. Except drink and type. YOU save the world, and I'll write about you saving the world, okay? Is that a deal?

J.-F. D: Do you meet other writers?
C.B: I stay away from them, entirely.
J.-F. D: Completely apart?
C.B: When I first started writing, they came around, and I would throw them out. And now, they know I don't want to see them. I don't like other writers, because all they do is talk about writing. And about poetry, and about publishers, and about royalties. They talk about everything but something real. I'd rather talk to a plumber. Or a man who catches his fish. Or a boxer. Anybody but a writer. Because they aren't going to say anything. Except how their books are selling in Hollywood, where their next reading is going to be. Writers here are much more of bitches than I am.
J.-F. D: Hey, but we spoke quite a little bit about literature, just now!
C.B: Oh, you're an interviewer, it's understood that's your job, that's a different thing entirely, forgive me, I don't wanna get you in a . . .
J.-F. D: Okay, what about sex? (*Showing a French paperback copy of* Tales of Ordinary Tales, *with a rosebud between the legs of a*

woman on the cover.) In France, they publish this kind of illustration on the front cover of your books . . .

C.B: The kind you find in supermarkets, yeah? (*laughs*)

J.-F. D: Well in bookshops too.

C.B: I know. That's nice to see one of my books . . . We never see them. Why don't I see it? Didn't I write it (*laughs*).

LINDA: Here is the original copy, published by Le Sagittaire in Paris.

J.-F. D: I hope you get the royalties, at least . . .

C.B: The writer is the last one to know, ha! ha! I'm sure I don't get all the money that's coming to me. I would be a rich man . . . No, I'm sure I signed some contract sometime. But they never send me a copy of the book.

J.-F. D: Okay . . . I asked about sex.

C.B: What do you want to know?

J.-F. D: Many people in Europe, who haven't really read your books, think you became famous for writing sex stories, especially *Tales of Ordinary Madness*. There is some misunderstanding about all that, I guess.

C.B: Well, you see, we go through phases of writing. For a while, I wrote about sex, I explored it. Much of it was done when I first started writing. Because I had to make money fast, because I didn't have any. I was fifty years old, and I quit my job at the post office, and I was in that room in Hollywood. So I drank and wrote sex stories for the sex magazines, who paid very well at that time. They have changed now, they are not very good. So I made my living writing these short stories for the sex magazines and they were very nice to me, the checks arrived continually, bing, bing, bing, and I kept writing sex stories. The only thing I did. . . . You know, most sex stories in the sex magazines were (*with a strong suggestive tone*): HE HAD A BIG THING, AND HE STUCK IT IN AND HE PUT HIS HAND ON HER ASS, etc. So, I didn't like that. I put sex in it but I would put a story around it, to please myself. I thought, well, they want sex, but I'll fool them. So this is how the sex stories came about. Even though they have sex, you will find sex is not the story; sex is in there, but there is another story going on. So it was never sex obsessed. But I had to put sex in to sell the story. I've nothing against sex, except . . . just the other day, this magazine, *Hustler*, they said: send us a story. It is a sex magazine that pays good. So I sent my story. They held it: great story! great story! Finally, they sent it back: not enough sex.

LINDA: They held it for five months!

J.-F. D: If sex is not such an obsession, what do you expect of a woman?

C.B: All I want out of a woman is peace and quiet. (*Linda starts to laugh*)

J.-F. D: What makes you laugh, Linda?

L. B. (*bursting out laughing*) He picked me!

C.B: (*laughs*) Maybe I met the wrong one.

LINDA: Oh!

J.-F. D: Who is the greatest living writer in the States, to you? If there is one . . .

C.B: He doesn't write anymore. He just vanished off the face of the earth. His name is J. D. Salinger. He wrote two, three books. Nobody has ever heard from him ever since. It's like he is gone. But he is not dead. The latest I heard, he said: I just write for myself. Now that is possible. That's a real saint. But if he says: I just write for myself, doesn't that destroy it? Just saying that? . . . So I don't know. Anyhow, this guy was so good, in his early books, and he just stopped all of a sudden. He is a complete mystery. J. D: Salinger. *Catcher in the Rye* is really great. You see, it's about young people going through their thing, but it's so well done. . . . Maybe when he got past the young people thing, that was all there was. . . . It would be sad if it was so.

LINDA: Didn't he write a book of nine incredible short stories?

C.B: He is not dead, is he, Linda?

LINDA: No, he lives in Connecticut.

C.B: Now here is an amazing man. Either he knows more than any of us, or he has just drifted off.

LINDA: He is an enigma.

J.-F. D: A little bit like Thomas Pynchon, have you heard of him?

C.B: I think he is on the bestsellers list, you know, the best ten.

LINDA: He was. You see his name on republished paperbacks a lot, and so forth, but nothing new.

C.B: I tend to be suspicious of bestsellers lists. If you need bestseller lists, it's just like voting for Reagan (*laughs*).

J.-F. D: What about women writers. Take for instance Joyce Carol Oates? Would you say she is a great American female novelist?

C.B: She is the human writing machine. Just pages and pages, She has an endless energy for putting words down. But I can't read any of it. Even though she says, I'm a great writer, I can't read her craft. It's almost like an endless flow of vomitive words that roll down. It's just like . . . There is a female poet in America who just keeps typing. You find her everywhere. It's like she wakes up in the morning and starts typing of joy, she will have a cup of coffee, and then (*breathing in and in one big blow, swelling his voice*) SHE'LL TYPE ANOTHER POEM AT ELEVEN-THIRTY, and then she'll wait a while, and then—all her divorced husbands, you know, sending her money, and all that—and then SHE WILL BRAND OUT ANOTHER ONE AT THREE-THIRTY, AND THEN . . . It's a sickness instead of . . . I guess the best of writing can be a sickness, and the worst too. So, what the hell is the difference?

J.-F. D: So there isn't any good female writer?

C.B: Women writers, there is one, Carson McCullers. She's dead now. She died of alcoholism. *The Heart Is a Lonely Hunter*. When you've read her talk about pain, you can feel the pain across each line. She was really . . . There was one story about a midget that is so painful and so hard . . . Carson Mc Cullers can really write . . . *The Heart Is a Lonely Hunter*, that's just the way she felt. So she died of alcoholism. I think, if I'm right, on a ship, on a trans-Atlantic journey. She was on her deckchair drinking . . . And they just found her there, stiff and dead. Great woman writer. Women can write too.

C.B: So . . . I can't stand Faulkner. You tried to read William Faulkner? The good thing about reading him is how difficult he can make writing seem. It's like each of his sentences is under a great strain to get rhythm down. You appreciate and you say: GOD ALMIGHTY, HE IS STRAINING LIKE HELL TO WRITE THAT SENTENCE AND THAT SENTENCE . . . IT MUST BE GREAT ART! Because he is straining his fucking guts out. How can it be bad art, when he is straining his guts out? So that's kind of a circus act too, you know. But he was a character. He drank whisky by the gallon. One time—he lived in a small southern town—there was a guy lying in the gutter; just along the gutter. And somebody said: who's that?—That's William Faulkner, a great writer. There he was . . . I don't see how a guy can drink whisky and keep writing. You must have a great brain for it all, because whisky, you know . . . you keep writing and, all of a sudden, man, you get a tear in your head, you can't see anymore . . .

J.-F. D: If it's just for one hour writing and the hour is good, it's worth it, no?

C.B: Yeah, you're right, whisky is good for one hour only, no more. But if you take it for six hours . . .

LINDA: Do you drink whisky when you write, Jean-François?

C.B: We're interviewing him now.

J.-F. D: Well, it happens.

LINDA: I mean, is it part of the process of writing?

J.-F. D: (*laughs*) Without a doubt!

C.B: I say!

J.-F. D: When you've got a deadline and . . .

C.B: Finish it? right? I like deadlines. I used to have a deadline for a short story a week. The deadline was there, I wrote for a newspaper, *Open City*, I'd lay around, I'd lay around, and I'd say, well, if you don't do it tonight, it's not going to get done. I was suddenly sitting in front of this white sheet of paper, and it would come. 'Cause the deadline was there. And you would just think, writing for a deadline, you get a piece of shit, right? And sometimes it's dead (*laughs*). But a lot of times, if the deadlines weren't there, I would never have written, and come up with something really lucky, you know? In fact, along time, the deadline was approaching, and I said, I can't write it, so I said, I'll just start with the title, to see up what happens, I'll make up a title. Suddenly a title, something like: Twelve monkeys carpet flying under a dead moon. The title is near that, I haven't it quite in mind. So I said: now I've got to write the story under that title. And I made up a story about twelve monkeys . . . so deadline can get you off your dead ass into rhythm. On the other hand, they can drain you, too. Anything and everything can happen at any given time. All of a sudden I can take care or I'm just ripped off. And just rolling my head through the outer window and . . .

LINDA: (*laughs*) Poor Jean-Fr . . .

C.B: Oh shit! I'm just trying to give him a little bit of jazz, for Christ's sake! He expects a little devious bullshit. I have to feed him a little bit of . . . you don't mind, do you? In my age, may I luckily rip my honor . . .

J.-F. D: What's your age, now?

C.B: Sixty-six.

LINDA: Sixty-five, Hank . . .

C.B: YES, sixty-five and still alive. We cleaned up our act now. Except, you know, when we first moved in here, the neighbors would say hello to us, they say, if you need anything, give us a phone. We would say yeah . . . Everybody liked these little children and said hello. We were here about a week, and there was screaming and drinking and crushing the bottles, and—it was four-thirty in the morning—the sun was just coming up, and Linda is running out there and I am naked, with my balls and my cock, I was throwing dirty clothes out and saying, you whore I'll kill you. So, after that . . .

LINDA: That was seven-thirty in the morning, after going all night long . . .

C.B: Oh, I thought it was three-thirty?

LINDA: No, seven.

C.B: Now, the neighbors, they say, well, you know, we heard things but we don't call the police. I said thank you . . . But we are not so bad, lately, are we?

LINDA: No, no.

C.B: There are just minor eruptions now. Just like . . . we were gently waiting for the big blow. (*laughs*)

LINDA: (*laughs*) Are we one volunteer or two?

C.B: I think you are the one (*laughs*). I'm sitting on top of it, waiting along.

J.-F. D: Do people around know who you are?

LINDA: Some of them.

C.B: Yeah, they are gradually finding out. The neighbor, when we first moved in, he says: "Hey, Charles, my brother read your stuff, he is crazy about you . . ." Well the brother was nice, he never showed up. And then, you know, we go to supermarkets and all of a sudden, there is all this cackling, we gonna (*he starts singing with a sharp opera voice*) OHOOH I WENT TO EUROPE, I SAW YOU IN A MAGAZINE . . . Until then, you know, we were the two old folks who came in a supermarket, getting our box of salt. They saw this almost tired old guy with this young woman, and they giggle: Wouahhhh. And suddenly! . . . So, we are hiding out of San Pedro, but now and then they discover a little bit. But generally, they'd leave us alone. Nobody knows who I am, I don't know who they are. Really nice people . . . You know, they can do whatever they wanna do, as long as they are not around me. They can burn cities, and go up in balloons, and go under the sea. As long as they don't do it around me.

J.-F. D: That's it, thanks.

C.B: Listen, we have to call your cab, right, the bottle is nearly empty.

J.-F. D: I think Linda is doing so . . .

C.B: I'm not trying to get rid of you, I'm trying to plan your future.

J.-F. D: And you're right, I've still some work ahead.

C.B: Oh! You are interviewing somebody else! I don't like that! Roaaar. You need somebody else to talk to after me!

J.-F. D: (*laughs*) Well, not tonight . . . Tomorrow.

C.B: Oh, tomorrow is better . . . Okay, that's not so bad (*laughs*). Well shit. Doing what you're doing, you know that beats the eight hours job, don't you baby. It beats the eight hours job, doing what you are doing. It's better than the eight hour job. Don't you think?

J.-F. D: Sure . . .

C.B: You're not in a factory. You play your game.

J.-F. D: My game? Which game?

C.B: Your game is to leech off the poor souls of writing (*laughs*). You're feasting off of other lives and going back to your country . . .

J.-F. D: Hey, that's not nice!

C.B: Oh, shit, I'm just playing with you. Don't you understand, I'm not serious.

J.-F. D: (*laughs*) Sure?

C.B: Oh, Christ . . . Relax, I'm just playing. I know you won't take me as serious.

(*Linda comes back*)

C.B: You know I started playing with him. He took me seriously. I said he is feasting off of other lives . . .

J.-F. D: I am only doing like you: looking for a book, looking for a man.

C.B: A new great writer? . . . It seems everything is so dark, I think it is occuring and it seems to go on and on, that's all faint sand, there is no new fresh blood. There is nothing to shape the trees. There is only me here. And I am bad, but I am not bad enough, ha! ha! ha! So we are hoping for better writers, better interviewers, and quicker taxi cabs! (*laughs*).

J.-F. D: What more could we say?

C.B: You asked me earlier: is there any hope for the human heart? Right? I said yes, but that was a very tiny yes. A very very tiny yes . . . I'll have another drink.

THE DEATH OF CHARLES BUKOWSKI

John Bryan

On March 11, 1994, the *San Francisco Chronicle* reported that Los Angeles poet and storyteller Charles Bukowski had died from leukemia two days before, at the ripe old age of seventy-three. His work was "rough-cut" . . . "sleaze" . . . "gritty" . . . "contentious" . . . "raw," and definitely "embittered."

Hank, said *Chronicle* Reporter and Cultural Attache Steve Schwartz, was a "cult figure" in America and a "literary superstar" in Europe, especially in his native Germany, where he'd sold more than 2.5 million copies. (Steve got several of the biographical facts wrong, but was probably right about really important things, like sales figures.)

The Chronicle obit ran thirty inches in the entertainment section—those nice, fat, 12-pica columns which escalate the advertising revenues but hyphenate so badly. It was an amazing give-away of space for the kind of raucous loudmouth the De Youngs and Thieriots and McEvoys have always hated in a paper which normally mourns the departure of kings and congressmen with six to eight parsimonious inches.

The March/April *Poetry Flash* reported Buk's death on page 2, noting that "people who don't normally read, let alone read poetry, suddenly found themselves picking up his books."

All too true. Hank was a pop commodity.

In the next *Flash*, the World's Favorite Drunk rated a page one lead-off and three inside jumps for a total of forty-six inches (19 picas wide and a lot better hyphenated than the computer-driven *Chronicle*).

Stephen Kessler did an awe-struck adios, noting that when Buk died he was "the largest-selling contemporary American poet." Kessler added that he'd never had the dubious privilege of interviewing Buk in person but suggested that the man just might have been a trifle "misanthropic" in his "immortal dotage."

Other windy tributes blew in from around the world and from all kinds of media. They spruced Hank up and permanently put him on display in the literary pantheon—right next to Keats, Shelley, and James Whitcomb Riley. Quite a showing for an anti-social scribbler from the back-alleys of L.A.

As an old friend, editor, and drinking companion, I'd like to make some well-considered comments about Bukowski—mostly about the very human being I published in two 'Frisco literary magazines named *renaissance* and *Notes from Underground* (1961–65) and in the L.A. underground weekly *Open City* for 92 consecutive weeks (1967–69).

He was my neighbor. We lived in the ruins of "Old Hollywood" together, down by its eastern-end near Normandy and Hollywood Boulevard, over by Western and Sunset before they removed the Daniel Boone sets and tore down the fascinating old Fox Studios to install a shopping mall.

I loaned Bukowski money, worried about his crazy Communist wife, babysat his blue-veined baby daughter, listened to him scream and curse the world all night, screamed back, wiped up his treacly vomit, believed in the crazy bastard and trusted him with my life.

He betrayed me and for twenty-five years I hated his guts but today forgive him.

I'm going to miss you, Dirty Old Man (a title I invented for his column). But not for reasons that Steve Schwartz or Stephen Kessler are likely to understand.

Putting aside all the Johnny-Come-Lately obituaries, all that polite and cumbersome adulation, why did Bukowski's death generate so much ink and why will millions of fans keep right on reading him no matter what the critics say?

Do all these respectable and well-washed writers of pretentious drivel really know what they're talking about?

Charles Bukowski was a great writer and a lousy human being. Maybe the two things go together like Ham and Eggs. Like Bush and Quayle. Like Bill Clinton and Sophomoronic Lust.

I helped to make Bukowski famous and, in return, he pissed on me quite publicly. (In a short story called "The Birth, Life, and Death of an Underground Newspaper" and appearing in an early 1969 issue of *Evergreen Review*, then reprinted and still being circulated in a City Lights collection called *Erections, Ejaculations, Exhibitions, and General Tales of Ordinary Madness*.

A lot of it was lies written for effect, but all too much was true. What hurt the most was that I went to Bukowski as a friend when I was fighting for my life and what I told him in strict confidence were my most hideous secrets and my darkest nightmares. I needed help. I was on the verge of self-destruct.

Bukowski laughed and sneered and told the world. For twenty-five years I hated him and had good reason.

Yet I was not totally surprised when Bukowski pissed on me. Two other friends and editors got pissed on long before I was drenched.

Their names were William Corrington, teacher of English literature at Louisiana State University and Jon Edgar Webb, New Orleans street poet, hand-printer and a naively adoring friend.

Actually, there were four of us who really got Hank going: Corrington, Webb, myself, and John Martin, the tactful and dedicated owner of Santa Rosa's Black Sparrow Press who devoted a quarter-century to publishing Buk—and made a lot of money in the process. The four of us were there during critical periods when the Old Man needed us. We got him going, spread the word in places where it counted, put in faith and energy when it did the most good.

He publicly pissed on three of us and I'm sure that Martin caught his share but bit his tongue while the profits flowed in.

Jon Webb died hurt and angry long before he could forgive Bukowski. I'm not sure how Bill Corrington feels these days but I forgive Bukowski. (The Devil may be less understanding.)

Bukowski changed my life in a number of ways. His columns in *Open City*—generally not-so-short stories or essays printed exactly as they shot out of his machine-gun typewriter—were undoubtedly the best material that we printed. They helped to make the paper a Minor League success.

For six weeks less than two full years, I promoted Bukowski on the streets of L.A., printed five to fifteen thousand copies every week and gave half of them away.

The paper cost ten cents. You could buy it out of vending machines on hundreds of street corners and in the most unlikely places—most especially around recording studios, publishing houses, the giant movie lots and television cities, up and down the Sunset Strip, in Santa Monica, even in Ventura and Orange Counties. We mailed it to a hip and literate following—lots of musicians, actors, writers, producers, artists, entertainment biz executives.

Bukowski leapt out of the shadowy, semi-private world of tiny litmags and burst upon a bright-lit, public stage.

Ordinary people who despised all poetry and its effete creators took Bukowski to their hearts. He suddenly became a Los Angeles celebrity and L.A. is the media-capital of the world. People bought him drinks.

He spoke their language. Using many lies, he told the truth. Life is a meaningless pile of shit, he said. It all goes nowhere but the grave. What's left are drinking, fucking, and playing the longshots. Take whatever you can lay your hands on. Save your own sweet ass. Fuck everybody else.

In 1968, Bukowski guest-edited an *Open City* insert called *renaissance*, a newsprint literary magazine whose contents he chose with no interference from me or anyone else on the staff. He selected a Jack Micheline short story about a red-haired New York girl who liked to fuck. It was called "Skinny Dynamite." It got me arrested for publishing "obscenity."

(Micheline showed up with testimonials that could be used in court from several dozen notables, including Norman Mailer. Lawrence Ferlinghetti phoned exultant. Recalling his own experience with *Howl*, he predicted that the roust would make us famous but it did not. An embarassed Beverly Hills judge dropped the charges one year later and no one knew the difference.)

After the arrest, Sheriff's deputies beat me up on the way to jail. My wife freaked out. The legal fees bankrupted *Open City*. All of this drove me out of the Los Angeles publishing game.

Bukowski played the editor but I went to jail. He felt guilty about it and handed over 100 bucks for the defense fund but the lawyers wanted $10,000 more.

Yet Bukowski unwittingly saved my life. There'd been bomb threats and I was shot at twice. The Minute Men kept sending me malevolent greeting cards. Our house was watched all day, all night. Undercover cops planted my car with bags of marijuana. The F.B.I. broke into our offices at high noon one day and copied all our files. The I.R.S. was getting interested. Creditors were closing in. My two children cried a lot.

Joan—my skinny, super-psychic wife—was sure we were all doomed if we didn't immediately get the hell out of L.A. and Joan was usually right about that kind of thing. We left.

So, thanks, Bukowski, you saved my life. Although you didn't mean to.

Jon Edgar Webb died before he could forgive Bukowski. It doesn't much matter how the other early friends and editors feel now that the Poet/Drunk is dead. It's been so long, all this time has passed, so many oceans of cheap Budweiser have flowed under all our burned-out bridges. And who gives a damn?

Corrington, Webb, and I were grown men when we got involved with a post office clerk named Hank Bukowski, when we spent night after night drinking ourselves comatose and listening to his fascist screams. We knew what we were getting into.

We knew the bastard was an asshole but we also knew that he was a GREAT asshole. Bukowski was born lucky. He had endless energy and style. He could produce unimaginable quantities of first-rate prose and poetry at a single sitting. He had a certain loathsome charm.

How can you hate a talent like that?

Bukowski had no real politics or beliefs. When he worked with the hippies at *Open City* he called us "commie scum."

He refused to fight during World War II and that took guts but it also may have been because he was a native-born German and didn't want to go into combat against his own people. Bukowski was sometimes accused of being a Nazi and he had many of the makings but it simply wasn't true. He hated all politics and all politicians equally. He had amazing good sense.

No one ever called Bukowski a pacifist. He had nothing personal against violence. Go see the movie *Barfly*, which is surprisingly accurate about his love for bloody fist-to-face combat.

He loved to fuck but was a total misogynist. In the first year or two that I was his neighbor he boasted like a high school kid about his boiling love affairs but never really got any.

He despised and mistreated all his women and attracted nothing but full-blown masochists.

Bukowski was a loud, impossible boozer. Even in the depths of Lower East Hollywood, he gave alcohol a bad name.

It's also pretty clear that Bukowski didn't like Bukowski much. It flavored all he did and everything he ever wrote.

Bukowski was a thorough-going cynic and had very little hope for the human race. Perhaps that's why so many "average people" still dig him.

For that's exactly how the "average man" feels today about himself and his rapidly-disintegrating society.

Despite all of this, the most intriguing thing that all of us saw in Bukowski was his amazing sensitivity. It was reflected in those sad, blue, poet's eyes of his, peeking out from behind that ugly, acne-pocked mask of a face—the tough guy hallucination which both Hank and the world insisted on.

That amazing sensitivity was well reflected in the following 1964 poem ("The Swan") which I first published in Issue No. 1 of *Notes from Underground.*

It's always been one of my favorites and, if Bukowski had never written another thing, it would have more than bought the ticket for his nightmare, self-destructive trip through a hostile world. Wrote Charles (Hank) (Buk) (Dirty Old Man) Bukowski:

"swans die in the Spring too / and there it floated / dead on a Sunday / sideways / circling in current / and i walked to the rotunda / as overhead / gods in chariots / dogs, women / circled, / and death / ran down my throat / like a mouse, / and I heard the people coming / with their picnic bags / and laughter, / and I felt guilty / for the swan / as if death / were a thing of shame / and like a fool / I walked away / and left them / my beautiful swan."

HIS WOMAN HIS PARTY HIS PRICE

Wanda Coleman

it was another great party
plenty of literary hangers-on at the ol' timer's
waiting for the clown show to jump off
a little lightweight repartee
jokes as old as grandma moses and beer, plenty beer
me in my wig hat, leotards and jeans
high heel sandals, checkin' out some gray boys
checkin' out the action
the ol' timer is swilling beer and spewing curses
he's been watching his lover, the curlicious blonde cowgirl
flirt with a hot aryan range rider
he's with it. he throws a bottle of beer
against the nearest wall. there are squeals
of delight. the party has started
and now his curses are louder and she boots over
to calm him down with no success and now everybody
spills out of the kitchen, bathroom and bedroom to watch
"hey" a fat young dilettante yelps,
spilling beer on his belly, "the ol' man's at it again"
i figure it's time to split, go home to watts

my friend bonnie who invited me to this farce
say adios and then slip out the front door.
the man's disappeared. when i get to the
driveway on the slope of the hill, i see him in his volks.
the ignition is whining. it won't start.
he looks sad. he looks frightened. he's drunk.
"hey, ol' man, you can't get out,
you're parked in," i yell as i saunter past
on way to my pinto.
the ignition stops. i look back
he's slumped over the wheel
a man in severe pain. a man bawlin'

CONFESSIONS OF A BUKOWSKI COLLECTOR

Al Fogel

I am a Charles Bukowski fan and collector. I became an avid fan with the first book I read by him; collecting his first editions took longer and evolved naturally—out of a desire to read everything I could by him, which led me into realms I never believed existed.

But let me backtrack a step.

One day in the late '70s I was walking the Florida streets when I ran into an acquaintance who had just returned from San Francisco. I noticed he was carrying a large oversized paperback with the face of a strange-looking man spread across its cover.

"Watcha got there under yer arms?" I inquired.

"A collection of stories that will knock you out!"

"Yeah?"

"Here, judge for yourself," he said, handing me the book and vanishing.

I looked at the heading: *Erections, Ejaculations, Exhibitions and General Tales of Ordinary Madness*. Strange title. It was written by a Charles Bukowski and was published by City Lights in San Francisco. I opened the book to the first story and began reading. I read and I read and I read. I was spellbound, speechless; I had never read such powerful stuff. I must have read half the book while walking the city streets, turning corners, bumping into strangers, sitting on bus-stop benches. Here was the real thing—honest gutsy stuff written by a man who evidently experienced much of the existential despair common to us all. And he made me laugh through all the pain. Nothing was held back, nothing spared. He hit the jugular and blood came pouring across the pages like bittersweet wine. I was so excited the next day I rushed to the local library looking for anything I could get my hands on by this strange and wonderful writer.

"Do you have anything by Charles Bukowski?" I asked the librarian.

"Bukowski?" she rejoined, more than a little perplexed. "What does he write? Mysteries? Gothic Romance?"

"No ma'am, the best stories of our generation!" She sat there, nonplused. Finally she pointed to the wooden card catalogue and told me to search yonder. I ran to the alphabetical files and began searching under the "B" headings, but there was no Bukowski to be located.

Next, I combined the local bookstores—but without luck. "If you'll leave us a deposit, we will gladly try to order some for you, sir. How do you spell his last name?" I thanked them all very kindly and departed. I wasn't about to wait six weeks or longer. I hungered for his stuff—now! So one evening a short time later I placed a long-distance phone call to the Black Sparrow Press in Los Angeles.

"Hey, I hear you publish Charles Bukowski. I want everything you got by him."

"Yes, Sir!"

Four days later I received a large package containing an armful of beautifully printed books and I began devouring Bukowski with the avariciousness of a man who had not eaten a good meal in years. The more I devoured the more I hungered. There seemed a perpetual tapeworm gnawing away. I didn't know it then, but what I had was an almost fatal affliction: the Bukowski Bug! I bought everything that was available at the time. Unfortunately, a lot of his earlier books were no longer in print. But I was determined to get my hands on them. That's what led me—headstrong—into the realm of the Rare Book market. I found out his earlier stuff was for sale—at a considerable premium! I didn't care. With every good score I made at the track, I was able to purchase another rare Bukowski book or chapbook. Sometimes I lucked out and was able to circumvent dealers and go directly to former friends of Bukowski.

"I hear you knew the Buk! Do you happen to have any of his booklets lying around?"

"Bukowski!? That no good two-fisted drunkard! Here, take them all!"

Before I knew it, a burlap sack of prime Bukowski material would arrive at my doorstep—at a fraction of dealer prices! On one occasion I was furnished the phone number of a lady who turned out to be former editor of *Epos* magazine and publisher of Bukowski's rare second booklet, *Poems & Drawings*. She was living in Central Florida (only a few hours drive) so I made arrangements to visit and after spending a pleasant afternoon at her wilderness retreat recounting stories of Bukowski misadventures, I departed with five copies of Bukowski's second book along with *Flower, Fist & Bestial Wail* & *Run With The Hunted*—two scarce early chapbooks!

Sometimes there were unexpected surprises. When I contacted William Corrington (an early friend and admirer) he sold me *Signature 2* (a rare booklet of poems, one of only five copies known to exist!) & *Longshot Poems For Broke Players* (a scarce early chapbook) When I opened *Longshot Poems* and began reading I noticed pages seven and thirty-seven were blank! I was able to contact the publisher (Carl Larsen) who informed me a few initial copies (maybe eight or ten were run off with the blank pages before the error was discovered and corrected! I was holding a first issue *first state* of a Bukowski rarity!

Soon I had quite a collection on my hands!

The next step seemed only natural. I decided to write Bukowski a letter! Thank him for all the pleasure he brought me with his mighty pen. But how to reach him? The year was 1979. He had become something of a legend and his address was one of the best kept secrets in the world—like Michael Jackson's facelifts. But then another turn of good luck. I was speaking on the phone to Jeffrey Weinberg—a rare book dealer in Sudbury, Massachusetts one late afternoon inquiring about an elusive Bukowski title that I needed to add to my burgeoning collection.

"I've got *Genius Of The Crowd*," he informed me.

"Great! I've been searching for that one for months." He quoted me a price and I told him to send it.

"Jesus, I wish I had his address." There was a moment's silence, then:

"I've got Bukowski's address. I'll give it to you if you promise to keep it to yourself."

"Mum's the word," I said, jotting it down and thanking him heartily!

The following day I sent Bukowski a long letter of praise, at the end of which I asked if it would be okay to send him books for signing. A week later I received the reply:

> *"O.k. Al, send books plus postage and I'll sign . . . my action at the Track has been cooled. Some punk broke into my BMW and ripped of my stereo and radio but I'll be back!"*

Over the course of the next year there was an exchange of about a dozen letters between us, me sending along books and him sending them back with lavish and generous inscriptions, usually accompanied by a letter with a discourse upon the Race Track—a subject of interest to both of us:

> *"The women who go to the Track look worse than the $5000 claimers. Luck, Charles Bukowski."*

By now, I had just about every book published by Bukowski, most of them generously inscribed. But as all serious collectors know, the hunt was not over. There remained hundreds of obscure little magazines and underground newspapers with Bukowski contributions that I wanted to own in order to boast a complete collection. Bukowski's popularity seemed to coincide with the proliferation of these "little magazines" that burst onto the scene in the '50s and '60s with their revolutionary overtones and protest against the "establishment"—a continuation of the 50s "beat" rebellion. Although these periodicals were not as expensive to purchase as his books, they were difficult to locate—many of them having long since ceased publication by the time the 1980s rolled in. These were the small literary magazines that literally launched Bukowski's career: *Nomad, Quicksilver, Wanderlust; Coffin, Coastlines, Galley Sail Review.* Slowly, they began to surface in dealers' catalogues and I began buying them. To tell you the truth, I was fascinated by them. Aside from containing the first appearance (the true first edition!) of many of Bukowski's poems, stories, letters, essays, artwork, and interviews that were later collected and published in book format, these magazines seem to capture the temper and flavor of the times—more thoroughly than books. I eagerly awaited the arrival of each one.

It was also during this time (early '80s) that I decided to publish a *Comprehensive Checklist* of Bukowski's primary publications and when I informed him of my intentions he graciously consented to sign a few copies for the limited edition, but when the time came to sign, he reneged—upon the advice of his publisher. I had already pre-sold the limited edition, so I was fuming. This was the only time we had a verbal flare-up. He eventually relented, and wrote back,

> *"I'm sorry and I apologize . . . Send me anything you need signed. To me, a guy like you knows a hell of a lot more about life than the first 5000 I follow on the freeway . . ."*

The man had integrity beyond reproach!

Well, my *Checklist* sold out and the magazines with Bukowski contributions were coming in so I was merrily on my way to a complete Bukowski collection when a series of personal events culminating in the loss of my job (and long-standing girlfriend) sent me into an emotional tailspin—putting an abrupt halt to my collection frenzy. Once again I was walking the city streets, bumping into people—but this time not out of Bukowski euphoria but like a zombie who had lost contact with reality. This went on for months. It was in this confused mental and emotional state that I made a decision that I regret to this day: I sold my Bukowski collection! A California dealer had made me a tempting offer and out of desperation and a need for cash I succumbed. The infusion of cash did help me slowly wean my way back into society and when I became a working stiff again, I vowed to continue to collect Bukowski magazine contributions and renew my correspondence but when I attempted to contact him he had moved (with no forwarding address). Time passed and I became engrossed in worldly pursuits until Bukowski was no longer a priority but relegated to "someday I'll finish my collection . . . someday." But days turn to months that lapse into years and suddenly a decade had flown and I'm in Borders bookstore leafing through a magazine (*Poets & Writers*) when I come across this: *"In Memoriam: Charles Bukowski."* I stared in disbelief. Bukowski . . . dead? Oh my God! There had been many prior pronouncements of Bukowski's demise (which proved unfounded) but now it was staring me in print from a reputable mag. Oh my God. An incomparable sadness descended upon me. With tearful and reminiscent eyes I envisioned Bukowski, alone in his room, surrounded by beer bottles and horse-race tickets, banging away on an old Underwood manual, pounding, pounding, spitting his words out like nails, nailing ME with his gusty words and warm inscriptions. I bowed my head and uttered a silent prayer. A literary GIANT had passed away.

But life goes on (for the living) and it wasn't until several years later when I was doing some general housecleaning that I stumbled upon a little magazine from the early '60s. I began leafing through it when I came across a poem by Bukowski. I had somehow inadvertently failed to include this magazine when I sold my collection. I thought to myself, this was an omen, a reminder of a promise I made almost two decades ago to continue my Bukowski collection!

Not long afterward, I purchased my first computer and quickly learned to surf the Internet. A friend had informed me about a site that contained millions of out-of-print books—many of them first editions. It was called *Bib-*

liofind. When I located the site and typed in "Bukowski" I was inundated with hundreds of Bukowski first edition books and broadsides. They even had a copy of my *Checklist* for $150! IT had become a rare collectors' item! I was hoping for magazine listings. As I scrolled down the list I spotted one, then another! Yes, interspersed among the expensive books and broadsides were the '50s, '60s, and '70s little magazines that I came to love so much. And they were reasonably priced! Here was my golden opportunity to continue where I had left off—almost twenty years ago. This would be my tribute, my eulogy to Bukowski—my atonement for hastily selling out on him.

My first purchase was four early '60s magazines with Bukowski contributions. They were offered by "Skyline Books." I told the proprietor, James Musser, to charge my credit card and send priority mail! I eagerly awaited their arrival and when the package arrived I was back in the hunt again!

So I now enter what I'd like to consider the final "phase" of my Bukowski collecting. The time-frame for completion could well be indefinite, considering Bukowski's prodigious periodical output (over three thousand original contributions in over one thousand periodicals!) But I am far too immersed (happily again) in the chase to ever give up until I find them all!

Looking back, it has been an exciting and fruitful experience, ever since that fortuitous encounter on the street twenty years ago. Somewhere along the way I crossed over that fine line between reader and collector and acquired a hobby (passion!) that is not likely to be relinquished in my lifetime.

EVERY TIME I

Todd Moore

walk into a junk
shop & see an
old typewriter
i think of
bukowski & his
typer his sub
machine i can
almost feel
the way his
mornings wd go
maybe a puking
session to
clear the pipes
then a little
hair of the
dog & by that
time he's got
a poem or at
least the first
few lines some

thing abt a
whore he picked
up in a bar
she's got a
nice shiny
ass & inside
the night runs
deep & pretty
soon he's flying
he owns the
wine the sun
light & the
alphabet's cunt

WHAT DID BUKOWSKI SMELL LIKE?

FROM BUKOWSKI IN THE BATHTUB

John Thomas and Philomene Long

PHILOMENE: What did Bukowski smell like?

JOHN: He had virtually no smell. For one thing, he would bathe many times a day without any soap. He would sit in a hot tub and sort of rub himself, mainly soak, get up and dry. Sometimes there would be, besides the beer smell, a faint vomit smell to his breath because he would go the bathroom several times a night to throw up. Because he was in somebody's else's house, he didn't have a toothbrush. All he could do was rinse his mouth out. So there would be this very faintest smell of stomach juice.

PHILOMENE: I wonder, if he smelled himself, why would he take a bath that many times a day?

JOHN: I don't know. He also liked to sit in the bathtub and jack off. He wasn't getting laid much in those days. Once in 1967 he was telling me about his most recent piece of ass. It was sometime in the late summer and he was saying it was the first time he had gotten laid that year.

PHILOMENE: Why didn't he get laid until late summer?

JOHN: That didn't come up: "This is why I didn't get laid . . ." I think he was shy. He was vain about his legs, though. He thought they were enormously thick and strong

PHILOMENE: He appeared to be interested in legs. Do you think there was a connection?

JOHN: No.

PHILOMENE: No? He just liked legs?

JOHN: I think once a long time ago a woman had complimented him on his legs. Yeah. The idea was that they were thick and strong, and I remember him talking about a woman wrapping her legs around him, him standing and fucking, holding her up. And she was saying, according to him, "Oh honey, your legs are so strong!"

PHILOMENE: So that left a lasting impression.

JOHN: I guess so. Somewhere on the tapes a woman was flirting with him and he was saying, "I'm ugly, but I have these great beautiful leeeeeegs!" And he pulled his trousers up to show off his legs.

PHILOMENE: And what was her reaction?

JOHN: She giggled and said, "To me they look like blue cheese."

PHILOMENE: Were there varicose veins?

JOHN: No, but his skin was very pale, so the blue veins were quite visible. She said then, "That's all right, my legs get gray. Sometimes they get green." And it went on from there to other things.

PHILOMENE: Interesting woman. What was her name?

JOHN: Carole Sides. She was a black woman. She was an artist and pretty good, also a film student in those days at UCLA. Not that it matters, but this is a little thing that popped into my mind. He used to talk, not infrequently, about how ugly he was. Joking, not moaning about it. One Halloween . . . you know those things, maybe they still do put them on the top of dash boards? The little plastic virgins, you know what I'm talking about.

PHILOMENE: Yes, I do.

JOHN: OK. One Halloween I was in a supermarket and wandering past the kids' toy section and there was a bin of little plastic toys, among them a toy Frankenstein, the same height as those dashboard things. So I bought it and glued a little disk magnet under the base of it and gave it to him as a present. So in the old car he had in those days, he always had it sitting up there on top of the dash.

PHILOMENE: Like the Virgin Mary.

JOHN: Yep.

PHILOMENE: Did he see his face in Frankenstein?

JOHN: I don't recall him making the connection. He always drove very slowly, by the way.

PHILOMENE: Do you think he was afraid of death?

JOHN: No. He was terrified of being pulled over for speeding and that the cop would take him to jail, so he drove very slowly . . . and sort of slumped down in the seat.

PHILOMENE: Of course that's exactly how he would be seen by a cop.

JOHN: Yeah.

PHILOMENE: Did he ever speak to you about death?

JOHN: One thing he used to say in his late forties was, "John, IF I LIVE TO BE FIFTY, I'LL LIVE FOREVER!"

PHILOMENE: Doesn't Frankenstein do that? Live forever?

JOHN: Frankenstein? They would periodically freeze him up. He would appear to die, but in the next picture he would come back.

PHILOMENE: Let's end with that, because he is an immortal now, so to speak.

DID BUKOWSKI EVER USE YOUR BATHTUB?

JOHN: Once he began coming on to a woman, who shall be nameless, saying, "Wouldn't you like to fuck me in a bathtub full of come?"

PHILOMENE: Did Bukowski ever use your bathtub?

JOHN: Sure.

PHILOMENE: When?

JOHN: He used my bathtub once when he was sneaking around behind Linda King's back with some Greek woman. The woman was crazy. She stayed at that place Laurel Ann Bogen goes to in Hollywood, that private nut hospital. She was a woman in her fifties, not very good looking. She may have been at one time. He asked if he and this crazy woman could use my place. I had to make the bed with clean sheets. They came over and I left. Afterwards he was telling me that it was very scarey to him, because that little bedroom had pornographic pictures covering the wall.

PHILOMENE: Yuk. I go along with him there. Did he bathe before or after sex, or both?

JOHN: Just before. If he bathed afterwards, it was in someone's else's bathtub. Not mine. But I even gave him clean sheets.

PHILOMENE: Do you have a sense of why he bathed before sex? Was he was washing off another woman's smell.

JOHN: No. The crazy Greek woman knew about Linda. Rather than bathe and primp himself, he did it at someone else's house.

PHILOMENE: Hmmm.

JOHN: He would bathe all day. He wouldn't even soap himself, but he would sit in the tub over and over again. Sometimes jacking off, sometimes not.

PHILOMENE: Doesn't that cloudy up the water, so to speak? What happens with the semen in a tub of water?

JOHN: It goes down the drain.

PHILOMENE: Then he should have smelled of semen.

JOHN: I can't smell semen.

PHILOMENE: It's a powerful smell. So he must have smelled faintly of semen.

JOHN: How much could there have been in proportion to the bath water?

PHILOMENE: Gallons, according to him.

JOHN: No matter how much male bragging you've heard, there's not much male semen.

PHILOMENE: So let me get the picture of Bukowski in the bathtub.

JOHN: The door was shut. I wasn't in there.

PHILOMENE: What did you hear?

JOHN: A little bit of delicate splashing.

PHILOMENE: Of delicate semen-scented water. Let's penetrate this further. Why was he taking a bath before? Isn't that unusual for a man? I've never heard of it.

JOHN: You must have had a tacky sexual past.

PHILOMENE: Tacky, yes. A shower, yes. But a bath? How did you find the bathtub after he finished? Immaculate?

JOHN: No. Not immaculate, because it wasn't immaculate before he got in.

PHILOMENE: You have to admit, it's a striking, incongruous image—Bukowski in the bathtub. Why?

JOHN: I don't know why.

PHILOMENE: How were the sheets after he finished?

JOHN: Actually the sheets were in pretty good shape, because he had taken several bath towels from the bathroom, and when they came down he had the towels rolled up in a ball under his arm. Put them in my hamper. I didn't inspect them.

PHILOMENE: It may be cruel for me to say this, but he could be cruel, too . . .

JOHN: Aren't we all?

YOU DON'T KNOW WHAT LOVE IS

(AN EVENING WITH CHARLES BUKOWSKI)

Raymond Carver

You don't know what love is Bukowski said
I'm 51 years old look at me
I'm in love with this young broad
I got it bad but she's hung up too
so it's all right man that's the way it should be
I get in their blood and they can't get me out
They try everything to get away from me
but they all come back in the end
They all came back to me except
the one I planted
I cried over that one
but I cried easy in those days
Don't let me get onto the hard stuff man
I get mean then
I could sit here and drink beer
with you hippies all night
I could drink ten quarts of this beer
and nothing it's like water
But let me get onto the hard stuff
and I'll start throwing people out windows

I'll throw anybody out the window
I've done it
But you don't know what love is
You don't know because you've never
been in love it's that simple
I got this young broad see she's beautiful
She calls me Bukowski
Bukowski she says in this little voice
and I say What
But you don't know what love is
I'm telling you what it is
but you aren't listening
There isn't one of you in this room
would recognize love if it stepped up
and buggered you in the ass
I used to think poetry readings were a copout
Look I'm 51 years old and I've been around
I *know* they're a copout
but I said to myself Bukowski
starving is even more of a copout
So there you are and nothing is like it should be
That fellow what's his name Galway Kinnell
I saw his picture in a magazine
He has a handsome mug on him
but he's a *teacher*
Christ can you imagine
But then you're teachers too
here I am insulting you already
No I haven't heard of him
or him either
They're all termites
Maybe it's ego I don't read much anymore
but these people who build
reputations on five or six books
termites
Bukowski she says
Why do you listen to classical music all day
Can't you hear her saying that
Bukowski why do you listen to classical music all day
That surprises you doesn't it
You wouldn't think a crude bastard like me

could listen to classical music all day
Brahms Rachmaninoff Bartok Telemann
Shit I couldn't write up here
Too quiet up here too many trees
I like the city that's the place for me
I put on my classical music each morning
and sit down in front of my typewriter
I light a cigar and I smoke it like this see
and I say Bukowski you're a lucky man
Bukowski you've gone through it all
and you're a lucky man
and the blue smoke drifts across the table
and I look out the window onto DeLongpre Avenue
and I see people walking up and down the sidewalk
and I puff on the cigar like this
and then I lay the cigar in the ashtray like this
and take a deep breath
and I begin to write
Bukowski this is the life I say
it's good to be poor it's good to have hemorrhoids
it's good to be in love
But you don't know what it's like
You don't know what it's like to be in love
If you could see her you'd know what I mean
She thought I'd come up here and get laid
She just knew it
She told me she knew it
Shit I'm 51 years old and she's 25
and we're in love and she's jealous
Jesus it's beautiful
she said she'd claw my eyes out if I came up here and got laid
Now that's love for you
What do any of you know about it
Let me tell you something
I've met men in jail who had more style
than the people who hang around colleges
and go to poetry readings
They're bloodsuckers who come to see
if the poet's socks are dirty
or if he smells under the arms
Believe me I won't disappoint 'em

But I want you to remember this
there's only one poet in this room tonight
only one poet in this town tonight
maybe only one real poet in this country tonight
and that's me
What do any of you know about life
What do any of you know about anything
Which of you here has been fired from a job
or else has beaten up your broad
or else has been beaten up by your broad
I was fired from Sears and Roebuck five times
They'd fire me then hire me back again
I was a stockboy for them when I was 35
and then got canned for stealing cookies
I know what's it like I've been there
I'm 51 years old now and I'm in love
This little broad she says
Bukowski
and I say What and she says
I think you're full of shit
and I say baby you understand me
She's the only broad in the world
man or woman
I'd take that from
But you don't know what love is
They all came back to me in the end too
every one of em came back
except that one I told you about
the one I planted
We were together seven years
We used to drink a lot
I see a couple of typers in this room but
I don't see any poets
I'm not surprised
You have to have been in love to write poetry
and you don't know what it is to be in love
that's your trouble
Give me some of that stuff
That's right no ice good
That's good that's just fine
So let's get this show on the road

I know what I said but I'll have just one
That tastes good
Okay then let's go let's get this over with
only afterwards don't anyone stand close
to an open window

THIS THING UPON ME*

Jack Grapes

It's 1964. Late spring, almost summer. In New Orleans, the maple trees hang their leaves and branches over the old cracked streets. I'm sitting in a classroom, about to take the first of two French final exams, and if I am to graduate, I'd better pass them. I reach under my desk and bring up a copy of Racine's *Phaedre*, pull an unopened letter from between its pages. It's addressed to me, a thick black scrawl. On the top left corner it says: Buk. Short for Bukowski.

A letter from Charles Bukowski. Racetracks. Whores. Fights in back alleys. Booze. The writer in the cheap room. And I'm sitting in a college classroom, having to focus on a French literature exam, in French. I'm dizzy with the two worlds swirling before me. Bukowski and the meat world of real poetry versus this academic rock pile of propriety. I know if I so much as slit open the envelope and read the letter, I'm a goner. So I slide the letter back into the book and put the book back under my desk and concentrate on Racine.

In 1964, few poets knew of Charles Bukowski. Except for the underground world of small press poetry, he was relatively unknown. At the time, I believed he was a great, unknown poet, and would never have predicted the popular success which came within another decade, mostly from his column of prose works in the *Los Angeles Free Press*, "Notes of a Dirty Old Man," and the poetry readings, which were more a spectacle of his getting drunk and the audience taunting him to get drunker. And then the series of books that Black Sparrow Press began publishing. In 1963, he'd had three small chapbooks to his credit. Some of his poems had appeared in an underground literary magazine called *The Outsider*, edited by Jon Webb. In 1963, Issue #3 included a special section devoted to him as "Outsider of the Year," and by the end of that year, Loujon Press brought out his first major book, *It Catches My Heart in Its Hands*, a limited, hand-set edition of 777 copies. I'd read his poems before in various little magazines, many of them cheap mimeographed productions typical of the sixties—"the mimeo revolution," it was called—but when Jon Webb and his wife Gypsy Lou brought out his poems and I held that book in my hands, I was convinced that Bukowski was a great poet. It was this book that convinced me that poetry was a real thing, that words come from a real world, about a real world, and can be sent out with dignity into this real, awful world.

Robert Lowell's *Life Studies* is often cited as the work that changed the idiom of American poetry. The natural, spoken, confessional lyric. Whenever I read that, I'm always a bit surprised. This Orwellian rewriting of history, as if what goes on in the academic world is all that goes on in the world. Lowell may have been the first poet of such academic stature to write in a more natural, so-called confessional idiom, but "underground" and "beat" poets had been slinging the spoken phrase across the page for a decade—much of it trite and subject to self-parody—but no one who had read the poetry that was being published in the little poetry magazines would have been surprised by Lowell's newer verse. Whether directly or indirectly, I suspect he was influenced by what they were doing, or by what he saw his own students bringing in.

The problem for me back then was that neither the academic verse I was reading in college nor the underground or beat poetry that I picked up in bookstores in the village rang with the kind of truth I was looking for. I wanted something without pretense. I wanted poetry that rose up out of the need to speak, not poetry whose subject matter was a mere excuse for shaping language in a lyric way. No one wanted to admit it, but it was like bad acting, all flourish and swagger, vocal histrionics, literary mugging.

As a college student, much of what I had read came from Oscar William's-mid-century anthology *The Little Treasury of Modern Poetry*. Looking back over it, many of the poems are rough and awkward going. Except for the great poets of the earlier part of this century, few of the ones anthologized as being modern or contemporary are read much today. The classic cast included Hopkins, Hardy, Houseman, Yeats, Edwin Arlington Robinson, Edgar Lee Masters, Frost, Vachel Lindsay, Wallace Stevens, Pound, Jeffers, Eliot, John Crowe Ransom, Cummings, Allen Tate, Hart Crane, Richard Eberhart, William Empson, Auden, Delmore Schwartz, Dylan Thomas. Among the more recent contemporary poets (that is, poetry of the forties) were Elizabeth Bishop, John Berryman, Karl Shapiro, Robert Lowell, Anthony Hecht, Richard Wilbur, Kenneth Fearing. Not one of the others has since been included in any modern anthology. I've gone back and reread some of them, to see if there's a forgotten genius, but no. Most of those poems are pretty bad, technically nice, rhythmically proper, quaintly elegant.

There was nothing nice or quaint about Bukowski's poetry. What was most startling was the persona the poet presented. This was not the melancholy romantic musing on some intellectual theme, observing the world from a scholarly distance, but a man who had worked in a series of low-paying, backbreaking, often humiliating jobs, and was now ensconced at the post office, living in a cheap room—an ornery and anti-social bastard who hung out at the track and in low-class bars, drinking, whoring, and coming home bloody from some back-alley brawl. He openly spit on any group of writers and their cliques. There was nothing "literary" about him. I can't think of another poet at that time who has presented such a lower-class persona in his writings to the world. The beatniks might have been bummed out and beat, but they were still literati. The blood in Bukowski's poetry was real, not metaphysical. The drinking and the fighting and the low-life set were real, not the weekend slumming of a writer gaining a bit of experience amid the lower depths. Out of his own despair and physical torment came poetry.

The book opens where it will end, in a run-down room in a seedy section of Hollywood, in a run-down world going itself to seed.

> I awakened to dryness and the ferns were dead;
> the potted plants yellow as corn;
> my woman was gone
> and the empty bottles like bled corpses
> surrounded me with their uselessness;
> . . . .
> I shaved carefully with an old razor
> the man who had once been young and
> said to have genius; but

> that's the tragedy of the leaves,
> the dead ferns, the dead plants;
> and I walked into the dark hall
> where the landlady stood
> execrating and final,
> sending me to hell,
> waving her fat sweaty arms
> and screaming
> screaming for rent
> because the world had failed us
> both.

This is a world without exit, the Waste Land, the Inferno, *Ulysses's* nighttown somewhat tamed. Not a failed world, but each person's own absurd failure, the tragedy of the leaves; the sad distance implied in the line that he shaves, not himself, but the man who had once been young, as a mortician would shave the body before burial. Bukowski turns Joyce's religious symbolism upside down: the baptismal razor that Buck Mulligan carries aloft in the opening of *Ulysses* (like a babe, Buck is "stately, plump") becomes the doomed last rite before "walking into the dark hall . . . to hell."

The last poem in the collection is titled, "Old Man Dead in a Room." This is where he begins, and this is where he ends, in a cheap room, dead.

> this thing upon me is not death
> but it's as real,
> and as landlords full of maggots
> pound for rent
> I eat walnuts in the sheath
> of my privacy
> and listen for more important
> drummers

Far worse than physical death is the spiritual death of the artist who has lost faith—not in the world without—but the world within, the integrity of his vision and the willingness to commit to its message. He will be found, he says, dropping "a last desperate pen/in some cheap room," and those who find him will never know his name, nor his meaning. It is in this poem that Bukowski transforms the image of himself dying into something larger, with a more comprehensive meaning. But at that time in my life, that image of a man, dead in a room, resonated with my own imagined life to come.

My father grew up during the Depression, slept in freight cars and when he had the money, a cheap room. He was a drunk, a man who "rode the rails" and lived in flop houses, who slept in libraries during the winter, covering his face with newspaper so it looked like he was reading. Perhaps my father exaggerated these tales of living on the road. Sitting in his den in his leather chair, he spun tale after tale of coming into the Philadelphia stock yards clinging to the edge of a freight car, or boxing for a dollar a round, or scrounging for a bite to eat, or—well, check out *Ironweed*. That might have been my father. Except at some point he landed in New Orleans, and got work in a gym, sparring and sweeping up at night, for which he could eat and sleep on the mats. Eventually, he got a job in a shoe store, and then a job in the optical business, and then married, and I was born, and within a year or two he opened his own business, Nu-Deal Optical. When I was six years old, we moved to a large brick home in a fine residential neighborhood. I went to a private school, with other kids from well-to-do families. We joined a country club, and I spent my summers swimming all day. But my two brothers and I loved to hear his stories, about the time he was in jail in St. Louis, about when he slept in a back alley in the rain under a box, about how he made shoelaces and sold them in office buildings, about how he came into New Orleans over the Airline Highway Bridge and spent his last nickel on a beer. "How could you spend your last nickel on a beer?" I asked, incredulous. "Where would you sleep, how could you pay for food?" He'd smile and say, "Oh, something always came up."

My father looked a lot like Edward G. Robinson. We have a photograph of him in a gangster scowl, wearing a fedora. I remember one time the newspaper headlined how three guys from Murderer's Row were being executed. My dad pointed to their pictures and said, "I knew these guys. We used to throw bricks at each other from the roof of the tenements." My dad hung out with guys from Murderer's Row?

Then one night I was watching a late movie on television in my room; it was about 2 A.M. and I was supposed to be studying for some Spanish exam the next morning. The movie was *Tales of Manhattan*, starring, among others, Edward G. Robinson. The film is a string of five anecdotes linked by the travels of one tail coat and the effect it has on its various owners. In one sequence, a gangster wearing it is shot and killed. The tail coat is thrown into an alley, riddled with bullet holes. Robinson is a down-and-out bum, in the same alley, sheltered from the rain by a cardboard box.

This is my father. And this will be me, I thought. If ever I am to amount to anything as a writer, all the advantages my father has given me—private schooling, college education, a car, etc.—will have to be discarded. I'll have to end up living on the streets in order to rise back up, on my own, out of the same hardship and poverty my father knew. The world might fail us, but who would choose to fail the world? It was a fearful proposition.

I would rehearse. Sometimes, when taking a shower, I'd scrunch my body down to the tile floor and let the water pelt me, even going so far as to turn off the hot and let the cold numb my body. I'd imagine it was rain, and that I was sitting in some back alley, nowhere to go, out on the streets, sheltered by a cardboard box.

When I was eleven years old, my brothers and I would take the streetcar to the old Joy Strand Theatre downtown to see a double feature on a Friday night for ten cents. We had to be sure to save a nickel so we could call Mom or Aunt Fanny to come pick us up after we'd finished in the penny arcade next door. One night, we spent all our money. I was the oldest, so it was up to me to figure out what to do. I probably could have asked the lady who sold popcorn, or the man who took tickets, to phone home. But no, there was this man without legs who sat on a little board with wheels that he pushed with his hands, and he had a spot down the street next to a hat filled with pencils. You took a pencil and dropped in a dime. I decided to borrow the nickel from him. Why not? This could have been my father. This could be me.

Not very many years ago I played the part of a writer in *The Man in Room 605*. He had once been the golden boy of the literary scene. Overcome by mental illness, alienated from his friends and supporters, he disappears from the literary scene, in the end to die in an obscure Broadway Hotel. It's Delmore Schwartz. In one scene, in a drunken rage, he throws his typewriter to the floor, then falls on it sobbing, "the tools of my trade." For me, this was better than rehearsing in the shower. I got to play the whole thing out.

There was nothing sentimental or poetical about Bukowski's poetry. Yet he was a man who, for all his drinking and fighting and whoring, wrote poetry. He was a poet. In "To the Whore Who Took My Poems," he grieves their loss. "Why didn't you take my money?" he asks. Because

> . . . sometime simply
> there won't be any more, abstract or otherwise;
> there'll always be money and whores and drunkards
> down to the last bomb,
> but as God said,
> crossing his legs,
> I see where I have made plenty of poets
> but not so very much
> poetry.

There it was. A truth I'd suspected but was afraid to articulate in all those college courses. A variation of "where's the beef?" All these poets and their fine phrases, and their fine thoughts, and their fine style, but where was the poetry, where was the life? The academics did it right, without heart, and the beats (for the most part) were banging the drum, without music. It was all one kind of posturing or another. But reading Bukowski as a twenty-year-old college student, I experienced for the first time in poetry the breath of a living person, and a persona that was more interesting than that of most of the other poets I'd had to read, poets who seemed to keep any persona at all from the poems, as if the poems were found objects in the earth. Here was a poet using persona as an integral part of the poem, as if the fossil is both poem and poet, locked bone to bone as one.

In "The Sun Wields Mercy," the narrator realizes that, in a world waiting for the bomb, "peace is no longer,/for some reason, precious." A kind of madness, a spiritual vacuum awaits.

> the painters paint dipping
> their reds and greens and yellows,
> poets rhyme their loneliness,
> musicians starve as always
> and the novelists miss the mark,
> but not the pelican, the gull;
> pelicans dip and dive, rise,
> shaking shocked half-dead
> radioactive fish from their beaks

It's a startling image, rich and full, a full-circle prophecy. To hit the mark, the pelican ingests radioactive food. The capriciousness of life, that at any moment something swoops down upon our half-dead selves and completes the job.

> has this happened before? history
> could be a circle that catches itself,
> a dream, a nightmare. . . .
> can't we awaken?
> or are the forces of life greater than we?
> can't we awaken? must we forever,
> dear friends, die in our sleep?

It's a sad kind of rage against the dying of the light. A nod to the power of the gods to take us away for good. A man who has worked in slaughterhouses, and bled from his own internal sickness, unable to distinguish the blood of his victims from his own. He loses at the track; the kids crash the empties he puts out back almost as fast as he can drink them; a down-and-out friend wants literary letters to soothe his publishing woes. "Write me," he says. And Bukowski responds:

> write you? about what, my friend?
> I'm only interested in
> poetry.

If he is to be saved, it is poetry that will do it. Though he's not above trying for love, or if not that, romance. In "A Literary Romance," he discovers a truth about both. He meets her "somehow through correspondence or poetry or magazines." She writes poetry, and shows him her life's work. The writing's pretty bad, but he tries to be kind. Then she tells him her secret. She's a thirty-five-year-old virgin. He takes her to the boxing matches and afterwards they return to her place, make some intimate contact, but when he leaves

> she is still a virgin
> and a very bad poetess.
> I think that when a woman has kept her legs closed
> for 35 years
> it's too late
> either for love
> or for
> poetry.

There is little redemption, if not salvation in the world. The man he shaved in the mirror, that younger twin, becomes the twin of his father in the last poem that closes out the first section of the book. My own father had died the year before the book was published, so the theme was fresh for me. The poem is titled "The Twins," and Bukowski goes home to collect his things. He moves through the house and looks at his father's "dead shoes,/ the way his feet curled the leather as if he were angry planting roses,/ and he was." Finally, he tries on his father's light blue suit:

> much better than anything I have ever worn
> and I flap the arms like a scarecrow in the wind
> but it's no good:
> I can't keep him alive
> no matter how much we hated each other.
> . . . .
> Very well. Grant us this moment: standing
> before a mirror
> in my dead father's suit
> waiting also
> to die.

The father is dead. The world is absurd, pain is absurd, there is no exit, we prepare ourselves for death the same way God might. Even in our father's suit, flapping its arms, we cannot keep him, or ourselves, alive.

If "The Tragedy of the Leaves" invokes the cul-de-sac of personal damnation, "The Priest and the Matador" takes the scope of this vision and braids it into the spiritual imagery of a godless universe. The matador and the landlady are both out for slaughter, and the priest, behind his window, is no less trapped than the man unable to pay his rent. But unlike the speaker in "Tragedy," this narrator stands firmly between the opposed conditions of faith and violence, only to realize that his opposition is an illusion and both lead to the same despair. Religion and ritualized violence are opposite ends of the same sword of hopelessness:

> set this to metric: the bull, and the fort of Christ:
> the matador on his knees, the dead bull his baby;
> and the priest staring from the window
> like a caged bear.

Each is trapped in his own dialectic of despair. And neither finds escape, neither can offer hope in the barren, ruined landscape.

> you may argue in the market place and pull at your
> doubts with silken strings: I will only tell you
> this: I have lived in both their temples,
> believing all and nothing—perhaps, now, they will
> die in mine.

If both face a spiritual if not physical death in the desolate temple of modern disenchantment, where is there "escape"? Is there some fabric of meaning that can survive the toppled wizard of twentieth-century existentialism? What lies between Camus's fatal sense of life's absurdity and the futile act of self-destruction?

The poem that follows "The Priest and the Matador" takes a moment to reflect, not just on experience, but the act itself of making poems about it. In "Love & Fame & Death," Bukowski's vision of the human condition is suddenly personalized, even trivialized, on purpose, as if to remind us not to take it all too seriously. He doesn't get very far in the poem (11 lines) before closing with

> the way to end a poem
> like this
> is to become suddenly
> quiet

He continues to move through a barren, ruined landscape, unable to make contact even on the phone, where every call is a wrong number.

> there is no church for me,
> no sanctuary; no God, no love, no roses to rust;
> towers are only skeletons of misfit reason,
> and the sea waits
> and the land waits,
> amused and perfect;
>
> . . . .
>
> I return the receiver
> and return also

> to the hell of my undoing, to the looming
> larks eating my wallpaper
> and curving fat and fancy in the bridgework
> of my tub,
> and waiting against my will
> against music and rest and color
> against the god of my heart
> where I can feel the undoing of my soul
> spinning away like a thread
> on a quickly revolving spool.

What made *It Catches My Heart in Its Hands* so powerful was the authenticity of this narrator, and the real (as opposed to metaphysical) truth of his pain, poverty, and despair. This was a persona quite unlike any I'd encountered in poetry. Bukowski's thing with the horses was not a gambler's addiction, nor was it a literary pose. His body was literally breaking down, and he believed the horses to be his only hedge against backbreaking labor. Learning to win at the track was a life-and-death matriculation. He wrote to Jon Webb in July of 1962 (a series of letters published in *The Outsider* #3).

> I have put in a lot of time in studying the horses, going to tracks, because when I got older like this I sensed that what was left of my thin soul could no longer take their pokes . . . the slow death thing, and I took the long dream: that the horses might save me.

What I haven't told you is how incredibly beautiful the book was. A hand-set limited edition of 777 copies. Handfed to an ancient 8-by-12 Chandler & Price letterpress; on Linweave Spectra paper throughout, in shades of white, winestone, saffron, bayberry, peacock, ivory, bittersweet, gobelin, and tobasco. A rainbow opening of deckle-edge papers under layers of cork cover and madras tissue and rice papers. The process of opening the book, turning the pages one by one, was both a spiritual and a magical exercise. I'd never seen anything like it, and in all the years since, no book design has ever come close to eliciting such awe, such wonder. It sold at the time for $5. I recently saw a catalog that listed it as worth close to a thousand. As beautiful as the book was, it came out of much struggle and labor and hardship. The struggle to write the poems was matched by the labor to create this book.

Here is what Jon Webb wrote in the colophon:

> The printing, all manual, was done thru the steamy months of June to September, 1963, in a slave quarters workshop back of a sagging ex-mansion in the French Quarter in New Orleans; and hand-bound in October—the workshop's windows gaping out into a delightful walled-in courtyard dense to its broken-bottled brims with rotting banana trees, stinkweed and vine, & moths, spiders, snails, bats, gnats; ticks, wasps, silverfish, ants, flies, mosquitoes, cockroaches big as mice & lizards, none of whom gave annoyance except accidentally: rats galloping overhead at night loosened showers of 1800's dust & plaster over completed pages stacked on every available level space, & seeping rainwater complemented the mischief so that pages had to be done over; bugs flew & walked into the running press to be ground up into ink; lovemaking rodents scattered alphabets in the typecases; fuses blew with awesome abandon; twice wiring in the aged walls caught fire; & thrice the press broke down, nesters mangled in the machinery or motor . . . the humidity burst open composition rollers, kept ink from drying on finished runs, & et cetera. But here is the book, written in blood, & printed in blood; but not like Bukowski's, more like the pseudo-stuff that bleeds from the madras tissue between pages 96 and 97 if you wet it and squeeze—for we've nothing at all to complain about: the experience was unforgettable, one that could not be bought for gold—nor sold to the devil.

The beauty of the book and the poetry were one. Each produced by the hardest of labor, emerging with the grace of a spiritual quest, out of the earth, as a farmer would work the land to yield its fruits. And yet, despite the book's beauty, it was hard to believe that Bukowski would end up any other way but a relatively unknown poet. When Loujon Press awarded him the Outsider of the Year with the publication of this book, the accuracy of that judgement was startling, for he was truly, at that time, an outsider, neither beat nor academic nor New York school nor San Francisco hip. Despite the rhetoric of his ranting, there was something traditional about the poetry's lack of avant-garde theatrics, and the simplicity of its honesty.

The Bukowski in the poems has come to his final room. And like the bull, he faces the final matador in the temple of the world. He thinks of Hemingway in the penultimate poem, who no longer touches his typewriter, who has no more to say. A year or so earlier, Hemingway had put a shotgun to his head. Now, Bukowski invokes his name, and his final act.

> I think of the form of the poem
> but my feet hurt, there is dirt
> on the windows.

This is almost comic. Contemplating form, he's faced with content. All the arduous formalizing that goes on in poetry, what Jack Gilbert has called the minor craft, "making the poem more presentable," is dismissed rather off-handedly because his feet hurt. The bulls of formalism charge, and Bukowski waves the cape as he bends to pick up a peach.

> I have a typewriter and now
> my typewriter no longer has
> anything to say
>
> I will drink until morning
> finds me in bed with the
> biggest whore of them all:
> myself.

He watches them outside his window fill up the holes in the streets, put new wires on the poles, and it rained

> . . . a very
> dry rain, it was
> not a bombing, only the
> world ending and I am
> unable to write
> about it.

We come to the fourth section of the book, and in it, just one poem, the last, "Old Man Dead in a Room." Bukowski, and my father, and Edward G. Robinson, and Delmore Schwartz, and Humbolt, and Dylan Thomas, and the ghost of my own Christmas future have at last come to rest. When Black Sparrow Press came out with Bukowski's selected poems in 1981, *Burning in Water, Drowning in Flame*, "Old Man Dead in a Room" was not one of the poems reprinted from *It Catches*. Since then, I know of no collection that has the poem. *The Penguin Modern Poets*

#13, published in 1969, which includes a selection of poems by Bukowski, Philip Lamantia, and Harold Norse, is the only place I've seen this poem reprinted.

OLD MAN DEAD IN A ROOM

this thing upon me is not death,
but it's as real,
and as landlords full of maggots
pound for rent
I eat walnuts in the sheath
of my privacy
and listen for more important
drummers;
it's as real, it's as real
as the broken-boned sparrow
cat-mouthed to utter
more than mere
and miserable argument;
between my toes I stare
at clouds, at seas of gaunt
sepulcher . . .
and scratch my back
and form a vowel
as all my lovely women
(wives and lovers)
break like engines
into some steam of sorrow
to be blown into eclipse;
bone is bone
but this thing upon me
as I tear the window shades
and walk caged rugs,
this thing upon me
like a flower and a feast,
believe me
is not death and is not
glory
and like Quixote's windmills

makes a foe
turned by the heavens
against one man;
. . . this thing upon me,
great god,
this thing upon me
crawling like a snake,
terrifying my love of commonness,
some call Art
some call poetry;
it's not death
but dying will solve its power
and as my grey hands
drop a last desperate pen
in some cheap room
they will find me there
and never know
my name
my meaning
nor the treasure
of my escape.

In this poem, the narrator/writer/persona/Bukowski has transformed the image of the futile death in a run-down room to a transcendent dignity. For all his suffering, this thing upon him (some call Art/some call poetry) is not death; its power is what grants him escape. Not an exit from life, but an escape from life's meaningless pain and despair. No more illusion. The soul rises above the steady erosion of loss and loneliness and finds spiritual triumph in the realization and creation of poetry. There is beauty even in pain and grief and loss when it yields such loveliness. The old man speaks against a world that has failed, but a failure he refuses to accept. The way out is not through the dark hall where the landlady, the priest, the matador beckon. It is through pen and paper, in creating the poem, the artifact, the fossil emerged from living skin.

WHEN BUKOWSKI MET COLIN THE JOCK

Ray Clark Dickson

Colin, the English jockey riding at Santa Anita
had a chin like a pear-shaped tea caddie;
tight, round little lock for a mouth
he kept shut for intolerable lengths of time,
particularly if he knew someone was going to ask
him for a horse.
"Who do you like in the third, Colin?"
He looked cautiously both ways before pointing
to himself.
"But you're on Devastator, the favorite,
in the third, man. There's no bet at two for one."
Colon offered a reluctant smile, tapped Hank's
latest personality signed book with his whip,
and like a small prancing horse, whirled away.
Hank spit, rubbed his pockmarked chin, let loose
a torrid stream of Old English oaths never heard
in salon or stable, finishing with, "I thought
everyone said the little limey bastard was a
collector of great literature."

Still cursing, he ended up at the paramutual window, bet a big chunk to win on Colin, doubled his money, still growling, "Fuckit, then—this will take care of him."

CHARLES BUKOWSKI SPIT IN MY FACE

David Barker

This story is neither fact nor fiction. It is a memoir, and as such, subject to error, distortion, and fantasy. While Charles Bukowski, Linda King, Gerald Locklin, John Kay, and myself are real persons, the reader should not assume that the events described herein actually happened in exactly the manner presented. Frankly, my memory isn't that good. Some of the dates and sequences may differ from historical reality. While many of the quotes are direct, others are only approximations of what was said. Nonetheless, the gist of the story is true. In the interest of fairness, I have changed the name of one character; "Dana Mill" is a fictitious name.

The 49er Tavern was dark and crowded. Charles Bukowski, the greatest poet of twentieth-century America, stood in the narrow aisle between the beer soaked redwood tables and the row of occupied bar stools. He was drunk and he was dancing, arms held above his head, a blind, weary smile of madness playing across his battle-scarred face.

It was a painfully alive face, like raw hamburger, all nerve endings and open wounds, showing the terror and agony of living with uncompromised genius in a land of fatheads. He was Lazarus, raised from the dead by the holy bleeding Jesus. He was Zorba the Greek, arms poised, gently swaying. He was Charles Bukowski, dancing.

I passed between him and the bar and he stopped me. I stood there transfixed, a frightened rabbit held in the hypnotic stare of a coiled rattler. His thick chest expanded and the powerful arms went higher, ready to strike, to come crashing down on me.

Then he spit in my face. The greatest poet in America, my idol, my hero. The saliva hung, slowly dripping down my cheek. I didn't wipe it away.

"Thank you," I said, and I walked back to my table.

Bukowski, the finest writer in the world. The Hemingway of his age, but tougher, realer than Hemingway. And he hated us saying these things about him, because he suspected it might be true. And he waved away his greatness like an annoying fly.

We called him Bukowski. Not Charles Bukowski, but just Bukowski. Close friends called him Hank, short for Henry, which is either his first or middle name, I forget which. And many of the little magazine editors during the '60s called him Buk, or The Buk (rhymes with puke) but I never cared much for that.

He was our god. We all wanted to be like him. Hell, we wanted to *be* him. We wanted the face, the beer gut, the receeding hairline, the acne scars, the bulbous veined nose like a swollen spade or the head of a prick, the booze ruined body, the sour flesh. We wanted his drunkeness, his hard women, his brutal poetry, his weeping soul. We wanted to live the legend too. But it was his alone. God knows he had earned it. He wasn't giving it away.

Charles Bukowski was born in Germany in 1920 and grew up in Los Angeles, California. Somewhere in his many stories, he mentions that his father beat him. As a teenager, Bukowski suffered from a horrible case of golf-ball sized boils all over his face and back which left him permanently scarred. Ugly and unsociable, he began drinking in high school and never stopped.

Bukowski attended L.A. City College for a while, dropped out and went on the bum and wrote hundreds of now lost short stories which he mailed off to the slick magazines at the rate of five or so a week. They all came back, rejected. Then, at twenty-four he published his first short story, "Aftermath of a Lengthy Rejection Note" (I could have the title wrong) in a 1945 issue of the prestigious literary *Story* magazine.

The same year, he stopped writing and went on a ten year drunk, drifting from city to city, flophouse to flophouse, shitty job to shitty job, whore to whore. He was beaten in gangster bars, married and left a Texan millionairess with a deformed neck, slept on trashcans in rat infested alleys, considered suicide.

In 1955, he was admitted to the charity ward of an L.A. hospital with bleeding ulcers from drinking. He almost died, but he didn't, and when he came out, he got a job at the post office, bought an old typewriter, and began writing the poetry which made his reputation as a hard-living poet of the streets.

I first read him in the '60s, when he wrote a column for the *L.A. Free Press* called "Notes of a Dirty Old Man." It was good prose, funny, shocking, freewheeling, but of course I had no idea then about the poetry he had already written, the immortal "the tragedy of the leaves," the love poems to Jane, his one true love who died young of alcoholism—"I TASTE THE ASHES OF YOUR DEATH," "FOR JANE: WITH ALL THE LOVE I HAD, WHICH WAS NOT ENOUGH," "URUGUAY OR HELL," "NOTICE,"—the saddest love poems ever laid on paper. Heartbreaking stuff. I didn't even know he wrote poetry, let alone that he was the most important poet to come down the line in the last 100 years or so.

I worked at the college library at Long Beach State. The only guy I knew who had even heard of Bukowski was a tall black man with one bad eye that rolled around his face when he smiled. His name was Tony, and he lived with a white girl who had a baby, his or otherwise. He was intelligent, but not very verbal, and he tripped up his words when he spoke.

I mentioned Bukowski's column to him one day as we were gathering returned books from the bin in the back room, and Tony's face lit up and he started yelling, excited beyond control.

"Ya! Ya man, I read that dude! That muther's crazy! He's great!"

But it was John Kay who told me about the poems. John and Leo Mailman edited a little magazine called *Mag*. It was a good mag, especially considering that it came out of a college campus. John had taste and he knew good poetry when he saw it.

John had just put out a book by Gerry Locklin called *Poop and Other Poems* around the time that I first got to know him. *Poop* was a best seller of sorts for a small press book, selling out the first edition of 500 copies in a month and eventually going into many printings. It was a popular book locally, because Locklin, a professor at Long Beach State, had a strong local reputation and the book was a natural, what with the title and the cover photo of Gerry sitting naked in the bath tub with a can of Coors and his rubber duck. It went over big.

Through John Kay I met Gerry Locklin and eventually Bukowski, both of whom in their own way turned me around from being a hopelessly shitty and obscure romantic poet and got me headed in the right direction toward the other thing; the poem as it must be if it is to be anything worthwhile at all.

I had only known John a month or so, but I already valued his literary opinions highly. He was obviously a man who had thought deeply about poetry and who cared about it as an art.

We were walking along between classes and I asked him who he thought was the best writer of poetry around. It was Bukowski, an answer that surprised me. I thought Bukowski was just some pervert in Hollywood, a primitive who lucked out occasionally and just happened to turn out a good dirty story now and then.

"Read his poems. His early poems, they're great," said John. I did; they were great. I'm still reading them now, twelve years later.

Because of John Kay and *Poop*, I began sitting in on Locklin's class. I wasn't signed up for it or even auditing, I just came along for the ride with John and sat in and listened. Locklin stood at the lectern and made it all up as he went along, telling jokes, asking what team had won which football game, asking his class trivia questions. He was funny and he didn't bore his students, so he was well liked. Sometimes he even got them to read a good book and like it, which was better than most professors could do.

One afternoon, Locklin brought in a stack of little magazines and small press books of Bukowski's: *Laugh Literary and Man the Humping Guns, Post Office, The Days Run Away Like Wild Horses over the Hills, All the Assholes in the World and Mine,* and others. He told us to read Bukowski and come back next time to discuss what we'd read. Most of the girls didn't like Bukowski. They said he was dirty minded and cruel and hated women, but all of the guys liked him because he was dirty minded and cruel and he hated women.

We started reading him, and that's what mattered. Then we found out. We knew. Not many did, but we did. We were the lucky ones.

John Kay talked the school into giving him $1,000 to put on an annual literary event, *Poetry Week*. The money was for paying the poets an honorarium to come and read, and for buying their airline tickets, meals, drinks, hotel rooms, and such while they were in town. He brought Lyn Lifshin and Brother Antoninus and other poets on campus. But most important, he brought Bukowski to Long Beach.

John had published some of Bukowski's poems in *Mag*, so he called him up and asked him if he wanted to read.

John imitated Bukowski's voice for me; it was a sly Tennessee Williams type of lisp, "Hey, John Baby . . ."

Of course, Bukowski wasn't interested in reading until John offered him $200. Then he agreed to do it.

This was in the fall of 1971. I had seen Bukowski read once before, back in 1969 or 1970. Someone had brought him on campus and he read to a class of about twenty-five students. He was not well known then, and he was still working at the post office or had just quit after fifteen years.

He looked younger then, he was thinner, his hair darker, and he looked like a boxer, like Humphrey Bogart. He read a short story about going into the ring with Hemingway and knocking him out, then going off with a society broad to glory and fame. Years later, I found that same story in an old issue of *Laugh Literary and Man the Humping Guns*.

He may have read some poems too. He was calm, cool, hard-assed. He was almost quiet. It was a low key yet impressive reading.

Two years later, during Poetry Week, Bukowski was more widely known and his reading was a bigger event. His first novel, *Post Office*, had just been published by Black Sparrow Press, and 75 or 100 people showed up to hear him.

The reading was during the morning, on a weekday. There was something classical and timeless about it. I got the feeling that it could have happened a hundred years ago or a thousand years ago. Bukowski came in sick, hung over. He looked ancient, a Greek god gone to pot. He sipped orange juice and vodka from a thermos and read some of the best poetry I've ever heard. They were things out of the early books, *Flower fist and Bestial Wail, Longshot Pomes for Broke Players, Run With the Hunted, Cold Dogs in the Courtyard, It Catches My Heart In Its Hands, Crucifix In a Death Hand*. The books were long out of print and few of us had heard the poems before. He read well for an hour and he earned his money. When it was done, the pretty little coeds came up in their short skirts and had him autograph books. He obliged them.

Afterwards, there was a little gathering at the local tavern, the 49er. Locklin and John Kay asked Dana Mill, another student writer, and I if we wanted to come along and meet Bukowski. Like myself, Dana was a great admirer of Bukowski.

I remember feeling ill at ease sitting at the table with him. John had a reason to be there as the guy who had brought him onto campus and allowed him to make a quick $200, and Gerry was his friend, but Dana and I were just hangers-on, eager for a chance to sit and drink with the famous man.

Not much happened. We drank beer and listened to Bukowski for about an hour. He made a couple of disparaging remarks to Locklin about his students, "The Boys from English 1A" or something to that effect, but he didn't persist and nothing happened.

Bukowski's girlfriend Linda King had just published a book of poems about their affair called *Suck Pluck and Fuck* or something close to that, and she was throwing a big publication party. Bukowski invited Locklin and Locklin asked if he could bring along a few of his students, so John and Dana and I were invited too.

It was 1972, the ragged tailend of the '60s cultural revolution, and most of us were tiring of the hippie thing by then. I had already cut my hair short a couple months earlier, and the evening of the party I shaved off the beard as well, then showered and combed my wet hair straight back so it would look like Bukowski's.

I drove over to Dana's little one bedroom cottage and we got a jump on the drinking. Dana poured the wine and talked about Buk, the Old Lion, just like Hemingway, the Old Literary Lion before him.

We were fairly drunk by the time we got to the 49er to meet Gerry and John. The four of us had several beers there, just to get into a party mood, and then we headed for Los Angeles in John's 1965 Mustang convertible.

I had to piss something terrible on the way there, so John pulled off into a black neighborhood and I relieved myself in an alley behind a gas station.

The party was at Linda King's house. I'm not sure what district it was in, but it wasn't far from Bukowski's Hollywood bungalow. The entire literary elite of L.A. was there by the time we arrived. Mostly it was young male poets and small press editors. A couple skinny hippie chicks and some very attractive and standoffish big city black women. Bukowski sat in an old easy chair in the livingroom, next to a big overstuffed bear of a poet. I won't mention his name, but he carried around all of his poems in a manuscript book which he read from in a rolling boom that sounded like fake Dylan Thomas. He told me that he used a pen name because he had abandoned his wife and kids and he was hiding from justice. I didn't like the guy at all; I thought he was a pompous ass. But Bukowski liked him. I couldn't understand why he would want this big fraud blowing off steam in his living room.

On the other side of Bukowski was a petite, pretty French woman of about fifty. At first I thought she was Anais Nin. She seemed like a fake too. Very refined, but phoney. What did he see in these people?

I almost expected to see Henry Miller come strolling out of the kitchen, asking for a corkscrew.

Copies of the new book were stacked on a table, for sale for $1. I didn't have a buck, so I passed. I looked a copy over. It was a crude mimeo production, with poems by Linda King and maybe also some by Bukowski too. I read a few; they were good. But I was broke. I had spent my last dollar at the 49er.

Locklin had brought a six pack or two of Coors, tall ones in cans, and Bukowski said there were plenty of bottles of Bud in the fridge. I polished off two of Gerry's Coors, then went on to find the kitchen.

Soon I was very drunk. I was standing in the kitchen with Dana and Bukowski, all three of us drinking from the brown bottles of Bud. Bukowski was telling us that he hated parties, that he couldn't stand to be around people. "I only do it for the girl," he said, refering to Linda King.

Dana asked him a lot of questions and he was very kind to us, tolerated our presence in the kitchen where he had gone to escape the crowd.

Bukowski lit a cigarette and pulled at his beer. He looked like a terminally ill man. I saw the tiny veins on his nose, the broken red lines crisscrossing the surface of mottled flesh. He said he had been sick, that he was cutting it down to a little beer and a little wine and staying away from the hard stuff. He hacked and coughed and spit a clot of blood striated mucus into the sink, then flicked the ash off his smoke into it and rinsed it away with tap water.

He opened another bottle of beer and offered us the same.

In Linda King's bathroom I saw the typical and usual paraphernalia of normal existence; the uncapped wreck of a tube of Crest; mouthwash, pink and joyful in an economy sized bottle, a spray can of Arrid Extra Dry, floral scented toilet paper. Drunk as I was, it seemed a grand revelation: Charles Bukowski brushed his teeth and gargled and sprayed and wiped just like the rest of humanity. Suddenly he didn't seem like such a giant. The Old Lion was just a tired old alcoholic who also happened to be the best poet around. Genius was just an accident that had happened to him. All over Los Angeles, a million men just like him in every other way were drinking and watching TV and fighting with their women. The only difference was the poetry. Nothing else mattered.

I began feeling claustrophobic. I needed to get away for awhile to get a grip on myself.

I stumbled into the back bedroom where Linda King's kids were watching an episode of *Star Trek* on the color TV. A cosmic demon in a shimmering silver robe was melting away under the unforgiving stare of the disenchanted space orphans. It was Dorothy and the Wicked Witch of the West all over again. I gave in to the fantasy.

Actually, I was hiding out. I didn't want to fall on my face or pass out or get into a fight. I was afraid I might say something rude to Bukowski, to intentionally provoke him just to see how he would react. So I stayed there in the back room with the TV and the kids nodding off in their pajamas until I had regained control.

When I got back out to the living room the party was in full gear. Bukowski and Linda were dancing to the Stones' "Honky Tonk Woman" and people were yelling and the room swirled.

On the fireplace mantle were numerous little twisted and sculpted lumps of clay, and beside them a large, rough hewn clay bust of Bukowski. Linda King saw me examining them and came over to tell me about them.

She was a good looking brassy southern woman of about thirty-five with long sassy brown hair and a voluptuous body. She reminded me in a silly way of my Uncle Duke's ex-wife, the one he met in a country-western bar. She wrote poetry (Linda King, not Uncle Duke's ex) and she was a sculptress as well.

I admired the bust, although really I thought it was a hunk of shit.

"It's going to a university up north," she said. "They have a Bukowski archive, they're saving all of his books and letters and manuscripts, everything he does, and they want the bust too."

"Did you make these?" I asked, picking up a gnarled clay breast.

"No. Hank made those. He makes a whole bunch of them and then throws them away if I don't save them in time."

We got off the clay and started talking about music. I mentioned Bob Dylan, one of my big heroes of the time, but she didn't like him at all.

"He's a phoney and he whines. He gives me a headache," she said.

Dana was leaning against the dining room table. Linda King went over and sat on the table next to him, her thigh against his. I saw Dana's hand on her ass, cupping, rubbing. They were talking in low tones. Soon they were dancing together, closely, romantically.

Out of nowhere it seemed, a roar, a deep bellowing as Charles Bukowski stormed across the room in a rage, screaming at Linda.

"WHORE!" he cried over and over, "WHORE!"

John Kay appeared from thin air, as if he had been waiting all night only to save us from the impending disaster.

"I gotta get you guys out of here," said John. He hustled us out to the night air, towards his car. He was more sober than Dana or I, so he drove. On the freeway home we talked it over. Dana couldn't understand what the big deal was.

"I was only dancing with her, that's all."

"No," said John, "He saw you patting her ass. He thought you were trying to make his woman, that you were taking it away from him."

We made Long Beach, dropped off Dana, then John and I went to the Christian halfway house where he boarded and both had a bowl of granola mix and milk to try and sober up.

The next day, a Saturday, I woke up with a terrible hangover. I was still too young to know the remorse, the regrets that later accompanied such mornings, but I was sick enough to not want to go anywhere or talk to anyone. That's when I discovered that I had somehow left my keys at the party, at Linda King's house.

I called Locklin and told him my problem. He filled me in on what had taken place after we left the party.

"Bukowski yelled some more at Linda and she said he was acting crazy. Then he stormed out the door and got into his car and roared off into the night."

Locklin gave me Linda King's phone number. I called her and explained my problem. She didn't remember me, but she said it was okay to come over and pick up the keys. I drove to her L.A. address with my wife. It was a bright day, the palm trees still against the sky. In the daylight, I saw for the first time that she lived in a relatively quiet and comfortable old residential neighborhood, unlike the battlezone where Bukowski lived.

I walked up to the door while my wife waited in the car. I knocked and Linda came to the door. Again, I explained.

"I left my keys last night."

"Sure," she said, "come on in."

"I'll just be a minute."

Bukowski, who kept his own place in Hollywood when he wasn't staying with Linda, was nowhere around. I was glad of that. I found my keys and beat it the hell out of there, afraid that he might show up after all. I imagined he'd be sicker and more hungover than I, and still angry. I had no desire to face his rage.

Dana was worried that Bukowski wouldn't forget the offense, that the Old Lion would hold it against him. Dana had a theory that Bukowski hated the young poets because he was old and he was afraid that the young would take it—the women, the poetry—away from him. The Old Lion was defending himself. Dana agreed with him in principle, but hoped to God that Bukowski had merely forgotten the whole incident. It worried Dana and he asked John, Gerry, and I if we thought it would present a problem if he should happen to meet Bukowski again. We told him not to think about it, that it was probably all an alcoholic blur by now in Bukowski's mind, but Dana was still worried.

* * *

The flyers were up all over campus: big 11×17 inch posters printed in stark black and white advertising the second annual Poetry Week. Bukowski's face was everywhere, in the Student Union, in the cafeteria, pinned up on the cork bulletin boards in the hallways of the Humanities Office Tower. John and I spent an entire afternoon sticking them up.

The night of Bukowski's reading, Locklin picked him up in Hollywood and John and Gerry took him to a Mexican restaurant for food and drink.

About a half an hour before the reading was to begin, I found Bukowski, Linda King, Locklin, and John Kay walking up the hill towards the lecture hall where about a hundred students were gathering. Bukowski said nothing when he saw me, and I joined them. Apparently he had either forgotten about Dana and I, or he didn't associate Dana with me, or he just didn't give a shit one way or another.

As always, he was a nervous wreck over having to read. John handed him his check and he stuffed it into his shirt pocket. Then he bent over and vomited in the parking lot near the Student Union Buildings.

"I always vomit before a reading. Steadies the nerves," he said. He and Linda walked arm in arm towards the building. I followed a short ways behind.

It was a vastly different reading than the daytime one I had seen last year. The crowd was lively, demanding and somewhat hostile. A long haired hippie in the back of the room kept calling out to Bukowski in the middle of the poems, heckling and asking rude questions. "Fuck off, mother!" muttered Bukowski in stride, not missing a line.

He was drunk and getting drunker. The more conservative professors were lamenting having spent university funds bringing him here.

He read new poems this time, not the classic old poems, and it was tentative and uneven. Some of the poems seemed inadequate, unfinished. He was trying out some recent work and it wasn't quite going over with the audience. He fumbled words now, his voice trailing off into inaudibility at the end of each poem. He insulted the audience between poems, saying: "You just want my blood, my bones . . ."

Then it was all over and he seemed very glad of that. I had suppressed an impulse to call out during the reading, to ask him how he got to be such an ugly man, and now I was glad I hadn't spoken. It was over and he was happy. He had the check in his pocket. He suggested to one and all that we go over to the 49er and get shit-faced.

I drove home first to clean up, figuring that I'd show up an hour later at the bar and not be so noticeable. My new copy of *Erections, Ejaculations, Exhibitions and General Tales of Ordinary Madness* was on the kitchen table. It was a thick white paperback with a brutally ugly photo of Bukowski on the cover. On impulse, I picked it up. Dana and I had talked about having him sign some books while we could. But we weren't sure we should; it would be an imposition and he might be annoyed. What the hell, I thought. I took the book with me.

Bukowski was on a barstool near the door, Linda beside him, a tall glass of beer before him, a cigarette with long ash burning. Students kept coming up to him and talking, asking him the obvious questions about literature, his books, and his life. They wanted a piece of him to take home, a hunk of flesh from the rotting corpse. He hated them, he tolerated them.

Dana and I sat in the back near the pooltables.

"Think I ought to ask him?"

"I don't know," said Dana. "I thought about it but I chickened out. Now I kind of wish I had brought a book or two along to have him sign. We'll probably never get another chance."

I had the book, but I couldn't get up the nerve to go through with it. We walked back and stood and watched the people playing the pinball machines.

"He's the Old Lion," said Dana, "he despises the young poets. He's afraid of their balls. He's afraid they'll take his place and he knows that someday maybe one of them will and he dreads that."

I went up to the bar with my copy of *Erections, Ejaculations*, etc. and said something to get Bukowski's attention.

"Leave him alone!" said Linda King, "You leave my man alone!"

"I'm not going to hurt him," I said, "I just want to ask him to sign a book."

Bukowski turned and looked at me with great weariness. I had been at the 49er for an hour and he had been there for two, and he was tired of the game. He was also much drunker than before, and he was getting ready to do something. When I saw the expression on his face, I wished I hadn't come over. I lavished praise on him, trying to mask my fear.

"I loved the stories, they really ripped my head off."

"Bullshit," he said.

He took the book, carelessly dropped it on the wet bar, and roughly opened the cover, pressing it open in a manner that suggested he had no regard for literary artifacts. With a ballpoint pen he made a wild, messy drawing of squiggles that looked like two big figures—he and Linda—with lots of little figures—the students and hangers—on and sycophants—beneath the big figures. On the facing page he wrote "2 U—FUCK OFFF!" and signed it "BUK". Then he scribbled all over his photo on the front cover.

I took the book, feeling like a fool, a worm, an unworthy insect. I took it back to the table and showed it to Dana.

"Damn, now I really wish I'd brought a book," he said.

It was an accident that I ran into him again in the bar that night. I was returning from the pisser and I had decided to stay the hell away from Bukowski for the rest of the evening.

He was dancing alone in the aisle, oblivious to everyone, celebrating his own drunken madness, rising above it all, above us, above the stupid occasion. Above all those who craved a bit of his remaining soul to cherish at their leisure. He was victim, we were carrion eaters. But he was Bukowski, Zorba the Greek, dancing in the midst of death and madness.

I didn't think he saw me passing him, but he caught me with his stare and held me there. I thought maybe he was mistaking me for my friend Dana. We were about the same height and age and both had longish dark hair and wire frame glasses. Maybe he thought I was the guy who had tried to steal his girl. Maybe he thought I was going to ask him for something else. Or maybe he just knew me for what I was, an eager, immature poet who needed to be taught a lesson.

When the arms went up higher above me I knew then that he wasn't dancing anymore and that he was getting ready to do what he had been thinking about doing all night. I knew he would do it and then he would feel better for awhile, he would triumph. I thought about hitting him first, in self defense. I am not strong and I'm not a fighter. If I was lucky and he was drunk enough, I might knock him out. If I knocked him down, he might hit his head. He might even kill himself in the fall. I would be responsible for the death of the greatest poet in America. If I didn't knock him down, he might beat the shit out of me. I decided to do nothing and just watch what happened.

I expected the arms to come down. They'd strike either my shoulders or my head. I might be hurt. There might be ambulances, police.

He hocked and snarled and got up a good one and he let me have it right in the face. I couldn't believe what was happening. He spit in my face.

I got back to our table. No one had even seen it.

"What was he doing over there, what did he say to you?" asked Dana.

"He spit on me. Charles Bukowski spit on me."

Word got around quick about Bukowski spitting in my face. Everyone blamed him. "He can be such an asshole," said Locklin, apologizing for Bukowski. Dana thought the attack was meant for him, and that I caught it by mistake. John was disgusted with Bukowski. Several of my friends claimed they would even stop reading his books.

Naturally, I blamed him not myself. How could he do this to me, a fan who had bought his books and read them, someone who believed in his genius? In time I began to hate him. I wished he would die. I threw away the posters with his picture from the reading. I almost threw away his books, including the one he had inscribed, but instead I put them away in a box.

Eventually, the books came out of the box. They begged to be read. No one else was that good. I had to read something.

With time I forgave him. And I forgave myself for being the guy who got spit on. As I got older and began to grow as an artist and a person, I also began to understand what he did and why he had to do it. And I even look at it as a good thing that happened to me. A sort of baptism by saliva, a cleansing in the blood of the lamb.

SLEEPING WITH THE BARD

Jill Young

Even before he died I was thinking
that I should have accepted the offer:
to meet him, and to fuck him.
My arms were taut then
without exercise—
skin firm and close to the bone,
my neck white, lineless, long.
I had sex for religious reasons;
for moritification of the flesh,
or for charity
not vanity.
I could have enjoyed
him savoring me
for my close grained skin,
for my youth and ignorance,
but I held out
thinking vertigris would gather over me
in a day and give me soul,
give me prominence,
make me woman and real.

If I'd known the bounty of normalcy
I'd have today,
I'd have done it,
that and more,
and recollected here couched in my birthing fat
and milkworn breasts
his pissy breath
his slubbed skin,
the autograph left inside me.

SUBJ: BUKOWSKI BOOK

by Pamela Miller Brandes
aka "Cupcakes"

Needless to say, I have not had time to make a contribution to your new book. What is the title? *Drinking with Bukowski*? I feel badly about that because it was an interesting relationship. I suppose in simple terms, you could liken it to the classic *Beauty and the Beast* syndrome. He had many qualities I wished to possess and vice versa. Anyway, it certainly was not mean-spirited, the way he has described it in his poems and prose subsequent to our break-up. Apparently, as I mentioned to you during our phone conversation, my splitting with him must have cut him to the bone. I had no idea how deep and intense his feelings toward me were at that time. Admittedly, I was quite young and self-absorbed. Hopefully, age has made me wiser and more compassionate. I did love Hank as much as I could love anyone at that juncture of my life and I know he loved me, too. I am very disappointed at the excessive negative hyperbole used to descibe my character in his later writings, but you know what they say about the "pen!"

In retrospect, maybe I deserved some of it. I suppose I should be flattered to have made an impact on the life of such a complicated mind. A genius in the estimation of many people, including myself.

LAUGHTER IN HELL

Harold Norse

Charles Bukowski first wrote to me in the spring of 1963 when I was living in Paris at the "Beat Hotel" with William Burroughs and other Beats. Another resident, Kay Johnson, corresponded with the unknown Bukowski. She said he admired my poems in *Evergreen Review* which kept rejecting him. His next letter was to both of us, followed by his book of poems, *It Catches My Heart in Its Hands*, inscribed to me with a flattering dedication. I was impressed and recommended him to Fred Jordan, Grove Press' editor of *Evergreen Review*. His poems were accepted.

That Spring the hotel was sold and I left Paris. In London I met the poetry editor of Penguin Books, Nikos Stangos, who offered to publish a book of my poems. They also ran a series of three-poets in one volume which sold better than the single-poet books. I chose the trio (Ginsberg, Ferlinghetti, and Corso were in the previous one). Surprised at my choice, Stangos was even more surprised when I chose Bukowski. "I never heard of him!" he said. "You'll hear of him soon," I replied and lent him *It Catches My Heart*. It caught his heart and the rest is history. He also agreed to my third choice, Philip Lamantia. I made a selection of Bukowski's poems and the book appeared a year later in 1969. We got great reviews and international praise.

I had repatriated in 1968, settling in Venice, California, where my mother had moved from New York but I had no idea it was only a short drive from Bukowski in Los Angeles. We continued to correspond and phone each other before we had met. Then, during the most violent storm in thirty years, he appeared at my door, soaking wet. He was polite and respectful, still reverent, and from then on we remained in close contact. We fascinated each other but I had to deal with his mood swings, fueled by alcohol. He admitted that he "tested" his friends—Bukowski-speak for offending them. I saw him as an American Céline, compelled to jeopardize his relationships.

He was working at the post office and phoned daily, drawling in a monotone full of despair, "Hal, I can't go on. It's destroying me." He said if he hadn't kept on writing he'd have killed a fellow worker or committed suicide. I gave him all the moral support he needed. Then I heard that he slandered me behind my back but praised my work. When I mentioned this I'd get an evasive response: "I have been faithful to thee in my fashion." If he put you on a pedestal he'd also knock it over. It was a bumpy ride on a roller-coaster. Though his admiration was genuine, ups and downs were the norm in his relationships. If he admired you he was also consumed with envy and jealousy—the real motive for his backstabbing.

The letters read like an epistolary novel or a play or prose poems. Confessions, feelings of elation, depression, angst or amusing and bizarre experiences pour out in a spontaneous cascade of words. Humor leavens the complaints. We always complained. It was our only means of catharsis. We pulled out all the stops and let go like two operatic tenors in a duet with our tragi-comic arias. I think the correspondence contains some of our best writing. But it's not for the squeamish. These personal letters were raw, candid autobiographical documents of self-exposure by two writers with their eyes on the prize. But our personalities couldn't have been more different.

Hank played games and stirred things up. Once while strolling on the boardwalk in Venice near the liquor store on Windward Avenue, we spotted an old wino yelling obscenities and challenging invisible demons to a brawl. Hank's face lit up. "Hal, let's have some fun with this guy!" he said. "Watch this!" Waving his small fists menacingly, Hank began teasing and taunting the wino, who swore in a thin, quavering, boozy voice and staggered off. "It's like bullfighting, Hal," Hank crowed triumphantly. "You gotta know the moves or you get gored." "Sure," I said. But I didn't find it amusing. I thought it was pathetic. While Hank callously gloated I felt sorry for the old wino.

Finally, thanks to his bad-mouthing, I quit corresponding. I knew he couldn't control himself but I was offended (I can't recall why). Then I regretted the silence and wrote him in March 1989 for permission to use excerpts from his letters for my autobiography, *Memoirs of a Bastard Angel*. He responded warmly but I was shocked at his condition. He was seriously ill. The thought of his mortality suspended all judgments.

> "Death, of course, is the ultimate relief, I have no problems there, it's just being half-assed that galls. I'm going to send the okay off to your publisher. Yes, I met Schwarzenegger a few times. The first few times he was almost modest. Then he switched over to this satisfied stupid slob thing. Saw him at a party once, puffing on his big cigar. I walked up behind him and said, 'Arnold, you used to be a nice guy but now you've turned out to be a piece of shit.' Luckily, I didn't get killed. You've got to be lucky. Even typing this I am getting drained. Luck with your book and if you say some nasty things about me, that's all right. Sure, old timer, Hank."

I assured Hank there'd be no "nasty things," only the truth. But truth *is* nasty and stranger than fiction. I often wondered if Bukowski knew the difference. Five paragraphs below, starting with "On one of his visits," I submit an example of the thin line he walked between fact and fiction.

Six weeks later, handwritten in large print, all capitals, his last letter arrived, ending twenty-six years of correspondence:

> HELLO HAL—JUST CAN'T WRITE. MORE HOSPITAL TESTS, SOME NOT SO GOOD. TOTALLY DRAINED. JUST TO SIT DOWN AND ATTEMPT TO PAY A GAS BILL TAKES A GREAT ACT OF WILL. TRY TO UNDERSTAND. YRS, HANK.

I understood. The booze, the lifestyle had taken their toll. Despite his depleted energy he enclosed a separate handprinted page for the publisher of my *Memoirs*, William Morrow, Inc., authorizing me to quote from his unpublished letters. Though "totally drained" he was considerate. This was the kinder, gentler Bukowski beneath the bluster. I felt acute remorse about my long silence.

His letters portray the early struggle for success in the midst of what grimly looked like certain failure. He had beaten the odds. But the one thing we can't beat was looming large. I didn't feel too good about it.

* * *

In the '60s Bukowski had a long row to hoe before his success. In one letter he called me his hero and I repaid the compliment. For me, I said, it was like corresponding with Van Gogh. His use of language conjured up in my mind, the mad Dutchman's use of paint, like a force of nature. Hank's insides were rotting away from alcohol abuse but through those terrible early years he had an uncanny ability to infuse ordinary language and situations with life and humor. Coarse and vulgar, yes, but he turned pain into pleasure and the commonplace into fantasy with style and imagination. For example:

On one of his visits to Venice, where I lived in an old red-brick apartment house on the corner of Paloma and Speedway, a block from the beach, he passed out on my living-room couch, dead drunk. About 3 A.M. I had to pass by him on my way to the bathroom. Slumped in a sitting position under the still lit floor lamp, his green eyes half-shut, he was chuckling and muttering to himself. When he saw me he yelled, "HEY, WHO THE HELL ARE YOU, MOTHER? WHAT'S THE NAME OF THIS SHIP? I GOTTA TALK TO THE CAPTAIN! I'VE BEEN SHANGHAIED GODAMMIT! I'M AN AMERICAN CITIZEN! CALL THE CAPTAIN!" On and on he raved, talking to himself and chuckling. He didn't know where he was or who I was.

Later that morning, hung over and cold sober, he grinned. "Hey, Hal, where's the cabin boy? The kid with the long blond hair? When did you sneak him in? Ah, you sly old dog! Buggery aboard ship, eh? C'mon, Hal. What did you do with the hippie cabin boy?"

"Threw him overboard," I said, smirking. "He was a bore."

Hank was convinced that I had smuggled a beach kid into the flat—or *cabin*. Only a delirious drunk or God or Hollywood could create two people out of one. A fifty-two-year-old brunet doubles as a teenage blond boy in a two-room seaside flat that's also a pirate ship at sea? This was serious. Was it delirium or madness? No, it was a hallucination. I had a sudden glimpse into the dark interior of his mind. In the silence of the night the waves could be heard and he *was* dead drunk. To him the ship and the cabin boy were real. The line between fantasy and reality was thinner than air. With or without alcohol or drugs, fantasies are a major source of material for writers. The line between fact and fiction is blurred. In Bukowski's mind reality and fantasy merged, giving everything an imaginative twist. This is what made his letters as fascinating as his fiction and poetry. But it doesn't make his relationships fascinating. For better or worse, he saw people through a glass, drunkenly.

* * *

I also corresponded with writers of the older generation, warm friends like Anais Nin and William Carlos Williams, until his death in April 1963, when I received my first letter from Bukowski. Williams was more than a friend, he was a surrogate father, a master, an influence. He singled me out as Bukowski did after him. In his letter of 7/6/66 Bukowski wrote: "old William C. Williams knew a poet when he saw one. I wish I could use the language like you. You have all the words and you use them exactly . . . I don't have the words, I am afraid of them. I work with black and white and dirty stick."

Well, hardly. That dirty stick was a magic wand. But it was good to know that, for all his bragging, Bukowski had moments of self-doubt. Maybe not moments. Maybe years. Those were his post-office years, the darkest. His letters were full of suicidal despair, but he was becoming a great writer, a one-man revolution. He always knew it. But if I hadn't put his foot on the first rung of the ladder would it have happened?

Rereading our letters I felt his presence again and contacted his widow and sole heir, Linda Lee Bukowski, for permission to publish them. He'd have liked that. She granted it and I was struck by her intelligence, warmth, and literary acumen. I had never been in contact with her but now we had long phone talks about this book. I said that though we had never met I felt that I knew her. She said we *had* met at a reading I gave with Allen Ginsberg in Los Angeles in 1977. She was there. She said we shook hands afterwards.

I believe Linda made Bukowski's last years worth living. Loneliness would have been a bitter irony. But, as he always said, he was a lucky man, though not so lucky in his suicidal post office years.

In his journals of the '90s I noted that the tone, though still insolent, had lost its attack mode. Dissatisfaction and insecurity were gone. Savage indignation was gone. Mellowness replaced bitterness. Still belligerent, scornful, and insulting, to be sure, but no more messy blood from open veins. No madness. No desperation. The style was smooth, the tone confident. The words flowed like wine, no longer vinegar or lava. They exuded assurance and satisfaction. He had a great wife, a home, a swimming pool, a BMW, nine cats, a Hollywood movie, world fame. He had found peace at last.

In a letter to Carl Weissner, our old friend and famous German writer/ translator of our work and the Beats, Bukowski writes (September 28, 1967):

> "our man Harold in London, as you must know. his physical self still low but his spirit will mystify Scotland Yard—received a 3-page letter from him on yellow paper. a literary masterpiece and no charge. seems strange, weird to be hooked up with these great souls of the universe. I am grateful."

Our letters were a dialogue, like a play or a movie. He hated Hollywood until he got rich and famous with his movie *Barfly.* It brought international stardom.

He was a kind of François Villon, a poet of the people who *lived* the life of the underdog—slummy bars, cheap whores, dingy furnished rooms, squalid tenderloin districts. The tone and language reflect this drab existence.

In 1969 he gave me an inscribed copy of *At Terror Street and Agony Way* where he writes: "You too have lived on the terror streets of our turdy world. To know you has been grace." This association copy sells for over a thousand dollars, a sum that would have changed Hank's life at that time.

The other day I found my copy of *Post Office* which Hank had sent with the tender inscription: "For Hal Norse—I wish your ass had been in the Post Office for 12 years. Keep the cattle out of the corn, Charles Bukowski—July 25, 1974. A belated birthday gift. I sighed at this touching reminder of his sentimental nature. And it's only one of many deeply-felt inscriptions like the poignant one in *The Days Run Away like Wild Horses Over the Hills* where he writes: "To Hal Norse—LOVE, LUB, LUB, LUB, TO YOUR ETIRETY [sic] OF YOU + WHAT HAS KEPT US BOTH, 1-8-70-." The first blank page he filled up with his pen-drawing of a big dog with a big dong and Hank's inscribed message. "BET HIM!" Bouquets and stilettos mixed with moaning and groaning a la Bukowski and his most admired friend and wordsmith.

In a brilliant essay on Gertrude Stein, Katherine Anne Porter wrote: "Who wants to read about success? It is the early struggle that makes a good story." That's what our relationship is about.

Bukowski was lucky but so was I. In the vanguard of a new way of writing, I had close ties with other poets and writers who changed the second half of the twentieth century in American literature and social behavior—the Beat Generation in particular. I knew them when we were young and unknown in New York's Greenwich Village in the '40s. Writing saved *our* lives.

"I'M PRODUCING STEEL, MAN"

Harvey Kubernik

I used to read his column in the *Los Angeles Free Press* when I was in college. Around 1972, I was published in that same paper. The *FREEP* ran an interview I did with keyboardist Brian Auger, and I was invited to some of their office parties.

In 1976, I went over to the *Free Press* Hollywood Boulevard location for a hang and nosh. Charles Bukowski was at this get-together. I checked him out, was given a brief introduction, but didn't talk much. As usual, I was too busy discussing records and helping somebody out with a problem. There were hardly any girls at this reception, and most of the people were over thirty!

I think it was Bukowski who suggested to a friend of mine to make a liquor store run across the street.

Then Bukowski started to make a move like former Dodger baseball player Maury Wills inching off first base. I monitored his actions like viewing a slow-motion Zapruder film. Bukowski approached my pal's wife. She had a ring on her finger. Then the guy did some dirty talk while pawing her with a rap. She was a big girl, could handle the graphic proposition, but still was shaken. Then the beer arrived. The man and wife, now a lawyer and author both wishing to remain anonymous, quickly split the scene. I had to hitchhike home to West Hollywood. Personally, I thought Bukowski was rude.

Tommy and Miles, who lived in East Hollywood down the street from him shrugged off his "actions" and informed me "that's the way it is."

His own interviews were revealing and candid. I will always thank him for introducing me to the writings of John Fante, one of his heroes and buddies.

In a twenty-five-year period before his death, I'd run into Charles Bukowski all over Los Angeles. One time, after visiting D. Boon, Mike Watt and Splat Winger in San Pedro, Boon told me to go to a restaurant Seven Seas for a meal. The place was closed, so I drove over to nearby Ports-o-Call to eat some chopino. Pulled my car into the vast parking lot, and right next to me came a black BMW and out popped Bukowski, obviously on the way to the racetrack. It was daytime. He nodded, with those blue eyes.

A few years earlier, we chatted at a screening of Ron Mann's *Poetry in Motion* documentary on Wilshire Blvd. at The Four Star Theater. I also saw Buk a couple of other times at film-related showings. He was very friendly in a movie lobby.

I also caught one of his readings in 1972 at Papa Bach Bookstore. Poet/actor Harry E. Northup was there, and I met the store's owner John Harris. Years later I recorded both writers on an album I produced. I did make it a point to thank John Harris for Papa Bach not just for presenting a forum for Bukowski, Wanda Coleman and others, but because the venue did provide pivotal free draft counseling advice for me right after high school before I obtained a student deferment.

In the mid '90's I produced a poetry reading in San Pedro at Vinegar Hill Books that featured Northup and Holly Prado. Linda Lee Bukowski came to our gig. At the time she was going to her husband's grave three times a week and was very sad. I felt her pain. She grinned when I told her I was keeping tabs on her and I heard that Dave Alvin had visited the day before. I was glad in 1995 when she attended a MET Theater series I curated and helped produce and then she was able to smile. We talked about Bono and U2. I recall her saying that Bono sent a car for them to attend a U2 concert at Dodger Stadium a few years before. I then ran into her at a Patti Smith Long Beach poetry reading.

And how can I forget a 1978 Troubadour appearance Bukowski gave on Santa Monica Blvd. I mean, Louie Lista was the bartender, Paul Body the door man, and Robert Marchese the club's manager. They sent a six pack of Heineken up to Bukowski and it went quick. Denny Bruce was also there.

1980. Friend and mentor, Denny Bruce, original drummer with The Mothers of Invention, was also a record producer who did albums with Leo Kottke, John Fahey, John Hiatt and The Fabulous Thunderbirds. He was co-owner of Takoma Records, a groundbreaking roots music independent label. Denny had met Bukowski a few times over the years, been to two of his Troubadour shows, and even saw a mid '70s "performance" in Culver City at the Robert Frost Auditorium with their mutual friend, Bob Lind of "Elusive Butterfly" fame. In 1978 or '79, Denny's label released *Charles Bukowski Reads His Poetry*, a live LP culled from a Bay Area reading CB gave. Excerpts of that same Berkeley playdate were utilized in the Taylor Hackford directed PBS/KCET documentary that had aired a few years earlier on public TV. When that album was issued, a small press party was held on Sunset Boulevard, down the street from the Takoma/Chrysalis office at the legendary Scandia restaurant. Bukowski got totally drunk, freaked out some of the restaurant people, and was tossed out of the establishment. Denny Bruce at the time was like a Jim Brown figure on the football field trying to demonstrate to everybody how the spoken word and audio poetry game should be played. His style and game preparation certainly influenced the way I eventually produced and created tough stuff and unique, pioneering sound expeditions.

Denny then arranged to produce another live Charles Bukowski session at the Sweetwater Inn in Redondo Beach. I was the production coordinator. That album, *Hostage*, was re-released a few years ago on the Rhino/Wordbeat label, and mysteriously, my name was removed from the new credits.

Anyway, Denny had done his homework, knew the Bukowski book catalog, and lent me some of the titles before we ran tape at the beach. A few weeks before, Joe Wolberg at City Lights in San Francisco had sent down to Denny the first treatment for the proposed film of *Bar Fly*, that director Barbet Schroeder was putting together that featured James Woods and Karen Black in the leads. We schlepped over to The Sweetwater in Denny's BMW. I was formally introduced to Barbet who was there setting up a film camera to capture the evening on celluloid. He was very impressed that I was aware of his movie *MORE*, which used the music of Pink Floyd live at Pompeii. I was given a full access pass and invited to look through Schroeder's lens while supporting Denny at the soundboard. I talked all night with the both of them, long before Schroeder filmed *Single White Female*.

The anticipation of this particular Charles Bukowski poetry reading reminded me of *The Last Waltz*. And, like Bob Dylan, circa 1966–1973, Charles Bukowski wasn't reading often in public, especially around

Southern California. Ninety percent of the crowd seemed to be literature students from nearby Cal State Long Beach. There were all sorts of people at this show that twenty years later I still see and talk to. Eddie Call, then in the Marina Swingers band, was the bartender. He and staff were instructed to serve Bukowski. No tip at the end of the night.

Drummer Phil Bunch sat at the front of the stage. During soundcheck we kept going back and forth covering Bukowski and Bob Marley. Jim Dunfrund, of KXLU-FM was there and is still on the air hosting "Surf Wave" at the beach radio station. I had a good time carrying tape boxes, sorting out reels, testing microphones. Denny Bruce oversaw the recording operation like General Patton. He had a hunch this "endeavor" extended way beyond the normal defined show time. I laughed when he said, "we might be going into an overtime game." I didn't realize immediately what he was talking about. I found out later. It was apparent, that over the years, Denny really wanted to do a proper recording with Bukowski. As an A&R man, he'd been in discussion with the old man for a decade.

I'm not here to review the "recital." The edited results are available on *Hostage*. At the Sweetwater event, Bukowski drank four bottles of wine out of a water tumbler. You can hear the clicks and glass noise on the tape. When Denny later prepared the CD version of *Hostage,* he did eight years of additional editing so the slurry speech and pauses could be presented in coherent form. To hear the album now, it's like a good heavyweight fight where performer and crowd went the distance. Years ago, Denny, Miles Ciletti, and myself did a whole week at Kitchen Synch listening to the show. We would laugh out loud as one of the engineers would cut tape on the splice block. "Who is this guy?"

It's too bad I didn't have my own camera or a supplemental cassette machine at the Sweetwater. There were a lot of geeks in the house. You know, guys with first edition books begging for autographs, frat boys shoving their own writings at Bukowski, "Check out my stuff on computer!" and a whole bunch of cooties with ancient columns, now yellow with age, wanting Bukowski to personalize the newsprint with a signing. I was amazed that there were some pretty good looking girls in the orbit who somehow came out of the woodwork, hugging Bukowski, congratulating him after this alcohol-driven engagement. A few grabbed him for hugs and kisses. He turned to Denny and myself and uttered "Why does all the cunt show up at 54?" Afterwards, Denny asked me to guard the master tapes and equipment as he and Bukowski went to another room with Richard the club's co-owner.

Then there was a hassle. We knew the money was taken care of well before the booking. In fact, the wad bulged out of Bukowski's front pocket. Bukowski then pulled a pen knife out and jabbed it right into the desk of the owner asking for his money, forgetting the bread had already been paid. Everyone tried to calm him down and then Charles reached for a smaller knife and proclaimed, "I'm producing steel, man." Bukowski's friend Joe Wolberg managed to put him into a headlock and then took him away. There was a lot of static in the room and Bukowski's final words of the night were "the only reason you booked me into this clip joint was that you could hit on Linda."

Before the first version of *Hostage* came out I thought it would be a good idea for German film director, Wim Wenders, to write the liner notes for a projected German territory release. He was very receptive, invited me to the set of *Hammett* that he was doing for Zoetrope Studios. Apparently, he had been a music journalist and critic, liked Bukowski, and we all understood the market for a German audience that existed for oral Bukowski. The liners didn't materialize, but nearly 20 years later I ran into Wenders backstage at a Tom Waits concert in L.A. We were reintroduced and he mentioned he still had the original disc I sent him. In the early '80s I eventually asked poet/writer Kenneth Funsten to do the liner notes for the album and he really delivered. His text augments the aural Denny Bruce production. Decades later, the recording still makes me laugh.

To this day, I don't own any books of Charles Bukowski. Close friends have full collections. Over the decades I've pulled them out and read sections and specific poems when it seemed like I had to at the moment. He always had the ability to make you laugh and make you sad within the pages of any book. His columns for the *Free Press*, and *Open City* were raw and regional. I felt he was talking to me. I went to Fairfax High, he graduated from L.A. High. However, we both worked different sides of Western Avenue I worshipped Ole Sole Mio Pizza parlor, he cruised past Stan's Books, and went inside bars.

His poems to daughter Marina were a sharp contrast to the darkness and Celine-type climate that permeated some of his work.

What I've really learned in reviewing and examining this L.A. public school system product, is of how much an impact he had on independent publishers, small magazines, and the pre-fanzine nation who printed his poems, writings and drawings. Sometimes a Charles Bukowski short poem or doodle could help a chapbook or an out of town little magazine survive until their last issue. He helped create a DIY circuit that both captured and documented himself as wordsmith. In addition, it's pretty obvious that the man sent stacks of mail out regularly, and bundles with poems going in and out every week. His hunger, desire, literary ability, poetic observations, and need to be acknowledged must be applauded. And, this neighborhood cat really hit for the cycle starting in middle age through the end of his life.

About twelve or fifteen years ago, I received a frantic evening phone call from Andy Paley, record producer, musician, and a Brian Wilson co-writer. I played on a Paley Bothers session at Gold Star that Phil Spector produced. Rodney Bingenheimer and I provided handclaps on the studio date. Anyway, Paley had been involved in the *Dick Tracy* soundtrack and needed to get a signed Charles Bukowski book for a wedding gift. On my message machine, he said he'd detail it later for me. So I called back and told him to go over to a book shop on Las Palmas in Hollywood owned by Red, a good friend of Bukowski, who carried some rare autographed Bukowski signed books. Andy later left a thank you on the machine and had gone to the bookstore for the item. I thought "What a cool wedding gift." I didn't talk to Andy for like ten years, but I recently ran into him at a birthday party for Rodney Bingenheimer.

"How did that book thing wedding present work out?" I asked.

"Well . . . let me tell you," he replied. "It was a wedding gift for Madonna and Sean Penn. And, months after the wedding, Madonna called one night "Thanks for that Bukowski book. It's contributing to the break up of my marriage. He wants to be Bukowski now!"

from

SPINNING OFF BUKOWSKI

Steve Richmond

First things first, he directs me to the fridge in his kitchen. He tells me where it is and says, "Put the sixpack in the fridge and open up two and bring 'em back out, kid." (I doubt "kid" was said so soon, but I'm sure of all the words before "kid.") I did as he requested. It wasn't an order. Hell, God, I loved being there.

I go to his kitchen and open the fridge door and note two more six-packs inside. I open two cans and bring them back out to his front room and hand him a beer. He sits on his old sofa and I in an old stuffed easy chair. I think we made a toast but can't remember. I start looking about his front room. It's about twelve feet wide and twenty feet long. Hank's sofa is against the south longer wall.

Ah these beers taste good. Everything is going fine. We have exchanged oral pleasantries and now we're both quiet and relaxed and drinking our fine cold Miller's or Hamm's. Right next to his sofa, to his left, are wooden shelves held up on both red bricks and a few cement blocks. Shelves are maybe three feet long and this setup rises about five feet high. All three shelves are packed with magazines, books, perfect bound, stitched, hundreds of them. Hank's work is published in every one of them. He began writing poetry when he was thirty-five and he was thirty-five in 1955.

I'm sitting in a sort of angle position, facing Hank but I'm closer to the short wall opposite the front door, I mean I'm about 15 feet from the front door.

A big old wooden desk such as one might see in an old post office building or business building is set against this short wall to my right. On top of this desk and along the whole back or so of this desk, Hank has placed an old wooden pigeonhole piece of office furniture. It's about three and a half feet tall and two and a half feet wide and it has about thirty pigeonholes set in three vertical rows of ten holes each. There are thinner and thicker packets of white typing papers in every pigeonhole. The top of this pigeonhole cabinet seems higher against the wall than the top of my head, since it's on the desk and the top of the desk is about two and a half feet high.

Papers and pens and paper clips, etc. are also on top of Hank's desk. It's all very very neatly organized. Immediately I can see Hank's extreme focus and self discipline, just by the way his working papers are so neat, so organized, perfect order. Hank is waging a campaign and his supplies and how he keeps them will definitely not be his undoing. He is taking over modern literature, that's all, he's taking over.

There is the H Bomb Sword and there is Hank's Pen as exemplified by his desk and pigeonhole cabinet on top of it and all those Bukowski writings and copies of submitted writings and letters to his many allies and also his typer against the opposite short wall next to his front door and on top of the little typewriter table. And don't forget Bukowski's authentic place/role in 1965 Modern American Literature, articulated a year or so earlier best by two Frenchmen (Sartre and Genet) who said, "America's best poet is Charles Bukowski." Did they really say it? I'll bet they did.

A couple feet to my left on the old rug is a barbell, maybe fifty pounds in weights overall. Hank sees me noting it and he jokes a little about his exercise routines with it. We're not talking much but we're each through about three beers. Hank gets up and moves to his bathroom, closes the door, and pisses, and several seconds later I hear muffled retch sounds. He comes out, goes right to his fridge and opens a new beer, walks back into the front room again and takes a seat on the sofa and lights his first cigar of the evening, or at least since I've arrived and looks at me and says, "You don't talk much do you?"

No, I don't talk much. What th'hell is there to say? The world's fucked up—the world's fucked up. That's all there is to say.

I didn't say this to Hank. I probably shrugged a little in the easy chair and gulped more beer.

•

Bukowski and I took three different liquor store runs that night. We would buy two sixpacks and on our second run it was I who treated. I think that night started about 8 P.M. and ended around 3 A.M. Drinking partners. We were drinking buddies that first night.

My car was a two-door Chevy II red wagon. I'm almost certain it was I who drove us to a liquor store. He directed me north a block to Sunset Boulevard and east a few blocks to Hobart Street, I believe it was. This was his number one liquor store. I remember us exiting my car and walking in and Bukowski immediately talking with the man behind the counter. Bukowski waved me off when I made a timid attempt to chip in for two more sixpacks. Right at this instant he was like a father. He became a father, taking care of expenses for a semi-son. That's how I felt. I think he sort of felt this too but he wasn't thinking about it. He was taking care of serious business, buying necessary beer. He gabbed a bit with the storekeeper and he was definitely liked in this store. The talk was uphearted and familiar banter between a very good customer and a store—liquor store—man.

Odd that I so clearly remember the liquor store being on the south side of Sunset Boulevard, that I remember distinctly the time being about 9:30 to 10:00 P.M. and the street lights and dark navy-blue night-time and he and I getting out of my car and walking on in the place. He's in charge, he's the leader, he's full of purpose and gusto and not a single speck of shrinking violet in him. He's Leo, he's th'Sun-Julius Caesar-King Lion—a setup for Cassius and Brutus and those sorts of back knifers because his *TRUE GRAND STYLE MAKES THEM CRINGE WITH VIRAL JEALOUSY/FILTH.*

Style—Gregarious Autocratic Beautiful Glowing Style. Am I Mark Anthony? Hmmmm?

In the store he's my father and I know what it's like to be with a father because my real father Abraham has acted just like this when I've been with him on fishing trips to th'High Sierras, and he takes me into a fishing-supplies shop/sporting-goods store maybe in Lone Pine and/or Bishop on our way to Convict Lake for rainbow speckled and cut-throat trout. My dad Abraham is in charge in those sporting-goods shops picking number ten hooks and three pound leader, etc.

Two Pops. Beginning at the liquor store I've suddenly got *two pops:* one for my Spirit (Hank), one for my Bank Account (Abe).

Lucky me. I mean it. Very lucky me.

We mostly sat and drank beer after beer. I didn't talk much at all because he was wise, a true sage, and I wanted to hear him, not me. He began selecting various copies of books and magazines that featured his work and one by one signed and handed them to me as gifts.

Now he gets up and walks to his head for a leak, or his kitchen for another Miller's. I'm sure we're drinking Miller's. There will be no Miller's Light for another decade or longer. He walks back into his front room. Before he sits again he goes into a bit of a boxer's crouch. Just part way though, not a full crouch. He subtly raises the topic of Creeley and Olson. He says something that is a slight put-down of Creeley/Olson. Immediately he raises his face in a quick glance my way, as if to see my reaction to his quite moderate criticism of Creeley/Olson.

I mention Creeley's *The Island*, a novel I'd read about one year earlier. I told Hank that I liked this novel. Hank's face is not glancing at me now. His face has returned to a thought reflecting expression. Hank isn't looking at anything in particular. He's thinking, relaxed, wise, eyes almost closed, face directed a little downward and to my side. It's a wonderful shot for me. I mean like a camera, his face is beautiful, particularly in that soft glow of low to moderate lamplight. I'm catching the greatest literature maker on Earth in relaxed contemplation. I'm not flattering him, he's dead now, why should I flatter him now? To make myself larger? It's possible. To me now, 1965 then, he hasn't changed in so far as he's Earth's finest literary communicator. That's fact. Not flattery. Not me going gaga over Hank. Take it or leave it—you will anyway.

Pardon me, it's better I describe like a witness under oath, rather than pontificate like a lawyer paid to horseshit. 1965—his three-quarter profile in orange-gold shadow—*alive*—there's th'word I've been seeking. He's *alive*, thinking a bit, amused in his reflections, contemplations, musings, now about Creeley/Olson and just how much I'm a believer in those fellows and their works. He's checking me out if I've gone over to Creeley/Olson, Creeley really. Creeley is Hank's real competing suitor for th'brass ring . . . *If I've gone too far over for Creeley, then Hank has no choice but to forego paying for the next two sixpacks*. I'm no fool. It's been a minute since any talk so I let go, "Eh Creeley, he's a condescending prig. Yeah I liked *The Island* but only because I actually finished reading it."

Hank looked at me now. He studied me, eyed deeper into my visage. Was I conning him? That's how he looked at me. Then he said, "Let's go," and we were off to the liquor store again. Maybe the store was up on Hollywood Boulevard instead of Sunset. We were both drunk. I think he drove this time. He drove slow, took side streets skirting the Hollywood Freeway. Yes, the liquor store was on Hollywood Boulevard and Hobart Street. The southwest corner. On the drive back to his place the streets were very dark. He drove very slow, very safely.

There was a phone call—it was Curtis Zahn calling. Zahn lived in the Malibu Colony. A year earlier New Directions Press published a collection of Zahn's short stories. I remember trying to read them. I couldn't get into his tales. His writing style seemed rather entangled to me and there wasn't room for me to squeeze in, find a comfortable spot to relax, stretch out, read his inner-gut vision. There wasn't an inner-gut vision at all, his mind was writing, it seemed to me. Cerebral web strands, thin. Anyhow every second or fourth Tuesday, I think Tuesday, Zahn hosted a literary workshop at his Malibu Colony beachside home. Three months into th'future I would attend one of these gatherings, but now Hank was on the phone with Zahn and the two of them were bantering, kidding each other some.

All I heard was Hank's side of this conversation; however I'll bet this is how it went:

CURTIS: "Well how's it going Hank?"
HANK: "Pretty good, Curtis. How's your book from N.D. doing?
CURTIS: "Oh they're not doing very good getting it out there. Eh, not so hot, Hank. How's *It Catches My Heart in Its Hands* doing?"
HANK: "All sold out! It's aahhhlll sold out, Curtis. OK! OK! See ya then, Bye Bye . . ."

Hank hung up and laughed, really happy, enjoying himself more than at any other time that evening of my first visit. He made obvious to me his satisfaction at getting th'better of Curtis Zahn. Clearly, Bukowski didn't care much for the Malibu Colony writer. I just watched, took a gulp of my beer, and watched Hank glow in happiness and some sort of debt paid back in spades—squared. Zahn was what I would call upper crust L.A. Literary. He and Hank were about the same age. I guess they were peers—competitors—seeking the Brass Ring of Modern Literature. Fighting each other and a thousand others over it. Zahn would disappear. You know what would happen to Charles Bukowski.

During the phone call Hank showed me his "rascal side." He was wonderful, an old delightful scoundrel. A master . . . a style . . . a confidence. One had better be with him because there was no beating this man, especially by someone as inexperienced as myself. I celebrated with him while silently realizing he was a tough son of a gun. That's why I was mostly reticent, keeping my yapper shut. What could he learn from me? Maybe something about what the young were up to. Maybe it heartened him a little to find out there was at least one among the young who could keep his mouth shut.

Hank had a good time. Not once during those seven hours or so did he show the least ire, sadness, disappointment, with me. Through the years he would, but not that first evening.

•

Hank and Neeli and myself were drunk one night. We'd been either at Hank's De Longpre pad or at my own cave, drinking, yammering, insulting all others except us three. Hank said, "Where are the girls? We need WOMEN! Let's go get some WOMEN! Where can we go? I need WOMEN now! What are we doing here? This is empty! Steve, where can we go for women? Girls? Hmmm?" (Now I remember we were here in my cave). I was just a few years out of UCLA and for some reason I thought of Lum's in Westwood, a college alumni beerhall plus lousy grilled food. There are always young blond billboard-like beauties at Lum's, I knew. So we drove to Lum's in Westwood. It was about 10:30 P.M., maybe 1968 or so.

Lum's was packed with huge muscled ex-UCLA football players and just as many Blond Pretty Billboard Spearmint Faced 21-22-23-year old white but very tanned ex-sorority girls. Neeli and Hank and I took seats at the one empty small table next to the open but metal-faced entrance area. I had my back to the UCLA campus—I was facing South. Neeli and Hank sat opposite facing UCLA; Hank sat to Neeli's left and we ordered huge schooners of good, cold, golden, deep-golden beer. The place was packed—th'place was *packed*.

Neeli, Hank, and I, not only do not fit in but we are so different than all those Beta UCLA frat alumni ex-jock types & Kappa Gamma & Theta & Pi Phi sorority all-American Cheerleader pom pom girl sorts that I'm seriously wondering why on God's Earth I was cretin-ish enough to bring Hank and Neeli and myself here.

Waitresses pushed through holding trays high with huge beer mugs and full pitchers jiggling above 'em. I looked at Hank and then I looked at various Hitler master race specimens both female & male all blue eyed & real blonds and then I looked at Hank—I kept glancing at him to see what he felt about this place & these *Christian* Revelers.

Hank didn't hide his feelings—he got that bored "what the shit" look which told me he felt all these young ones were shallow billboard zeros and looked seriously at me—in my face he looked—and I thought I heard him say, "What th'hell we come here for?"

". . . what'd you bring us here for?"

And I was asking myself this same question—it was a mistake—but this was Okay with me because the general rule about Richmond was all's well unless *he doesn't make a mistake.*

Hank kept looking back over his left shoulder at various amazing tan blond young women and then he would face me again and he'd grab his mug/schooner and take a huge Bukowski-chug-a-lug. He was getting higher, drunker, more rambunctious. All the blonds seemed to know each other and also seemed to be *happy!* Maybe they were celebrating something—a UCLA football victory earlier that night? A win over USC at the L.A. Coliseum? Maybe it was something else out those hundred-plus tanned blond UCLA handsome/pretty young ones were simply *joyous* and they all absolutely treated Hank and Neeli and myself as if we were *in toto invisible.*

Hank got drunker and started swinging his left arm out behind him at some of those ultra-perfect tight girl asses which were well within his reach. I got anxious! These fuckers were violent: these were Hitler's people and they could suddenly pick us three up and carry us, pass us from claws to blond tanned claws over their heads to Lum's Kitchen Gas Oven and nobody would know a thing. We could be cooked with wieners and burgers and chips and secreted out Lum's backdoor and stuffed in garbage cans and . . . but fortunately this didn't happen that night.

Hank was going even more sort of ape-crazy now swinging his left arm and graspy fingers out behind him, behind to his left, precisely ass level with the standing blond tan girls trying to squeeze through the Aryan college crowd. Then Hank would face front and face me and grab his big mug and gulp again longer and deeper. I was pissed at myself for bringing Hank and Neeli to this place. I was getting more scared. Hank began making palm/fingers contact with real beautiful young tight girls asses and ". . . oh my . . ." I thought, this is it.

I was wrong. When Hank grabbed and squeezed a girl's butt/gluteus maximus/buns each time the girl would sort of look around and down and see Hank and *then* (I tell you this is completely true) proceed to give forth a small yet moderate, toothy-warmish-cute smile sort of vaguely in Hank's direction. It was as if she really liked it and enjoyed such fingers/attention/touch of the authentic Apollo Sun God/master scribe magic pet-touch-caress, and what was peculiar to me was that when this girl (there were about five different girls) looked and glanced vaguely toward (level and downward glance) Hank, it was as if she didn't see him and was sort of looking through *whoever did it and whoever did it* was invisible to her. But this was just a wee side experience, a small warm enjoyable tangent, practically unnoticeable by her and within two or three seconds she looked ahead of her trying to find a crack in the standing meshed bodies so she could squeeze deeper into Lum's Beerhall. *Amazing amazing absolutely Grace* is what I thought to myself. For me it was surprise and paradox and one more miracle of Hank's unique Magic, this time while out in th'public unlimelight.

Jesus man, I tell you I was stunned. After this same exact thing happened with blond tan cutie #3, I lost my fearfulness. Neeli? He sat in his chair occasionally gulping his beer and kind of huffing and puffing in place and mumbling a little about what a group of shallow unappealing young folks we were in th'midst of. I think Neeli didn't react at all to Hank's moves. Neeli hung out with Hank about fifty times more than I and so Neeli probably knew full well there was nothing, nothing at all to get scared about. Hank was Magic and Neeli was Hank's door-stop. Hank wanted Neeli to be more than a door-stop but Neeli didn't seem to want to be promoted beyond his expertise.

I don't remember us leaving Lum's, nor which of us drove, but I have a blurred trace of memory that Neeli was the only one of us to order some food. Neeli took care of business first when food was served him. I knew there was no way or anything I could say at all to Hank to restrain his left arm grab/swings.

•

I asked Hank for advice—once he said, "DRINK, WRITE, AND FUCK."

This came right after I complained about being bored about something. "Only the boring get bored," he commented. He was about nine feet from where I now type . . . his back to me as he was headed to my head—for a beer piss.

Another time, at his De Longpre pad, I believe, I was leaving and heard his last words to me, "Never under-estimate th'woman . . ."

He also included this phrase in a letter. I could be wrong about whether a letter or in person or . . . No! I know he said it aloud right in this room as he moved to the head because I remember his back. "Only the boring get bored."

Then me, ". . . so what should I do?"

"DRINK, WRITE, AND FUCK!"

AN AFFAIR TO REMEMBER

Karen Finley

"Charles, I'm pregnant." I said while sitting on the edge of the bed unwrapping my baguette from the cafe.

He didn't turn around but continued doing the crossword puzzle in the *National Enquirer*. "What was Geena Davis's first role on television?" he muttered.

I stared at him again and wondered if I should repeat the news, cry, or become even more emotionally distanced than him.

"The show was *Buffalo Bill*," I said blinking.

"That doesn't help me. That's the show title I want the character's name . . ." Charles puts the pencil down but still doesn't look up. "Go to Mexico. I know a doctor there."

"Chuck, abortion has been legal for over a decade. Besides, we're in St. Barths and nothing happens between Christmas and New Years. We're supposed to be on vacation." I reminded him.

Bukowski was sometimes disorientated from his years of drinking but that wasn't the issue here. The issue was Brautigan.

"You went to Mexico when you got pregnant with Richard," he said hissing. I could see the spittle spray on to the newsprint image of Mary Tyler Moore.

I sprayed back. "Yes, and that was when abortion was illegal! You can't let him go can you? Besides he's dead! He's dead! I was only a kid."

"Yeah, Frieda Kahlo was a kid when she met Diego Rivera and SHE NEVER LET HIM GO! Her entire life's work was about having babies, not having babies, Diego Diego. Diego is present in Frieda's work. Richard Brautigan is in your work. It never leaves a woman," he theorized.

"I don't think Richard has influenced my work," I said because it was my turn.

"You both write bad poetry."

"You're wrong Chuck."

He turned toward me now for I called him CHUCK. Calling the great, brilliant writer CHUCK always got his goat. No one called Charles Bukowski "CHUCK." Not even Sean Penn. And for greater impact I called him CHUCKEE when one of his many wives called, to let them know I was in charge. "CHUCKEE! Linda is on the phone. FrancEyE is on the phone.

I know what you are thinking. You think I'm a bitch. But I had to call him CHUCK and deflate him a bit for I couldn't depend on the BRAUTIGAN ISSUE to get his attention that was reserved for special occasions.

Take Note----------THE BRAUTIGAN ISSUE

Trout fishing in America, The Abortion. Oh, that Richard Brautigan.

I met Richard Brautigan at Enrico's cafe on Broadway Kearny down the street from the City Lights Bookstore in San Francisco in 1971. It was 1:30 A.M. and I had just ended my shift as a cocktail waitress at the infamous strip club The Condor. Enrico the owner of the bistro wanted me for I was underage and looked it. HE promised to set me up in my own apartment. HE never had me but would rub my knee while I ate my club sandwich and drank my hot cocoa. HE would always give the taxi driver ten dollars to take me home.

Enrico intriduced me to Richard Brautigan in mid January and it surprised Enrico when I told the table that I had written a term paper on him the year before as a sophomore in high school. That is when Enrico stopped wanting me, for the turn on was that I knew nothing and now that I revealed myself I would have to pay for my own damn sandwich. I knew Brautigan's poetry by heart and when I spoke Richard became enamored. Richard was drunk, despondent, depressed, and disillusioned but I was a devoted fan.

So that is how I met Richard Brautigan. I later met Kathey Acker as my teacher at the San Francisco Art Institute, who introduced me to Gregory Corso, who introduced me to Bukowski at Brautigan's funeral.

The Brautigan issue for Bukowski was that I became pregnant with Richard and had an emotionally, high charged, dramatic illegal abortion in Mexico. A conflict and intimacy that Charles grew envious and jealous of as his feelings for me deepened. The fact that I actually read Brautigan and never read Bukowski made matters worse. So now you know. I had an affair with Bukowski and never read any of his goddamn books. I loved him for the man and not for the writer and it tortured him.

Charles had returned to his daily crossword habit and I watched him spell Geena Davis's name in twelve down and I tried again.

"CHUCK, we need to talk . . ."

"Karen what's Jim Rockford's father played by?"

"Noah Barry."

"Is that with an E or an A?"

"Chuck you are a goddamn Polock."

Charles put the pencil down and this time he glared at me with that man testosterone look like he's stronger than me, smarter than me, bigger than me, own the whole goddamn world more than me. At that moment I realized Bukowski was in my work, in a reactionary way. Hell if I was ever going to let him know.

He looked at me with his eyes bugging out with the pupils dilated so big they lost all meaning and color. He could do this at will. This look was just as important as his craft with the word. And he kept reminding me of this. "A writer is as important as their reputation." He believed this so sincerely that he sometimes isolated so he wouldn't appear too happy or content. I tried to remember this while looking into his eyes as he said sternly "If you have that baby I'll change my identity and leave the country."

I turned over to give him back some of his own medicine and said, "Who do you think you are? Jack Kerouac? Jack wouldn't have to say it. He was man enough to just do it."

Oh, this made Charles mad. And he was trying hard not to show it. So I turned the screw more.

"Why don't you have a vasectomy or become a faggot like Burroughs."

Many homes have rules that are just left unsaid—no ball playing in the house, no hat wearing at dinner but in this house it was no reference to Burroughs. I used the word faggot before he could because every other word out of his mouth was faggot. I think it was more generational than actual homophobia but I never let him get away with it.

My morning sickness had worn off so I unwrapped the egg salad baguette. I didn't even get it in my mouth.

"You're eating egg salad? Do you know what that cholesterol will do for you? Mayonnaise! On white. Karen, this is awful for you."

"What do you want me to eat? Ham on Rye?" I answered with no expression.

"Charles, it's Christmas. It's Christmas. Yes, I'm eating egg salad. I'm in St. Barths. We're on a French Island. They couldn't wrap the salade nicoise. So what. No one tells me what to eat. I feel like I'm in *Pygmalion*. I don't think I want to be in this relationship anymore."

"OK. OK. I'm a noodge. But you are going to end our six month affair over a sandwich." He explained.

"Charles, it's more than that. You are so controlling. Cleaning up after me. Refolding my clothes. Restacking the dishes. Reclosing the lids after I do on the Chinese takeout containers. And last night you woke me up at a quarter to four to ask me why I wasn't as successful as Laurie Anderson! Karen, Karen why can't you be like Laurie? It was fucking Christmas Eve."

"Karen, and what did you answer?'

" 'Cause I don't play the stinking electric violin." I chuckled.

"Well, Lou Reed probably wakes up Laurie and asks her why she can't be like Karen Finley, take off her clothes and stick a yam up her ass."

I had to laugh at that but I had thrown my egg salad sandwich away and it was hard to stay in character. I was an emotional wreck. I wanted the baby. I wanted this repulsive, neurotic, drunken slob genius's baby. He stood up and said, "Let's get Peg and go for a ride."

Charles had a dog at that time named Peg. The dog had only three legs but could run like any other dog perhaps even better. I would hold the dog in a little knapsack as we rode on the motorcycle going through the traffic in St. Johns. We let Peg go off on his own through the tourists begging back in his own turf. He loved that little three legged thing. I don't know what this has to do with the story but I felt I should tell you that Charles was an animal lover.

Charles also believed in plastic surgery. And before he died he was seriously considering a facelift. Charles loved to make fun of me being a feminist. And one night while we were still in St. Barths listening to Mozart—I think the Magic Flute was on—I commented on our hostess's beauty and he reminded me that she had had a facelift, maybe two. We both agreed that she was beautiful to begin with but I knew he was looking for an argument. And did we have one. We fought over the aesthetics of fake breasts. Our argument was always the same that I felt beauty was in imperfection and he always felt that was insincere intellectual rubbish. That he had seen both pleasing natural breasts and ugly natural breasts and pleasing fake breasts and ugly fake breasts. And that he had had sex with women with fake breasts and liked it. It went on and on till we reached the topic of nursing and La Leche League. He ended the argument with accusing me of being so politically correct all the time and that I was so conventional and that I was a conventional beauty and that if I went into a shop no one thought I was a shoplifter but when he entered a store they wanted him out.

I answered with, "They want you out of their store 'cause you smell like the bottom of a beer cooler." He laughed. He was endearing.

I only saw Charles get angry in public once and that was when he wanted his bottle of Perrier on the table with his dinner and the waiter would have nothing of it. The waiter was new at Elaines and for some reason the waiter liked to keep the Perrier off the table and do the refilling himself, like champagne. The waiter probably thought he'd get a bigger tip. But Bukowski was on the wagon and liked his water on the table like his scotch. What was funny was that Charles was stoned sober but he grabbed the waiter by the neck and gave him what his reputation was built on.

On the last day on St. Barths we somehow got locked in the villa. The inside lock broke and all the windows had hurricane shutters. It was simple and complicated. We had to call the United States to get the phone number of our hosts so they could send the servants to let us out. But Charles became obstinate in his machismo. Issues about his father. Things I learned later that I was insensitive to, should have been more empathetic to, were being triggered. And I just laid in bed laughing like I was on an episode of the *Dick Van Dyke Show* and I rolled in laughter with tears streaming down my face. Charles continued to refuse to call for help and the more he refused the more I laughed. I couldn't help it. He just refused to call for help.

"I'm Charles Bukowski and I'm not calling to have some servant open a door for me. No one opens a door for Charles Bukowski. I've opened every one of my own doors." I'd never seen him so sincere in protecting his reputation at all costs, at any means necessary. That was when things fell apart for us. We enjoyed life differently.

But there is one thing I regret in not telling Mr. Bukowski. I never wanted Brautigan's baby but I wanted his baby.

THE POEM WILL SAVE YOU

Raindog

"even their nightmares are ringed with tinsel"
—Charles Bukowski

It's the middle of May and a warm tropical rain is falling
turning dusty streets into greasy ones.
I'm reading the newest book of poesy
from my favorite, now dead, poet
and marveling at his clarity and the strength of his lines.
He said it
"The poem will save your ass from madness"
The poem will save you
while fat drops of acid rain descend
while the bills pile up
while the paint peels
while you wait and wait and wait
for something to change
it doesn't matter what it is
as long as it's something
The poem will save you
while your auto insurance climbs

while the phone screams your name
while the pipe calls to you
from the other room
while your heart considers the pros and cons of retirement
while the beer goes flat
while the women come and go
while you jerk into the hollow memories of their brief
laughter, with legs spread wide
while someone lets the air out of your tires
the wind out of your sails
the joy out of your days
while the life seeps out of your windows
while the warranty on your vcr runs out
while the internet sucks you off
while the open grave waits patiently
and the orange waits to be peeled
and the lights flicker
and the ground moves
and the really important stories wait to be t/sold
and the needle crawls across the floor
like an inch worm
while you wait for its promise of happy stupidity
while you binge on lollypop dreams of power and glory
while you starve to death
twisting in the wind
The poem will save you
The poem will save you.

from

NOTES ON A DIRTY OLD MAN

Neeli Cherkovski

Bukowski called. "I've got the blues, baby, the deep blues. Can you make it over?"

"Sure," I said. My apartment felt like a steam bath. Bad air hung over the city like a sheet of iron. Before leaving, I glanced over to the shelf holding Bukowski's works. I let those old titles, the ones printed on the book spines, tumble through me: *Run with the Hunted, Confessions of a Man Insane Enough to Live with Beasts, All the Assholes in the World and Mine, Crucifix in a Deathhand, Notes of a Dirty Old Man, and At Terror Street and Agony Way.* The poet's originality came through, even in his choice of titles. Looking westward from Los Angeles, he would not think of Japan and China across the wide expanse of the Pacific. His vision would stop at the Santa Monica Pier, where some old guy might be throwing his line into oily water while a cop beat on the head of a wino on a landing under the pilings, his badge illuminated in a glint of moonlight.

Charles Bukowski. Henry Charles Bukowski. I drove to see him as stucco fell off the windmills of Mykonos. The sky was the same color as the face of the man dying in the window across from my place on Alta Loma. I paid sixty-five dollars a month to surround myself with death.

I passed Sunset Boulevard, heading east, passing the Hollywood Memorial Park, where I had snuck in one night to fall asleep, done in by cheap vodka, on Tyrone Power's benchlike tomb. Then I took a turn north on Normandie, arriving at De Longpre, a street lined with huge palm trees that have been there since the days of Fatty Arbuckle. In the middle of the block sat an old Ukrainian Orthodox Church, its spires rising toward the sun, and across from it a low, pink building. Hollywood Rest Home, which provided Bukowski plenty of opportunities to fantasize. He would say, "One day I might be sitting in one of those cold, sterile rooms, helpless. Then you can come in and dance around my body as I sit there trying to raise my arms."

I pulled up to his place, the first apartment in a shoddy court, rented from one Peter Krate, a short, bullnecked man who liked to drink with his famous tenant.

"He's in," Krate said, as he watered the thin strip of grass between the driveway and his units.

I stepped up to the porch and knocked. Bukowski called out, in that slow manner of speaking he had, "Hold on, baby, I'll be right there." A voice strong and resonant, not unlike that of Humphrey Bogart.

A few minutes later, the door opened and there he stood, Henry C. Bukowski. Hank. Beastbuk. The Outsider. Good time Charley. Charles. Never Chuck. That is one name he would always run from, quickly. He looked like an iguana, taking one step at a time, eyes leering from side to side. The only soft thing about him was his hands. He used to say, "Look at my hands, kid. See how delicate they are." He was old-time L.A.: cool, slow to praise and slow to censure, yet quick on the rejoinder. His hair was carefully combed straight back; a casting director looking for a character in a screen adaptation of Raymond Chandler's *The Big Sleep* would have gone no further than Bukowski.

"Come on in, kid," he said, "I'm on the cross, tricked by mere horses. It was murder out there. Nothing was right. Even the grandstands lost their edge of glory and the once-beautiful ladies looked like subnormals."

I stepped into the cavelike front room filled with cheap furnishings. The most important item in the room was the manual typewriter on a stand adjacent to the front door.

"Forget the track. At least you're making it with the writing," I said.

"If you call getting an invitation to submit poems to some mimeo magazine in east Dallas success, then I've really made it," he said. "These magazines appear out of nowhere. Any kid with fifty bucks can purchase a mimeograph and crank out forty pages filled with typos and call it a magazine. I mean, sometimes there's good stuff in these babies, but mostly . . ."

"But you have books out," I said.

"You do have a point there, kid. I can imagine some coed back East reading *Terror Street* and forming my name slowly on her lips, Bu . . . kow . . . ski. Bukowski. But where the hell is she and where are the moneyboys, for Christ's sake?"

He was in his bathrobe, a beer in hand. I saw a sheet of paper in the typewriter with a few lines typed out. He had been writing a poem when I knocked on the door. I felt a little guilty, but he was the one who had phoned.

"Grab a beer," he said. "When you get back in here from the kitchen, maybe you can tell me, when does the pain end? I want to know, when does it finally cease?"

"Jesus, Hank, you're supposed to have the answers . . ." I responded.

Bukowski worked for the U.S. Postal Service back then. It was housed in a huge, Spanish–style building, downtown, next to the old Union Depot where trains from the East came in. It bore the graceless American title, Terminal Annex Post Office.

"They got me on a treadmill," he said as I came back into the small living room, carefully avoiding the beer bottles scattered on the floor. "I stand there and sort these letters into their appropriate slots. What a dead-ass job. Me. Bukowski. Tough guy."

"You might make it someday with your prose," I said, "and then you can quit."

"I hope to hell I can, Neeli. By the way, they have openings for the upcoming Christmas season. I have pull down there. Do you want a job? Might do you some good. Look what it's done for me."

He always tried to make me suffer in one way or another.

"Thanks, Hank. Some other time."

Rachmaninoff blared out of his cheap radio, against which a half-dozen books, all written by him, were propped.

Henry Charles Bukowski was born on August 16, 1920, in Andernach, Germany, a small town on the Rhine River. The son of a German mother and an American GI father from Pasadena, California, who met his bride-to-be during the World War I, he was brought to Los Angeles at the age of three. His father held small-time jobs, and the family lived on the edges of the middle class. Speaking of the period, he said, "I remember the kids at school whose families had money. These kids would go on to the universities. All I looked forward to were shipping clerk jobs, road crews, and loading docks. Exactly where I ended up. Hell, I used to go down to Skid Row just to check on what the future held in store for me." The closest he ever came to big money was his one-year marriage in 1956 to Barbara Frye, a poet and heiress to a Texas fortune.

I first heard of Bukowski in 1960 from the poet Jory Sherman, who arrived in San Bernardino from San Francisco with crazy Beatnik stories. He had a packet of press clippings on his sixty-five unpaid parking tickets. He told me about a man in Los Angeles named Charles Bukowski who had just published a chapbook of poetry, *Flower Fist and Bestial Wail.* I liked the title. Sherman said, "He's not one of the Beats. This guy is totally his own man. Hardly anyone knows about him except a circle of writers who contribute to the small-press scene."

Bukowski was just over forty years old. He had grown up in the Depression and World War II. The Beat scene bored him. Sherman kept promising to introduce us. Finally the day came when I was told that Bukowski would be coming to visit. I was fifteen and Bukowski was forty-two. When he arrived, I feigned sleep. He walked into my bedroom with my father who said, "Wake up. Bukowski is here." As I got out of bed, before me stood this large man with a ravaged face, broad shoulders, and deep, penetrating eyes.

"Okay, little Rimbaud. I heard you wanted to meet Bukowski," he said. Then he looked at the photos of some of my literary heroes on the wall and said, "Jesus, how come there are none of me?"

We went into the living room. I handed Bukowski a handmade book of poems I had written about him. He took one look at it, reading the first few lines, and threw it into the fireplace where my father had made an inferno.

I dove in after the book, managing to save it. Only the fringes were burned.

Bukowski took it from me, saying, "I'll read your little poem, but no one has ever written about me. I'm sorry, kid."

Fifteen minutes later he was in the kitchen trying to make love to my mother. "Come on, Clare," he said, "I'm more of a man than Sam. Let's make it."

Two years later, a small press in Florida published a collection called *Poems and Drawings*, followed in the same year by *Longshot Pomes for Broke Players*. I carried those books around everywhere. Occasionally I would call Bukowski. Having noticed that we appeared opposite one another in *Epos*, a small magazine, he said, "Hey, kid. Are you going to crowd me out of the journals?"

I thought of him as a weathervane of the human condition. He hadn't bought the Eisenhower decade, nor did the Kennedy cult of youth and glamor impress him much. In Bukowski's view, a blanket of doom lay over the country. In "the house" he put it simply:

> It seems people should stop working
> and sit in small rooms
> on second floors
> under electric lights without shades;
> It seems there is a lot to forget
> and a lot not to do
> and in drugstores, markets, bars,
> the people are tired, they do not want
> to move, and I stand there at night
> and look through this house and the
> house does not want to be built;

I began picking up the literary journals and found Bukowski represented with increasing frequency. There was a tough edge to the poems I had never seen before. I felt the way he did. When I read him, it was as if he had pulled me over to his side from the rotting hulk of school and everything else that oppressed me. It wasn't so much what he said, but his attitude that crept up on me slowly. Unlike the Beat poets, his declamations were subtle. They were interwoven with storytelling in the classic sense of the word. I loved the deliberate misspelling I found in the title of *Longshot Pomes for Broke Players*. Another book from those years, *Run with the Hunted*, he signed, "For Neeli Cherry. I hope I have awakened some of your young sleep, Charles Bukowski." Next to it was a picture of a man smoking a cigarette with a postscript beneath: "God, you should have heard some of Franky Roosevelt's fireside chats."

In 1969 I received a late-night call from Bukowski. "Listen, kid. We're going to be rich and powerful. I met an old school friend who wants to invest some money in a literary magazine. You'll edit it with me. I've even got a name, *The Contemporary Review: A Non-Snob Compilation of Active Creativity Now*."

"It doesn't fit. We need a tougher, wilder title, something different than the others," I said.

Less than forty-eight hours later the phone rang.

"This is Bukowski. I got the title."

"Go ahead," I replied.

"*Laugh Literary and Man the Humping Guns*, publishers, Hatchetman Press."

"You got it," I said.

The promised investment, however, was not forthcoming. We had to find the money ourselves, producing a photo-offset magazine of forty typewritten pages. We took poems from writers we knew in the L.A. area. After the first issue, hundreds of submissions began pouring in. Most were attracted by the idea of having something published in Bukowski's magazine.

"This is frightening," he said. "All this shit arrives in the mail, to my address. It's depressing."

Often we'd only read the first poem in a five- or six-page manuscript and then send the entire thing back without going further. One drunken night Bukowski wrote, "These won't do," on a rejection slip and returned it to a prominent professor of creative writing. Then I wrote, "We wouldn't publish these if our lives depended on it." After that Bukowski went into the kitchen, got an egg, and cracked it into a dish. He crumpled a manuscript and dipped it into the dish. I added beer. Then we went to work on another manuscript, burning tiny holes in it. Next we wrote obscenities on various rejection notes. By the end of the evening we had disposed of forty-five manuscripts.

The following morning we both felt a tinge of guilt, which grew over the ensuing weeks. Always, Bukowski hoped for a new discovery. He wanted "that tough e.e cummings in bronze" to break on through. One hot summer night he thought he had made such a discovery. He called, saying, "I have a great writer here. You must come over, immediately."

"Hank," I said, turning on a light and glancing at the clock, "do you realize it's 3:00 A.M.?"

"Doesn't matter. I have been reading these poems for hours. They have power. This is what I have been waiting for."

"Can't it wait a little longer?"

"No, it cannot," he said with finality.

I drove to De Longpre Avenue and soon found myself standing before my co-editor and a poet named Tracy Gross. He sat across from Bukowski, his eyes glazed over with impotence. And yet, I thought to myself, what do I know? Perhaps I had been mistaken when I heard him read at the Bridge in the Saturday poetry series.

Bukowski sat in an overstuffed chair next to the radio stand. Empty beer cans littered the dirty rug. He handed me Gross's stack of poems. First, I wanted to relax. We drank and talked about women, poetry, and ourselves for a few hours. Finally Bukowski asked me to do my job as an editor of *Laugh Literary*. I took a poem from the stack and began reading. The first poem was called "Twilight L.A." It began:

> The ravens call
> from streets of light

where darkness darts
and women rape the wind
I stand aside
to dream wonderful dreams
of where the raven pecks
at life

It did have something in the first four lines. Then I read another poem, worse than the first.

When I finished, I looked up at Gross and then over to Bukowski. They were smiling at one another, hardly aware of my presence. I handed the poems back to Bukowski. "Why don't you do a second reading?" He began to read. And, as the first rays of dawn entered through the curtains, forming a perfect halo around his head, Bukowski said, "Jesus! This stuff is horrible! They don't make it. Not one of them. There is hardly a line with backbone enough to stand up until noon."

Suddenly Gross shot out of his chair, grabbed his manuscript from Bukowski's hands, and turned to me as he left: "You ruined it. Things were going fine until you showed up. He loved my poems."

Bukowski leaned over in his chair and said, "I'd like to thank you for saving me from those poems," after which we drove to Norm's, an all-night restaurant on Sunset that served a $1.49 breakfast special. We would go there often, laughing at ourselves, one another, and the customers. This morning it was Bukowski's treat.

but this thing upon me
as I tear the window shades
and walk caged rugs,
this thing upon me
like a flower and a feast,
believe me
is not death and is not
glory
. . . .
this thing upon me
crawling like a snake,
terrifying my love of commonness,
some call Art
some call poetry;
it's not death
but dying will solve its power

Bukowski's "love of commonness" is what held him together and forced him to stay with his stories, and eventually led him to poetry. He wanted to communicate what he perceived as an intensely personal, wholly original vision. Yet he could never rid himself of the Romantic myth of the artist.

> and as my gray hands
> drop a last desperate pen
> in some cheap room
> they will find me there
> and never know
> my name
> my meaning
> nor the treasure
> of my escape.

He sees himself as the tough guy from the streets, but that self-perception masks a vulnerable, sensitive writer unable to shake off feelings of being somehow different. Yet being different, and his embarrassment about it, is a theme to be dealt with: "I apologized for the beer cans, my beard, and everything on the floor," he writes in "I Am Visited by an Editor and a Poet."

There are few writers as unaffected by the idea of demonstrating their proficiency, the number of tricks in their respective bags, as Bukowski. Los Angeles, which he celebrated for the common sights, sounds, and banalities others made light of or used as reasons for sociological essays about the profanity of modern civilization, had sunk indelibly into his consciousness. His novels, *Post Office, South of No North, Ham on Rye,* and parts of *Women,* offer keen insight into the life of Los Angeles. Bukowski's deadpan style and humor come through as a saving grace, making Los Angeles the perfect atmosphere for his characters, most of whom struggle at the low end of the social scale.

Humor, which he once told me had been part of a dialogue he held with himself as an adolescent, was his secret weapon against the dullness he sensed around him. "Humor kept me alive. Being able to laugh at others, but also myself, helped make me a writer. This, with commonality of tone, is my strength," Bukowski said.

One of his recurrent themes in conversation centers around the image of men being turned into hamburger, working in factories or in deadening office jobs. Through writing, he became a voice for those who lived oppressed lives. People who didn't normally read, let alone read poetry, suddenly found themselves picking up his books and reading them. The humor in his work served to make him even more popular and accessible. There was no program for social action on his part. He took life and hammered it down onto the page, almost always with himself in the foreground, so that his writings became a kind of ongoing journal. A reader can pick up Bukowski anywhere, at any point in his life. "When people read me," he said "I want to think of them as not reading literature, but actually participating in life."

His narrative poems place him outside of the mainstream of post–World War II non-academic poetry. This was not a problem for him. He had built his reputation in hundreds of small poetry journals that had published him from the late 1950s on into the early 1970s. The weekly column, "Notes of a Dirty Old Man," in *Open City,* a Los Angeles weekly newspaper, made his a well-known name throughout the city. The columns were collected in a book with the same title, becoming an instant underground classic.

By then the man who had been named Outsider of the Year in 1963 had clearly defined himself as a nonpolitical, working-class man who just happened to write poetry and prose. His motifs—centering around the battle of the sexes, the impossibility of maintaining a sane and rational relationship, the crises with landlord and boss—had been poured in concrete. Ezra Pound, T. S. Eliot, William Carlos Williams, W. H. Auden were all internationally known literary figures. The first two had fled what they saw as the vulgarities of America for European values, embracing the literary past while, paradoxically, inventing their own radically new forms of expression. Williams stayed home and spent his life insisting on "American Speech," yet he steered clear of street lingo. Eventually in *Paterson*, he began utilizing his own specialized literary techniques, formulating a virtual "policy" for the direction of contemporary American poetry. Auden fled Europe for America, but rarely stepped far beyond his rational sensibility. Even the Beat poets, from Allen Ginsberg to Gregory Corso, often weighted their work with traditional literary devices and language. Ginsberg leads us back to Whitman, Christopher Smart, William Blake, and, eventually, the Hebrew prophets. Corso continually evokes the spirits of Keats, Shelley, and Poe. Bukowski rarely goes much further than the Los Angeles city limits. The poem "the tragedy of the leaves" captures the life Bukowski celebrates:

> and I walked into the dark hall
> where the landlady stood

execrating and final,
sending me to hell,
waving her fat sweaty arms
and screaming
screaming for rent
because the world had failed us
both.

Bukowski chooses Los Angeles, swimming in it. In an anthology of L.A. poets edited by myself, Bukowski, and Paul Vangelisti, Bukowski wrote in the foreword: "You know, I can't think of another city that takes more mockery than Los Angeles. It is the unloved city, it is the target. We contain Hollywood—and in a sense, Disneyland . . . we are corn. We are mistakes . . . I think it is important to know a writer can live and die anywhere." And, indicative of his deep personal feelings about life and literature: "The true Angelo also has a certain sophistication—he minds his own damned business."

Bukowski's writing celebrates the aroma of hamburgers frying in the pan, the generalized daily life of the American. In his short stories he pries apart the eternal struggle between male and female, exposing the whole agonizing process while turning it into a mad, nonstop comedy. For him, the comedy of life is ever present. He grew up reading James Thurber, and echoes of Thurber's "battle of the sexes" can be seen throughout his opus. With Bukowski, people aren't so much destroyed as pulled along their varied paths of the tragic and comic, always managing to blend in with the urban landscape without succumbing to it. Even as they drown in back rent, cheap booze, lousy sex, and cars that stall as they are backed out of the driveways, they are bathed in a certain glory. The Bukowski of *Ham on Rye* is last seen playing a game in a penny arcade with a young boy. There are two boxers; one is missing an arm. The boy chooses the one-armed boxer. He wins both games. It is a bit sentimental, yet taken as a whole, a sweetly humorous snapshot of Bukowski's charm.

Poetry brought Bukowski closer to his feelings more quickly than prose did. He had tried climbing to the summit of literary success with short stories and had not succeeded. In the poem, he wrote with ease, never laboring over lines. After a full day's work at one menial task or another, he would come home and begin typing. His solace was beer and classical music. The many years spent gathering stories for his prose gave him plenty of material for his poetry. As he began corresponding with editors and other poets, and then meeting them, he wrote about the literary life, most of it humorous. What he excelled in the 1950s and 1960s was a poetic style devoid of pretension. It was tough, hard, with a Hemingway-like ease of expression:

> the girls shift buttocks,
> and the Hollywood Hills stand there, stand there
> full of drunks and insane people and
> much kissing in automobiles,
> but it's no good: Che sera, sera

There were also poems dealing with whores and life at the racetracks (Santa Anita, Hollywood Park, and Del Mar). *Longshot Pomes for Broke Players* was dedicated to the jockey Willy Shoemaker. When Bukowski worked at the post office, he would often take a day off, feigning sickness, only to be called and told that he was being docked two days' pay. "Can't you make it a week?" he'd ask the supervisor.

There we were, sixteen of us, all L.A. poets, on the steps of the church on De Longpre Avenue down the block from Bukowski's place. John Thomas and I were the only ones standing. Off to one side was Bukowski with his girlfriend, Linda King, sitting on the steps. Big John Thomas was wearing a Western hat, and his arms were folded. I thought of him as the best poet in Los Angeles after Bukowski, though he kept giving public readings and publishing the same poems over and over again. Paul Vangelisti was there, in the center, a translator of Polish and Italian, book publisher,and poet. Sitting close to Bukowski was Gerald Locklin, a heavyset, bearded poet who taught at California State University at Long Beach. Steve Richmond, author of *Hitler Painted Roses,* sat on the far side of the steps, dark hair spilling over his shoulders.

Bukowski reigned. When the other poets came together, the conversation usually turned to him. This day, as we assembled for our photograph to go with *An Anthology of L.A. Poets,* it was the same. He always had a new book coming out. Some of them, like *All the Assholes in the World and Mine* and *Confessions of a Man Insane Enough to Live with Beasts,* were mimeos badly stapled together, but considered gold to collectors of contemporary poetry. Bukowski's publisher, Black Sparrow Press, had come out with several Bukowski books by the time of our group photo for the anthology. The press's founder, John Martin, understood Bukowski's importance in American literature from the first time he read his poems. He became friend, editor, and agent, literally shaping the poet's career and book projects while promising him a secure future. Martin delivered on that promise in a big way, helping to make the poet a fixture in the American poetry scene and a best-selling writer throughout Europe. Bukowski wrote a warm description of their dealings in an informative introduction to *Burning in Water Drowning in Flame, Selected Poems, 1955–1973*. He used to tell me, "Martin's my man. Anything he wants."

Another photo, of Bukowski and me with an eighty-five-year-old window washer in front of his place on De Longpre, appeared on the cover of our little magazine. My father was taking a photograph of us when Bukowski called the old man over with his washing tools. He wore baggy pants held up by suspenders and was happy to stand between the two literary lights of *Laugh Literary*.

One night in 1972 he invited me to a party for a book he and Linda King had written together, *Me and You Sometime Love Poems*. The party went well at first. Linda's ramshackle rented house in Silverlake was a perfect place for a get-together. The house was surrounded by thick foliage and had a country feel. We were crowded into the small living room with plenty of beer, dancing, and loud conversation. That's when the trouble began. Linda, a pretty woman, shapely and vivacious, seemed to be everywhere at once and always with a different man. Was every male in the room dancing with Linda? Bukowski drank with increased frequency as the evening wore on and shot forth a few warning signs. Finally, when the party had boiled down to Big John Thomas, Paul Vangelisti, a poet named Tony Quagliano, Linda, and me, Bukowski said, "Okay, I've had enough. Linda has been asking for trouble all evening. She can't seem to keep her hands off anyone, including you guys."

Linda yelled, "Can't I have any goddamned fun without you getting jealous?" Her cheeks turned crimson and she fell back against a table stacked with copies of their joint publishing effort.

Bukowski picked up an empty beer bottle and held it by the neck in a threatening manner. "Okay, which one of you guys is first?" he asked, backing against a far wall and looking each of us directly in the eye.

Tony stepped forward, a massive man with a thick neck and gigantic hands.

"You want her, right?" Bukowski asked.

"No, I don't," Quagliano said, holding his ground as Bukowski took one step in his direction.

"Bullshit," Bukowski roared.

"You calling me a liar?" Quagliano asked, shifting his weight from right to left and readying himself for an attack.

Just then Big John moved in on Bukowski from one side and Vangelisti from the other. Bukowski suddenly threw the bottle to the opposite wall, where it shattered. He turned and stormed out of the house. Moments later we heard his engine rev up and he was backing out of Linda's driveway.

Linda ran after him, managing to get close enough to his car to bang on the hood and scream, "I hate you. Oh I do. I hate you, you son of a bitch."

When she returned, we settled down for more beer as Quagliano said goodnight, leaving with a copy of *Me and You Sometime Love Poems* under his arm.

Half an hour later, the phone rang. I was sitting near it, so Linda asked me to answer. "Hello?" I said.

"This is Bukowski. Put Linda on."

"Linda, it's Hank."

"I don't want to talk with him!" she said loudly enough for him to hear.

"Tell me, who's with you there?" Bukowski asked.

"John and Paul. Tony just left."

"Which one of you is going to end up with Linda tonight?" he replied.

"None of us," I said.

Then he hung up.

We finished drinking and Paul went on his way, leaving Big John, and Linda, me.

Bukowski called again.

"Yeah?" I asked.

"Who's left?"

"Me and Big John. Why don't you come back? We're only talking."

"I want you guys out of there," he said, hanging up before I could say anything in response. I glanced at the clock and noticed it was one in the morning.

Five minutes later, the phone rang. "*You sons of bitches better clear out. I'm real mad*," Bukowski growled.

"Hank, I . . ." But he had already slammed the receiver down.

Linda laughed and handed me another beer.

It wasn't long before he pulled up in the driveway. When he entered the room, Linda bolted from her chair, ran to him, and began scratching his face. "You ruined my party," she bellowed.

"Yeah? Well, I can ruin more than that if you want," he shot back.

Big John had slipped out unnoticed. I managed to get their attention long enough to say goodnight. As I drove down the San Bernardino Freeway I realized that I'd left my copy of their love poems back in Silverlake.

September 20, 1963, Bukowski to Neeli Cherry:

> I remember your bedroom and you asleep in there like a sick frog, and pictures of Hem on your wall, pictures of Hem and maybe Faulk and so forth, well, this is better for a kid than Henry Ford and almost as good as ice hockey . . . but look, someday the pictures have to come down . . . and paeans to a minor poet, c.b., must stop. It is pretty hard as you might guess, not to die before the last supper of your thirtieth birthday in our American society, and then you are never safe, you can go at any time like any Mailer, although I do not know their ages nor am I interested. The novel nowadays has become the guillotine. You can last longer in and around the poem although it isn't any news you won't make any money . . . this is stale advice from an old man to a young man

And a few months later:

> Writing is painting and the sooner people realize this the less dull crap will dull the market . . . Picasso does with paint what I would like to do with words . . . a good style comes primarily from lack of pretentiousness, and what is pretentious changes from year to year and from day to day, from minute to minute. We must be ever more careful. A man doesn't get old because he nears death, a man gets old because he can no longer see the false from the good Enough of speech making.

In the summer of 1968 Bukowski and I were going to a party up at Crazy Jack's, a small house perched on a hillside in Silverlake. For the previous two days we had been on a continuous drunk, buying sixpacks and making runs for greasy chicken-to-go on Hollywood Boulevard. Mary, Crazy Jack's girlfriend, had called to invite us. "It's a celebration for Jack's new drawings," she said. "Everyone will be there." For Mary, everyone meant an assortment of hippies, addicts, and small-time hustlers. But I loved her and I loved Jack's drawings. They were done in pen and ink and often dealt with Biblical themes.

Bukowski kept drinking on the way over, but somehow seemed perfectly sober. "Jesus, kid, I hope these people don't bore me," he said.

"You like Mary."

"I know, and Crazy Jack is wild enough. It's the others that worry me. I'm not much with crowds."

"Unless you're the center of attention," I said.

"Well, you have a point, Neeli."

We started up the steps on the narrow sidewalk leading to the house. As we walked, we were called over by a man working in his garden, separated from us by a white picket fence. He turned the earth with a tiny spade and had done a good job for an entire flotilla of petunias.

"I'm all alone," the gardener suddenly blurted out. "That's right. There is nobody left."

He was balding, with a large indentation running across his forehead. His eyes were pale brown and his lips thin. Something about his face made him suspect.

"What the hell," Bukowski said. "Why are you alone?"

"My parents died. Now there's just me. All alone in this house. All alone in the world. Where are you guys going?"

"A friend is having a party up the street," I said.

"Can I come, too?"

Bukowski said "yes," immediately.

"Hold on a minute," the man said, dropping the spade and running in the front door of his house. A moment later he reappeared in a tattered coat, his hair haphazardly slicked back.

"Thanks for letting me come with you guys. I don't get to talk to many people. I get so lonely," he said.

A few minutes later we were at Jack and Mary's door. Mary greeted me with a hug, then turned to Bukowski. "Mary, baby," he said, handing her the six-pack we had brought along.

Our lonesome guest shook her hand and walked inside. He sat on a sofa between two beaded hippies. Bukowski and Crazy Jack were huddled in a corner with Marv Conners, a poet, and Mary. I went into the kitchen to forage through the refrigerator.

Somehow, the conversation got around to the Vietnam War. Mary said it was all madness and nobody should take sides. Crazy Jack, high on pot, began chanting, "Ho, Ho, Ho Chi Minh, the Vietcong are gonna win . . ." As the talk went on, the tempo began to shift. Mary said that the United States had no business there. Others agreed. Bukowski cut in with "who gives a sacred fuck," and I said we were earning the enmity of the Vietnamese people. It was about then that the lonely man from down the street sprang up from the sofa, where he had been quietly sitting. He announced that he had killed ten men in Korea.

"So what?" Bukowski said.

"So I could kill ten more if I had to," the man said.

"That's sick," somebody shouted.

"Yeah!" Crazy Jack said as he threw some of his drawings onto the coffee table.

The lonely man suddenly ran toward the door, turned, and pulled a gun that he waved back and forth. "Okay, now listen up," he said. "I am a killer. It really doesn't much matter to me who I kill or where."

I tried moving slowly toward the kitchen, hoping to escape out the back door and go for help. But he saw me and motioned me back to where I had been standing. "Don't nobody try any shit," he said.

"Yeah? Who the hell do you think you are?" Bukowski retorted.

He ignored Bukowski and said to all of us, "You people never been on a battlefield. You don't know what killing is all about."

Bukowski said, "I don't think you're man enough to pull the trigger."

"Oh yeah?"

"Yeah," said Bukowski as he walked up to the madman, stuck his belly into the gun barrel and challenged him to shoot.

"Go on, baby. I'm ready to die. Shoot," Bukowski said, taunting him.

The man began to cry as Bukowski reached out and took the gun away. After emptying the bullets, he handed it back and told him to leave. The man did not want to go and began pleading to be allowed to stay at the party. "I was just kidding. I promise to be good. I didn't mean nothing bad."

"You could have killed someone," Mary shouted. "Get out of my house."

I opened the door and watched as he walked down the street to his place. Bukowski rejoined the party. The man with nothing to lose.

In 1985 *War All the Time* appeared. It included selections of poetry written between 1981 and 1984. Reading like one long poem, the tone of the book is focused into tight, proselike lines, sustaining the image of a hard-edged observer victimized by mundane situations but never trapped into sentimentality. The speaker in the poems is somehow triumphant in his knowledge of the traps laid before him. Looking through the book, I found a poem about Linda King in which Bukowski accurately brings her into focus:

> she had long hair
> and wild, wild eyes, and
> she danced and pranced up
> there with her poems,
> overdramatizing,
> but she had a great
> body
> and she
> twisted
> it
> and read and waved her
> poems

These loose sections, sparser than his earlier work, are a further affirmation of Bukowski's original impulse to write freed from preconceptions about how a poem should be shaped. The newer work is skillful, yet often lacks the lyric depth and emotional desperation of the earlier poems. With that said, it is still easy to flip through the pages and find brilliant poems and passages:

> I watch the falcon glide
> gracefully
> above the telephone wires,
> it is a beautiful
> thing
> that falcon
> from this distance,
> and, of course,
> it makes me think
> of death
> and death is perfectly
> proper yet I throw my cigarette
> down
> stamp it out,
> look up at the bird:
> "you son-of-a-bitch . . ."

Bukowski and I were involved in one of our wild, drunken escapades. Hours earlier we had come to Shakey's Pizza Parlor up on Sunset, a few blocks from his place. We started at the table nearest the door with a pitcher of beer and a basket of peanuts. After finishing the pitcher and the entire bowl of peanuts, our table was a mess. We ordered another pitcher, thereby earning the right to yet another bowl of peanuts. Rather than return to our table, we went to the next one. Three hours later, eight tables had been messed up by the two of us. Having run out of clean tables, we left the parlor to make a beer run. Returning to De Longpre, we began again, only this time throwing our empties on Bukowski's rug. We talked about literature. "Steinbeck, *The Grapes of Wrath*, think of it, man. Old John S.—*Cannery Row*, a touch of the sentimental, granted, flawing the work, but still . . ." Bukowski mused as we sat in his living room amid the clutter of a twenty-hour drunk. The tape recorder had been turned off hours ago. We now had no imaginary audience to play to. It was one on one, "the old man," as he called himself, and me, "the kid."

"It gives you the chills just to say his name," I said.

"You're sure as hell not kidding, man. Those guys could lay it down . . . blood on the line. Think of them. Think of Hemingway running on home for the touchdown."

"How about Saroyan?"

"A tough daddy. You should read *The Daring Young Man on the Flying Trapeze*. It was revolutionary in its day."

"Wolfe . . ." I said.

"A giant. Jesus, they were the ones I read as a kid. They stood eighty-feet tall, immortal. That's how it seemed back then. If I read them now, I wonder?"

He dismissed most of his contemporaries, especially the poets. "They all fall into the literary trap, even the ones who are supposed to be rebels. It's the same old literary con game."

"Where do you fit in?" I asked.

That was an easy one for "the old man." He took a long swig of beer, leaned back in his chair, belly protruding, and said, "My contribution is obvious. I opened things up to a clear line, so that an auto mechanic without an education in literature or a dock worker in Seattle can read me."

I didn't like it when we drifted apart. I began working a political job in San Bernardino in 1972, imprisoned in a coffinlike building downtown on a federal grant as an assistant to the mayor. From time to time I would read about Bukowski. Once he sent me an invitation to a documentary on his life. I drove to L.A. and saw John Thomas, Linda King, all the old gang. There we were, gathered in the lobby of a municipal building off Hollywood Boulevard, waiting to be called into the civic theater for the film.

Amid the larger crowd, Bukowski seemed unaffected. He and I joked with each other about looking older and things like that. "They're going apeshit over me in Germany," he said. "You got to remember, I'm the hometown boy." A bell rang and we filed in to see the film. I was going off to find a seat when Bukowski motioned me over to sit with him and Linda. When the film began, he took out the bottle of vodka hidden in his jacket. We shared a drink as the film credits flashed on the screen. Larger than life the poet stood, as he bought beer and cigars at the liquor store on Normandie where he and I used to go on our beer runs.

"How are they running at the track?" he asked the man behind the counter.

Thinking of those days when we first met, I remember him saying: "Someday, I'll make it. It's just a matter of time."

But back then, being only fifteen, I had no fix on time or the future. Nor did I have any idea of the long history Bukowski already had behind him: those years in rooming houses, the dead-end jobs, and the loneliness. When he was my age, his face was covered with boils. Other kids were going on dates, he would tell me: "I was on the outside by your age. The ugly kid. Maybe that's why I'd hide from people later on." He could always deliver a clear image of his aloneness and how a poet could grow through and beyond it:

I got somewhat larger
and took my first boxcar
out, I sat there in
the lime
the burning lime
of having nothing
moving into the desert
for the first time
I sang.

6 POEMS

FrancEyE

JUST BROWSING

There you are on the cover 25 years younger with your hair slicked
    back
and your tiny, shapely hands that used to stroke our shoulders
        they stroked Jane's shoulders that are under the ground now
        and Barbara's shoulders and her neck that wouldn't turn,
        and they stroked my shoulders and Liza's
        and Cupcakes's and all the Lindas's
while you told magical stories to put us to sleep—
the world's handsomest man, with scars,
masquerading as Mr. Ugly—
and all I want to do is kiss you and stay with you forever.
Forget I have tiny pig eyes and like to go to workshops
and never sweep the floor.
Forget you called me a whore,
puked in the bushes,
always passed out and had to be dragged to bed.
Oh you sweetheart, there on the jacket, thank you for kicking me out,

and for these magical stories to put me to sleep.

September 7, 1989

TO DRINK DRIVEN

He moves the way a rock
would, if it could
and like feathers.

He smiles the way the sun shines,
when it does,
and cries like rain.

He talks like a hammer,
but when he listens
he hears
what no one hears.

What breaks him, then?
Fury
inside out,
as echoes
will break
fine glass.

CHRIST I FEEL SHITTY

Christ I feel shitty.
For the last two or three days
I've been reading
Screams from the Balcony
and reliving
things that happened 30 years ago
and you know it is when you love someone
so much
and you want to tell them about something amazing
that happened to you
or that you witnessed

and you don't understand
and you think that when you tell them they too will be amazed
but perhaps will know the explanation
but anyway you know they will want to hear about it
because it is just the kind of story they themselves love to tell
and when you tell it they say
"That makes me want to puke"
and you realize you have been insensitive
and burdened this poor suffering beaten-down creature with something
he was not in the mood for
and now 30 years later you read in a letter to DOUGLAS BLAZEK
what he thought the story was about
and you want to give him a good shake and say "Listen!"
"That's not what it was at *all!*
"It was two white people!
"Where did you get this black-white thing?
"and it didn't happen at a meeting!
"I never said that!
"I was *all alone!*
"in the *bus station*
"in the middle of the goddam night."

But you can't do that.
The guy's dead.

At least it's clear now
He hated me
for being somebody I never was.
Maybe I loved him
for the same reason.
I thought he would want to hear amazing stories
when all he wanted was somebody to clean up the kitchen,
just like he said all along.

April, 1994

OUTSIDER

People ask me
sometimes
what it was like

living with you.
Thinking back,
I recite facts, like
. . . drunken quarrels
. . . I was a shrew
. . . the baby never slept . . .

All I really remember:
One day
a white cat
with a bent tail
walked in out of the sun
totally covered
spilling over
with five-pointed
pale blue flowers.

April 4, 1969

STILL THE OUTSIDER

The *New York Times* calls Charles Bukowski the "poet of excess."
Excess?
I guess
this just means the East coast establishment
still has its high hat on,
but like the high hat I saw on top of an automated piano
playing away by itself in a hotel in Sacramento,
the hat
is empty.

March 16, 1994

P.S.

P.S. I like to imagine that Hank, wherever he is now, has Sandburg and William Stafford to talk to and I can imagine them arguing forever. I think in heaven you just stay drunk, you don't puke and get stupid. (Hank used to say, "The People, No!")

November 16, 1994

THE OUTSIDERS

Julia Kamysz Lane

The houses dotting North Boulevard in Slidell look alike: small, dusty brick ranches with front lawns an almost surreal green. The dirty blond sidewalks are empty, the April humidity having herded everyone inside to air-conditioned living rooms, and the television keeping them there.

But inside one household, the TV has been momentarily turned off. Instead, the people who live here—two widowed Italian sisters—are embroiled in a cat fight. The elderly women stand their ground on mustard-brown shag carpet, filling the air with one verbal hiss after another.

The sisters' animosity has surged since 1993, when Lee, the oldest at eighty-five years old, insisted her lung cancer-ridden sister, Gypsy Lou, leave the French Quarter to live with her in Slidell. Lee, who refuses to tell her last name, is a retired housewife. She is dressed in slippers and a billowy, faded housecoat, and her wavy, chin-length hair is streaked with white.

The younger sister will tell her last name, but not her age. She is Louise "Gypsy Lou" Webb, a legend in small press publishing. While living in the French Quarter in the late '50s and early '60s, Gypsy Lou and her late husband, Jon, created Loujon Press to publish subculture auteurs like Henry Miller, William Burroughs, Jack Kerouac, Diane Wakowski, Allen Ginsberg, Jean Genet, and Lawrence Ferlinghetti. Their literary magazine, *The*

Outsider, started as a quarterly but only ran for five issues from 1962 to 1969; today, copies are collector's items nearly impossible to find.

Long ago, Louise earned the nickname "Gypsy" because of her exotic looks: luxuriously long black hair, olive skin, and colorful, hand-made dresses and jewelry. Now her bobbed black hair fans out around her face, and a deep red beret is balanced on one side of her head. She wears a loose Victorian blouse, the high lacy collar unbuttoned below her neckline, a navy and white polka dotted and striped skirt swirling around the tops of her scuffed white cowboy boots, the leather tassels curled with age. A sweating beer can rests comfortably in her hand.

The sisters were born and raised on a farm in Euclid, Ohio (a "ghost town, like here," Gypsy Lou says). But only Lee preserves the family's rural Midwest values, openly disapproving of her sister's past Bohemian lifestyle, and making it clear that she herself does not drink alcohol.

"You don't like the way I dress," Gypsy Lou says to her. "You hate these damn boots."

"I like them," retorts Lee. "I like them for a cowgirl!"

Gypsy Lou rolls her eyes. "I don't know how we stand it," she says.

Lee's eyes widen. "Because we're *sisters!*" she replies.

Travels with Charlie

If Gypsy Lou seems an outsider in her own home, it's in keeping with her long, storied life. The Webbs were always drawn to iconoclasts, and foremost among their friends was Charles Bukowski. In fact, they were so impressed with Bukowski's poetry that they named him their first "Outsider of the Year," putting his picture on the cover of the spring 1963 issue and giving him an honorary plaque.

The unexpected kudos lifted Bukowski out of a particularly bad depression, and he proudly hung the plaque on the wall of his Los Angeles apartment. More importantly for scholars and fans, as part of the award the Webbs published *It Catches My Heart in Its Hands*, the first collection of Bukowski's work in book form.

The Webbs' place in the poet's career is acknowledged in Howard Sounes' new biography, *Charles Bukowski: Locked in the Arms of a Crazy Life* (Grove). Writes Sounes: "Of all the small press publishers Bukowski dealt with in these early years the most significant, by far, were Jon and Louise 'Gypsy Lou' Webb and their extraordinary Loujon Press."

The couple's devotion to underground literature came with a price.

Sporadic income came in from Gypsy Lou's paintings, which she sold on the street in the French Quarter, and anything else they could do to keep going. "They sold every stick of furniture they had," recalls Edwin Blair, a former close friend of Jon's. "I can't begin to tell you how they lived during that period."

Gypsy Lou clearly remembers the day she and Jon waited at Union Station to meet Bukowski for the first time. It was 1965, early spring, and the Webbs had been publishing Bukowski's poetry for three years.

The Webbs believed the poet's honesty set his work apart from any other writer at the time, including the Beats, whom Bukowski deplored. "He was real," says Gypsy Lou. "He would write stuff about whores and race tracks and nobody except Bukowski would write [about] drinking and all that, like things that go on everyday."

At the time, Bukowski—known to friends as simply "Buk" or "Hank"—was working fulltime at a Los Angeles post office, had a new live-in girlfriend, and a baby daughter, and needed a change.

"All the different people were getting off, and Jon and I were hidden behind a post in the station, looking to see which one's Bukowski," says Gypsy Lou. "Then a guy staggered, and I said, 'That's got to be him!' Sure enough, it was."

The Webbs did not have enough room to host Bukowski in their small French Quarter apartment at 1109 Royal Street. However, their friend, Minnie Segate, lived in a spacious shotgun house only a few streets away. Gypsy Lou asked Minnie if she could spare a room for Bukowski, adding that he was a great poet. "She didn't give a damn whether he was a great poet!" says Gypsy Lou. "She liked men, you know. Oh boy! She got the right one."

Bukowski brought a six-pack of beer to Minnie's place and the two immediately hit it off. As the owner of Country Kitchen restaurant on Chartres Street, Minnie knew how to cook a good meal. "She fed him that first night they were together, and he had the best of everything," says Gypsy Lou. "He'd eaten like he'd never eaten before in his life. And she drank like he did, so everything was perfect."

(Local legend has it that during his stay, Bukowski inscribed his name in the sidewalk outside the current location of the R-Bar on Royal Street. Although the words "Hank was here" can still be seen, nobody can say for sure if it is the handiwork of Bukowski or an enthusiastic fan.)

Bukowski viewed the trip to New Orleans mainly as a social call on his publishing patrons, but Gypsy Lou says her husband was determined to get some work out of him. A routine soon was established during the two-week stay; upon waking well after morning, the poet would come by the Webbs' place for a beer. Jon would ask if he had any finished work. Gypsy Lou says Bukowski always replied no—because he was too busy fooling around—then repeat his request for a beer. Jon would shake his head and say the poems come first.

"He was tough with Hank," says Gypsy Lou. "So [Bukowski] would say, 'That damn Jon Webb,' then he'd go." After sitting at the "typer"—Bukowski's term for the typewriter—for a few hours, the writer would return, verse in hand. "When he'd bring his poems, six or seven," says Gypsy Lou, "Jon would sit down, take out two or three he especially liked, and then he'd say, 'Okay, go get a beer in the box.' "

Miller Time

Charles Bukowski was as renowned for his non-stop drinking as he was for his offbeat writing. In Sounes' book, Bukowski's widow, Linda Lee, insists he wasn't an alcoholic because he was productive during even the worst of binges. Friends like Gypsy Lou say he was a gentle teddy bear, but when drunk, Bukowski often looked for fights and destroyed anything and anybody in his path. "At one time or another," Sounes wrote, "Buk managed to upset almost everybody who was close to him."

Miller Williams—poet, University of Arkansas professor, and father of musician Lucinda Williams—remembers witnessing one such incident while Bukowski visited the Webbs more than thirty years ago.

"We were pleased with how naturally he moved into the New Orleans scene of that time," says Williams by phone from his office in Arkansas. It was fairly Bohemian, laid back, and at the same time questioning, intellectual and joyful. He seemed to feel that it was very close to the world he lived in in his part of L.A.

"We spent long afternoons and evenings far into the night in their living room in the French Quarter, just talking," Williams says. "It was as rich a time as I've ever spent with people in poetry; just talking, not necessarily all about poetry, just the world. It's one of the moments I always stop at when I'm looking back at my life."

It wasn't unusual for friends to drop by during these all-night rap sessions, such as when Louisiana academic John William Corrington drove from Baton Rouge to the Quarter to meet Bukowski, with whom he had been corresponding since 1961.

The visit proved disastrous. Williams and Corrington soon became engaged in a discussion about academic life. Bukowski remained silent, either too intimidated or bored by the topic to add to the conversation.

Soon Bukowski was snickering at everything Corrington had to say. Their friendship was over by the end of the night. In the Sounes' biography, Williams places the blame mostly on Bukowski; Corrington was just one of many friends and fans who became disenchanted with the great poet when faced with the belligerent man himself.

When asked about his favorite moment with Bukowski, Williams politely declines to comment. "Young lady, I can't tell you," the seventy-year-old poet demurs. "It's funny but a little too salacious. I can't even tell you my most second or third favorite moment! I wouldn't want to embarrass anybody still living."

Gypsy Lou admits that she, too, didn't care for Bukowski when they first met. "[But] I got to like him," says Gypsy Lou. "It got so I talked like him, all the swearing and everything, because we went around a lot together. He grew on you. In a way, he was a beautiful, ugly man."

Great Expectations

As Loujon Press, the Webbs published five *The Outsider* magazines—three in New Orleans and two while they briefly lived in Tucson—and two books each by Henry Miller and Bukowski. Miller's books included *Order and Chaos Chez Hans Reichel* (1966) and *Insomnia or the Devil at Large* (1970), both of which have been long out of print. Bukowski's poetry anthologies, *It Catches My Heart in Its Hands* (1963), and *Crucifix in a Deathhand* (1965) also are out of print. At *www.bookfinder.com*, a Website listing rare books for sale, the former lists for $600 to $1,000, depending on its condition; the latter ranges from $200 for a damaged copy to $1,500 for a book in excellent condition and containing a personalized inscription from the author.

Book dealer Joseph Cohen, owner of Great Acquisitions in the Riverbend, says several years ago, he sold a complete set of *The Outsider* magazines for $600. "I haven't seen a whole set since," he says. "I suspect there would be copies at university libraries, but locating one to buy would be a chunk of cash." Presently, Cohen has an August 1935 *Story* magazine with a story by Jon Webb. "Night by Night" is an account of Webb's incarceration after taking part in a failed burglary of a jewelry store in Cleveland. It was while Webb was in prison that the future publisher developed a love of literature and edited the reformatory's weekly paper. The *Story* magazine now sells for $100.

The Webbs' beautifully illustrated and hand-bound books were a labor of love. Jon Webb Jr., an Army veteran and retired chiropractor, occasionally helped his father and stepmother with the printing. "They had a little press, I think it was an 8-by-12 hand press," he says, speaking by phone from Stockton, California. "Every page you had to pull the handle." Originally, the Webbs patiently hand-fed the pages into an old Chandler & Price letterpress donated to them by a group of Chicago writers who had heard of their cause. "Tulane University gave us the small handpress," says Gypsy Lou. "Then Jon said [to one of the Chicago writers] Douglas Blazek that it would be nice if we had a nice motor press, so they raised enough money to buy us one. Jon was very resourceful."

He also was a perfectionist, remembers Jon Jr. "He'd say, 'You're pulling too hard, too soft, you're going too fast!' He was the driving force, a tough taskmaster. He was harder than my first sergeant!"

Indeed, Jon Webb had high expectations for Bukowski's first book—wanting it to be more substantial than Bukowski's previously published work in chapbooks and obscure magazines—and was driven to perfect every last detail. For starters, he insisted they use expensive, "deckle-edged" paper and bind the book pages with an ornate cork cover. Writes Sounes: "Jon Webb wanted to sell autographed copies so he mailed unbound pages to Bukowski to sign with a silver deco-write pen, giving precise instructions on how hard he must press, how long the ink took to dry, which side of the paper to work on and how many inches in from the margin he should write." Amused, Bukowski did as he was told.

Gypsy Lou says the grueling process practically drove her crazy. While working on both Bukowski anthologies, they couldn't even take a bath because the pages for the books were drying on boards across the bathtub before being collated. Edwin Blair, who was introduced to the Webbs shortly after moving to town in 1963, remembers the deplorable conditions under which the husband and wife team worked. "I'll never forget, when you walked in, the yard was covered with dog shit and they had a walkway of boards," he says. "The building was very ramshackle, and they had the little press in back. [Jon] was just finishing *Outsider* three and working on the first Bukowski book."

Sounes' book also lists other inconveniences, including rats that ran along the roof and caused ceiling plaster to fall on finished pages, bugs in the ink, blown fuses, flammable wiring, and the summertime humidity, which destroyed the composition rollers.

"They were a lot of work, oh honey, I'll tell ya," says Gypsy Lou. "I was painting, making the money, buying the type. Jon loved it." Initially, the Webbs hired Wally Shore to do the typesetting, but the ever-observant Gypsy Lou soon got the hang of it. "After doing it for a while,

I got the knack of it, just like that," she says. "And I was *good* at it! So I had to let Wally go, because I was saving money, and I did it better than he did."

Odd Couple

The typesetter's apprentice, Gypsy Lou, and her sister, Lee, still are not speaking when their New Orleans visitors rise from their chairs to leave. One of the guests, Kelley Edmiston, whose mother was an old friend of Gypsy Lou's, attempts to patch things up between them. She says they're lucky to have a nice home, and offers that the nearby senior citizen's center gives them a place to socialize.

"She doesn't like it," accuses Gypsy Lou. "I love it because I like people. When I was selling paintings in New Orleans, I was talking to the public for seventeen years. I liked everybody!"

Lee is speechless. "Well, I . . . I . . . She's talking as if I hate everybody," she says in exasperation. "*Some* people I don't like."

"I don't hate anybody," says Gypsy Lou. She turns to her sister. "I don't even hate you, Lee."

"Well, you told me plenty of times, Lou!"

"Only once."

"Lou! You've told me that lots of times."

Gypsy Lou shrugs. "Hate and love, you can't tell the difference," she says, showing her guests to the door, her white boots padding noiselessly across the shag carpet.

I MET HANK IN 1968

Michael C. Ford

I MET HANK IN 1968
HE WAS PUBLISHING A PROSE COLUMN IN A NEW ORLEANS
PERIODICAL CALLED
NOLA EXPRESS
AND CONCURRENTLY EXPERIENCING A CERTAIN LOS
ANGELES UNDERGROUND
REVERENCE FOR HIS DIRTY OLD MAN STORIES PRINTED IN
OPEN CITY

OPEN CITY AT THAT TIME WAS AN ALTERNATIVE TABLOID
ON A LEVEL WITH
ART KUNKIN'S *LA FREE PRESS* OR RICK MERLIN'S *LOS
ANGELES IMAGE* PAPER
IT WAS LOCATED ON MELROSE THEN
PRACTICALLYIN CITY COLLEGE'S BACKYARD

IT WAS EDITED BY JOHN BRYAN WHO EDITED AND
PUBLISHED A BEAT LITERARY
MAGAZINE *RENAISSANCE REVIEW* IN THE EARLY '60S
HE WAS SORT OF A SELF-STYLED RADICAL

VERY SINCERE AND A VERY HIGH ENERGY GUY
HIS OLD LADY WORKED THE *OPEN CITY* FRONT DESK
AND SHE CALLED HERSELF SUPERMOTHER
SO THERE WAS THIS PRE-DATED FEMALE LIBERATION VIBE

INTERESTING PEOPLE AND BUKOWSKI LIKED THEM VERY
MUCH
ANYWAY THERE WAS THIS BRIGHT INDIAN SUMMER
AFTERNOON: OCTOBER OF '68
JUST A FEW WEEKS BEFORE THE DEMOCRATIC CONVENTION

BUKOWSKI HAD COME BY TO DROP OFF COPY
I GUESS I'D COME BY TO DO THE SAME
AFTER PUTTING THE PAPER TO BED APPARENTLY THESE
ABBEY RENTS CHAIRS HAD BEEN
SET UP
AND THIS HISTORICAL MEETING WAS ABOUT TO TAKE
PLACE

JERRY RUBIN WAS THERE TOM HAYDEN ABBIE HOFFMAN
PEOPLE

LOCAL HEAVIES WERE THERE
LEVI KINGSTON; WONDERFUL CAT WHO RAN A VERY WITH
IT COFFEEHOUSE SCENE
NAMED POGO'S SWAMP IN THE MID-SIXTIES ALSO ON
MELROSE

AT ANY RATE BUKOWSKI AND MYSELF ENDED UP CACKED
OUT IN THESE SEATS LISTENING
TO WHAT TURNED OUT TO BE ONE PLANNING STAGE OF
THE YIPPIE INVASION OF
CHICAGO WHICH WAS IN ESSENCE DESIGNED TO MAKE A
MOCKERY OF THE DEMO CONVENTION
SO IT WAS THIS HISTORICAL OCCASION
KIND OF HYSTERICAL TOO WHEN YOU STOP TO THINK
ABOUT IT
WITH THESE VOICES SUPERCHARGING THE AIR WITH NEWS
OF
THIS MOCK INSURRECTION
THIS CARNIVAL OF ANARCHY

THIS BLUEPRINT FOR CLOWN-SHOW REVOLT

AS A MATTER OF FACT SOME WERE TAKING IT VERY SERIOUSLY
IN THE MIDDLE OF THIS ELECTRIC DIALOGUE, SOMEBODY IMPROVISES ANNOUNCING:
"WE'RE GONNA HAVE A REVOLUTION THIS IS THE BEGINNING OF A NEW AMERICAN REVOLUTION"

FOLLOWING THE MEETING BRYAN REQUESTED THAT EACH OF US CARRY OUR CHAIRS
BACK UP INTO THE LOFT
AND I SAID: HEY, BUKOW WHADDAYATHINK?
BUKOWSKY ANSWERED: WELL KID I GUESS THE REVOLUTION IS OVER

A PERCEPTION VERY SIMILAR TO THE KIND APPROPRIATE TO SO MUCH OF HIS WORK
WHEN IT CONCERNED OBSERVING AMERICAN DELUSION DESPAIR FOIBLES AND FAILURES

BUKOWSKI ON THE MIC

Barry Miles

The tapes I made of Bukowski were the result of an abandoned, but not forgotten, recording project I began in 1968 about which the less said the better. I had been an admirer of Buk's work since 1965 and finally had a chance to record him. So it was in February 1969 I pulled up at 5125 ½ De Longpre Avenue in a slummy part of East Hollywood near the 20th Century Fox Studios on Sunset in a rented green Mustang which looked gleamingly conspicuous in the shabby street. Slums in Los Angeles are not like those of other cities. During the Watts riots a few years before, the foreign press had driven straight through Watts looking for the slum because to European eyes these are reasonable houses: Everyone seems to have a large car and a television, it's always sunny and there are palm trees lining the streets. It is not the South Bronx, it is only a slum *in contrast*.

De Longpre was made from large slabs of concrete, chipped at the edges, lined with utility cables and tall scruffy palms, some of which had died and rotted. The single story wooden-frame houses had peeling paint and there were holes in the screen doors. Bits of cars lay in front yards and rubbish blew about. A '57 Plymouth was parked on the ruins of Buk's front lawn. Beer cans overflowed his garbage bins.

The screen door opened straight into his living room. The shades were drawn. Rickety bookshelves were overloaded with books, magazines, old newspapers, and racing forms. The settee had a hole where the stuffing was bursting out. There was a pile of car tires in the corner and many empty beer cans, and in another corner was Buk's desk. Here was Buk's typewriter: a prewar, battered, sit-up-and-beg, black cast-iron Remington; dusty but for the carriage and keys which were polished by use, surrounded by cigar butts and ash, crumpled paper, extinct beercans. Hundreds, perhaps thousands of poems had emerged from that old machine; countless stories, columns for *Open City*, the local underground newspaper which had been running his "Notes of a Dirty Old Man" column since May 1967, and letters to every little mimeographed poetry magazine editor who contacted him, from Germany to Japan, midwest farm-boys to slick New Yorkers—hundreds and hundreds of them.

Bukowski seemed happy to see us (I had my assistant Pat Slattery with me), but immediately after finding seats for us he was off, slipping like a shadow through the door, across the porch and away. Soon to return with another six-pack. Now he had a smile on his face and a bottle of Miller Light in his hand. He found a glass for Pat in the messy kitchen in back, talked about the race-track and about his publisher John Martin, from the Black Sparrow Press, about little poetry magazines and his worries and fears about trying to make it as a professional poet. Essex House, the pornographic book publishers, had just released a collection of his pieces from *Open City*, called *Notes Of A Dirty Old Man* as a mass market paperback, (or as mass market as a company that published books with titles like *Thongs* was likely to get) and he was encouraged by this latest development.

We talked about the record. He was casual, relaxed, and said that he had made a lot of home recordings before: "Sure, just show me how the machine works and come back in a few days. I'll just curl up on the rug with some packs of beer, my books, turn on the machine, and . . ." I wired up an Ampex 3000, arranged a microphone stand and microphone, headphones and twelve reels of blank tape. He refused to allow me, or anyone else, to be present to supervise the recording, claiming to be too shy. Some of the problems he had with the equipment were caused by his attempt to record on "both sides" of the tape which wiped what he had previously recorded.

Nine days later my assistant from San Francisco, Valerie Estes, and I pulled up in a blue rented Mustang. Buk was there, a bit hungover, and so was a woman, middle aged, wearing black fishnet stockings and a black slip. She disappeared into the bedroom without speaking, emerging some time later, ready to leave, looking tired and worn. Buk crushed some bills into her hand. "Carfare" he said, as much to me as to her. Nothing in the room had changed. The Ampex was where I had left it but it was done; every reel was filled with Buk's careful selection from his writing—six hours of his favorite pieces. He said to be sure to listen to the one called "The Firestation" as he liked that best of all. Then he told us a long story about his '57 Plymouth and about his landlord, flirted with Valerie, and eventually we got everything packed up and he helped carry it out to the car.

The tapes had that mixture of tenderness and toughness, understanding and acceptance which characterise Buk's best work. They were recorded before he became a "professional" writer. He had made a few tapes before, but these still have the conversational quality of someone who had not yet read his work in public. There is no attempt at performance other than getting the poem across.

It happened that this was a turning point in his career. A few weeks after making the recording he gave his first poetry reading. A year later, on January 2, 1970, at the age of forty-nine, he finally quit his job at the post office and devoted himself full time to writing. He couldn't get away from the post office, however; it became the subject of his first novel, called, unsurprisingly, *Post Office* published by Black Sparrow in February 1971.

Most people discovered Buk through the novels: *Post Office, Factotum* (1975) and *Women* (1978) with their gritty, erotic, uncompromising, and above all, honest, portrayal of life at the bottom. They are in the tradition of Jack Black's *You Can't Win* or John Fante's three-volume saga of Arturo Bandini (a major influence on Buk). His work stands alongside William Burroughs' *Junky*, Herbert Huncke's *Guilty of Everything*, the humor of Lenny Bruce, the growled vocals of Tom Waits, solos by Chet Baker or Art Pepper, the Beats and the deadbeats, the drop-outs and the freaks: white American males living in the underside of society, telling their experience with compassion and humor.

Bukowski started afresh, made a new life, got a new wife, began to drink fine wines instead of six-packs. He left De Longpre. He gave readings on smart college campuses and his books appeared in signed limited editions with paintings by him on the half-title. He was still writing. He was doing all right.

from

THE HOLY GRAIL: MY FRIENDSHIP WITH CHARLES BUKOWSKI

A.D. Winans

There was a particularly memorable time in San Francisco when Hank paid me an unexpected visit. Hank said he wanted to see what it was that people found intriguing about North Beach.

I parked my car just outside North Beach and took Hank for a walk up Grant Avenue. We passed the Cafe Trieste, a popular gathering place for the literary crowd and the pretentious elite. Hank paused outside the Cafe Trieste, and peered inside at the small crowd of people gathered around the intimately arranged tables. Suddenly he leaned inside the doorway and without warning blurted out, "Look at all these people waiting for something to happen, only it never will."

His remark was met with stunned silence. Hank seemed almost embarrassed as he hurried away without waiting for me. Before catching up with him, I heard a skinny young woman sitting near the doorway make an insensitive remark.

"God, did you see all that acne? And what a drinker's nose. He'll be dead before you know it." Her remark was met with a smattering of laughter as she continued drinking her espresso. The woman was dead wrong. The acne the woman referred to was really childhood boils, and he would live a relatively long life for a man who abused his body like he did. I managed to catch up with Hank. We didn't talk about the incident. I sensed it would be inappropriate for me to do so. We wandered down the street to City Lights Book Store, but Ferlinghetti wasn't in. Hank shrugged his shoulders and said it was probably just as well.

We walked back to where I had parked my car and had a long conversation. Hank talked about his dislike for the kind of people who hung out at places like the Cafe Trieste. He said that Los Angeles had the same kind of haunts, but that he made it a point to stay away from them. He described coffee houses as haunts for talentless poets and pseudo-intellectuals whom he referred to as "soft-boiled egg and parsley eaters."

The conversation shifted to the brawls Hank had gotten into as a teenager, when he said he had been forced to defend himself because of his pock-faced looks. Later he lived in the slum streets of Los Angeles where survival meant being able to take care of yourself. "Not unlike Hell's Kitchen in Chicago," he said.

Hank said that the amazing thing was that he "liked the impact of knuckles against teeth, the rush to the brain when a blow landed to a man's body, the feeling of having to shake loose and nail the other person before he finished you." But he confessed that he was too old for that kind of life anymore.

We left the car and walked up Grant Avenue. I showed Hank the old Beat haunts: the Coffee Gallery (now the Lost and Found Bar), and what had once been The Place, San Gottardo's Hotel and Bar (now a Korean bar and restaurant), Mike's Pool Hall, and other former Beat hangouts, long since closed down.

I walked him past the bars still in existence: Vesuvio's, Gino and Carlo's, Spec's, and the 1232 Club. As we walked along Grant Avenue, it was inevitable that we would run into poets and North Beach regulars I have known since the Fifties and Sixties.

Paddy O'Sullivan was standing inside the doorway of the Camel's bar, located on the corner of Grant and Green. Hank and I stopped to chat with him. Paddy was a legend in North Beach, having, among other things, lost his arm to a pet cheetah. Whatever may have happened to Paddy, he never lost his Irish charm. When Paddy left for the men's room, Hank said it was people like Paddy who gave poets a bad name. I disagreed, remembering how Paddy had saved my ass from a severe whipping one evening, when stone drunk, a local bully decided to take me on.

Paddy had grabbed the bully around his neck, holding him tightly in a choke hold, turning him nearly purple before throwing him out of the bar and on to the street. Paddy had more strength in his one good arm than most men have in both arms.

When I told Hank this story, he said, "Well, maybe he can't write poetry, and maybe it's all a con game, but he sounds like the kind of guy I'd like to have watching my back at a bar."

We left the bar before Paddy returned from the men's room, turning the corner, and walking down Green Street to Gino and Carlo's. Gino and Carlo's was owned by two Italian brothers, Aldino and Dinado. We stopped outside, where I exchanged words with Carl Eisenger, a sad figure of a man. Carl had been a poet, but hadn't written in years, after his life work had been destroyed in a hotel fire.

Hank and I entered Gino and Carlo's, where I was greeted by Dinado. Looking down at the floor, we saw Cheap Charly lying in a drunken stupor. Cheap Charly had earned his name because of his habit of mooching free drinks at North Beach bars. Hank and I watched Dinado bend over Cheap Charly, pouring whiskey down his throat through a funnel. The patrons cheered on the action. Cheap Charly would do anything for a free drink, including making an ass of himself. I would later write a book, *Tales of Crazy John,* based partly on the crazy antics of Cheap Charly.

"Are all the poets in this town crazy?" Hank asked.

"Not all of them," I said.

We departed the bar and headed down the street, stopping in front of the 1232 Club where Shoeshine Devine was standing outside. Shoeshine was the only man in the area with his own custom made shoeshine box. Shoeshine was different from other people shining shoes. For one thing, he didn't sit on a stool, but instead squatted in front of his customers, bouncing up and down like a yo-yo. I exchanged a few words with Shoeshine, whom Hank would remember as having a wild look in his eyes.

Shoeshine left our company to ply his trade down the street when Bob Seider happened by chance to come along, asking for spare change. Hank reached into his pocket and emptied his change. Seider thanked Hank and weaved his way down the street in the direction of Chinatown.

Hank said he didn't make it a habit to give street bums change, but that he had seen something in Seider's eyes that made him different from the rest. I told Hank that Seider had once been a jazz musician, back in the Beat era, but that one day he had pawned his saxophone and quit playing forever.

I tried to convince Hank to have a beer with me at Vesuvio's, located next to City Lights Bookstore, which had been a favorite meeting place of the Beat poets and writers, but he declined. He told me he was hungry and wanted to grab a bite to eat before leaving the beach, and I suggested Chinatown, which I knew would be free of other poets at this time of the day.

I decided to take Hank to Sam Woh's, a restaurant that required one to walk through the kitchen in order to make it to the upstairs dining room, where the food was brought to you on a dumb waiter.

Sam Woh's was, at the time, the most popular "in" spot in Chinatown, after the famed Herb Caen mentioned the restaurant in his newspaper column. But it was a waiter who went by the name of Edsel Ford who made the restaurant unique. As we walked through the kitchen, filled with non-English speaking Chinese cooks with meat cleavers in their hands, Hank said, "I hope the hell you know what you're doing."

"Don't worry," I said, leading him upstairs to the dining area, where we were greeted by Edsel Ford. Edsel was part entertainer, part waiter, and part madman. Edsel told the patrons where to sit, and what to order, and few people had the courage to challenge him. He was that big a man.

Edsel waved to me in recognition as Hank walked at my side. Suddenly Edsel turned and shouted at Hank, "Single File. Single File. You stupid?"

Hank was completely caught off guard, and at first appeared angry, but the look of anger soon changed to a smile as he realized it was all part of an act. Edsel escorted us to the back of the restaurant, seated us at a table, and thrust menus in our hands. I don't recall what Hank ordered, except that he wanted a bowl of steamed rice. Edsel glared at Hank. "No white rice. No white rice. You order noodles."

"Who ever heard of a Chinese restaurant doesn't serve rice?" Hank bellowed. He finally settled on a plate of noodles, which Sam Woh's was famous for.

We spent a considerable amount of time talking about Hank's favorite subject, women. I don't recall much of the conversation, but when I told Hank about breaking up with a woman I was in love with, and the loss I felt, Hank grew serious. "You don't know what it's like to really lose a woman," he said. "When Jane died, I knew I would never again be the same. It's too painful to put down in prose. I try to put it down on paper, but it doesn't come out right. I never want to bury another woman again."

Hank talked to me about fame and said that becoming famous was not important to him, but that he wanted someday to own a place of his own, even if it was only a shack. Hank felt it was durability that counted and boasted that he had outlived many of the editors who had rejected his work early on in the game. We talked about the small presses. Bukowski said that *Wormwood Review* and *Nola Express* were among the best of the small presses. He also spoke highly of *The New York Quarterly* and my own magazine *Second Coming.*

We talked about drugs and whether they were good for you or not. My own experience with drugs was limited to grass, uppers and downers, and single experiences with peyote and LSD. Hank admitted to having used drugs, but spoke negatively about cocaine, which he felt was destructive. Hank said the only drug he was addicted to was alcohol, but found that, unlike other drugs, it didn't interfere with his writing.

Hank and I finished our meal and left Sam Woh's, heading back to my car. I drove him across town, where he was staying, and promised to keep in touch with him.

There would be but one more meeting between us, which took place when I drove to Los Angeles to meet Hank at the home of his lover Linda King. I arrived in Los Angeles early in the day, stopping off at several bars to pass the time away. When I arrived at Linda King's home, it was just beginning to grow dark. I was in the company of a writer acquaintance named R.B. who lived in downtown Los Angeles, and who had expressed a desire to meet Hank.

Hank greeted me and R.B. at the front door. The look in Hank's eyes immediately told me he didn't like R.B. Hank had seen something in his eyes that had eluded me. Hank showed us into the living room and asked us what we wanted to drink. The drinks flowed freely, and it wasn't long before I was deep into a drunk. I was surprised that both Hank and Linda abstained from drinking, being the heavy drinkers they were. We spent the next few hours in heated literary conversation, with Hank playing the role of the Devil's advocate. Every poet I seemed to like, Hank attacked, and the poets I disliked, Hank defended. It wasn't until much later that I learned Hank and Linda were trying to see where I was coming from, and had remained sober for this purpose. I don't like being dissected at length, and if it had been anyone else I would have gotten up and left. But as the evening wore on both Hank and Linda mellowed, and the atmosphere became more relaxed.

Hank, Linda, R.B., and myself spent a great deal of time discussing Jack Micheline and his work. I argued that Jack had been largely ignored and that his work was as good or better than many of the Beat writers who had gained a measure of success. Hank readily agreed, referring to him as "Brooklyn Jack, a hustling, romantic poet of the streets." Hank talked about how Jack would pay him a visit, and how they would get drunk together, but complained that Jack had a bad habit of bringing his poems with him, and expecting him (Hank) to listen to them. Hank said he didn't want to listen to poets read their poems, not even Jack. However, he said Jack was the only poet who had inspired him to write not one, but two poems about him.

"Two of them," Hank laughed. "The bastard got two poems out of me." Hank said many of Jack's letters were poems in themselves. "How can I not like a man who enjoys going to the race track as much as Jack does?"

Linda King occasionally broke in with a laugh, throwing her arms around Hank, and saying, "He's all right. He's all right. He's no Buk, but he's all right."

The remainder of the evening became a drunken blur. There were some comical stories Hank told about his early relationship with Neeli Cherry. Hank said that Neeli would follow him around with a note book, writing down whatever he said, or taping it when he got the opportunity. Hank said in a somber tone, "When I'm dead and buried the kid will get rich off me."

Hank spoke about Neeli having worked for a politician writing campaign speeches, and walking around with his bank book in his pocket.

"This is what money does to you," Hank said. "It's driven him mad." Hank felt that Neeli had sold out, but said that he still held out hope for him.

I felt Hank was being a bit harsh about Neeli. It was true Neeli worshipped Hank, but I doubted if he was as bad as Hank said, and when I asked Hank if what he said about Neeli was true, why had they remained friends over the years? He quickly changed the subject.

As the evening wore down, Hank and Linda said they were retiring for the night. As I recall things, Hank simply stood up and said, "It's time to go." I felt like I was being dismissed from the King's court. R.B. asked to stay the night, but Hank turned him down, only to whisper I was welcome to stay and use the sofa once I got rid of R.B. I thanked Hank for the offer, but had already rented a cheap hotel room for the night.

As I prepared to leave, I paused to look Hank in the eyes. I told him Harold Norse had warned me that someday Hank would turn against me, as he had done with Norse and others. I told him Norse had told me he (Hank) couldn't stand to be loved, which drew Hank's famous impish smile. Without hesitation, he said, "And I will."

"No, you won't," I said. My remark seemed to catch him off guard. He wanted to know what made me think I was any different from the others.

I said, "What you said about the others was true. You don't know anything bad about me."

"You're right," he said, embracing me at the door.

5 POEMS

Joan Jobe Smith

BUKOWSKI BOULEVARD

For years before Bukowski died, just
to feel Bukowski's vibes, Fred and I'd
drive across the Vincent Thomas Bridge
to San Pedro to Santa Cruz Street we
named Bukowski Boulevard where Bukowski
lived in a big house with blue awnings
we'd drive by again and again and on
the way we'd say what would happen this
time: this time Bukowski'd be standing
on his sidewalk and he'd wave at us
and yell. "Fred Voss. Joan Jobe Smith
I've been waiting for you. Come on in.
I've got your favorite beer, Fred, and
Joan, some pouilley-fuissé for you"
and we'd go into Bukowski's big house
where Bukowski'd offer us his softest
chairs, he'd tell us his secrets, why
he REALLY wrote poetry, he'd show us

his limited editions and when Fred
admired "*Crucifix in a Death Hand,*"
Buk'd say, "Take it, kid, it's yours
Yeh, I know Red Skodolsky's priced it
at two-thou, but it's yours. Fred, for
I've always admired your work. And for
you, Joan, here's an ode, an apologia
for all the times I've insulted you."
Then he'd lead us to his dining room
for the feast he'd prepared just for us:
Peking duck, prime rib roast au jus,
chocolate chip ice cream and then on
our way home, Fred and I'd say. "Man,
that Bukowski, he's gotten soft. From
now on we're hangin' with Micheline."
But since Bukowki's died, we hardly
ever drive by his house anymore, and
when we do, it's hardly any fun at all

"This is a great house, bring my bottles up to the 2nd floor & type until 5 A.M . . . fights with women, cars roaring out the driveway at sunrise It's great. The house & me. I love my 3 cats."

—C.B.

LIFE'S ONE BIG ROTTEN TOOTH AND WHEN IT'S EXTRACTED YOU CAN'T CHEW ANYMORE

Bukowski once had a crush on me, maybe, but
that's like saying I once saw a pink sunset. How
many pink sunsets are there in the first place that
makes the one you last saw the most significant?
And Bukowski kissed me, once, as he was leaving
my party I'd given in his honor, the one-millionth
party a little mag editor had given him, and the
worst one, for I'd invited my fellow law students
and some assorted poets. Poetry and jurisprudence:
a living bunch of mixed metaphors and diverse

adversity as there'd ever be, and Bukowski said
his usual Wildman things, plus told near-libelous
lawyer jokes, pretended to urinate in a wine bottle
and, worse, pretended to drink it, and the law
students shriveled in horror and poets took notes
for future Bukowski poems while Linda King
hollered. Bukowski, you're fulla shit. Party vibes
made of barbed wire. Pearl Mesta I was not. Pearl
Harbor more like it, and finally everyone went home.
Bukowski the last to leave because there was beer left
and Linda King wouldn't let him take it into her car
because she didn't want no open-container charge
against her if some red-necked Orange County cop
stopped them, so out of a smoky-room dud of a party
Bukowski grabbed me like a grizzly would something
not as fuzzy, he squeezed the breath out of me and
kissed me, and while he murmured Mmmmm, I,
terrified Linda watched, peed my pants warm all the
way down my faded, patched bellbottom jeans, into
the décolletage of my worn-out Dr. Scholl's wooden clogs
Ah, memories, memories.

". . . at the end of feet
the blackbird walks."
—C.B.

NOTES OF A DIRTY OLD MAN

My kids didn't like it when Bukowski
called me late at night, sometimes on
school nights, waking them up. Mom!
one of them would yell up to my bedroom.
it's that dirty old man again, none of them
old enough or well-read enough to know
then about his writings called "Notes of a
Dirty Old Man," them calling him
that because of seeing him at the
party I gave in his honor, watched
him pretend to piss into an empty wine
bottle. Why does that dirty old man

call you all the time? they asked me.
Why do you talk to that dirty old man?
they asked me. Bukowski was hard to
explain to them, especially hard was
explaining to them how fascinating he
was, even when he was drunk, blathering
on, not knowing most nights he called
who I was, sometimes calling me Linda
or Jane, one night saying, Hell, all
you women are either named Linda or
Jane or Smith. It wasn't until my son
took English 1A in college and saw the
Taylor Hackford film on Bukowski that
at least one of my kids understood, or
at least almost understood Bukowski.
Wow, Mom, my son said, Bukowski's famous.
My teacher said he's a genius. And Bukowski
was right here in our house. He sat in that
chair. But then my son remembered the
wine bottle. But Mom, why, if he was such
a genius and was so famous, why did
Bukowski have to be such a dirty old man?

". . . 3:30 A.M. typer on floor.
Been working on immortal . . ."
—C.B.

EGGS OVEREASY

I was frying eggs overeasy when
I heard Bukowski had died and
suddenly the yolks came alive,
grew to the size of heavyweight
Golden Gloves smashing my spatula
and jaw while the kitchen swelled
shut around me like a big, blackened
eye. His obituary was in the Thursday
newspaper, my favorite paper of the
week for the Food Section, the recipes
(this week sickening ones of what to

do with peanuts), the supermarket ads
(this week St. Pat's Day specials,
corned beef for eighty-nine cents a pound,
cabbage for nine, rye $1.69 he'll
never eat agin, if he ever did,
or the wine I later drink with my
husband who mourns more than me
as he listens to a Bukowski Live tape
and reads over and over the only letter
Hank ever wrote him. Hank never knowing,
too busy to care, that his life changed
ours, that we'd come to know his mojo
poetry as well as the backs of our hearts
where manna and mortality are inscribed.
We'd wanted him to live to be 400,
after all, he was 200 at thirty, he was
supposed to keep telling it like it is
forever, our Poet Man, nexus and
code breaker of nether worlds. But
no one ever dies when you want
him or her to, death seldom an Ides
of March or hemlock time for which
you can set your alarm clock as, as he
was quoted in his obituary, you carry in
one hand a bundle of darkness that
accumulates each day. The eggs
overeasy were the coldest I ever ate,
a March ninth wind blowing in through
the window turning them to ice.

March 9, 1994

"We have everything and nothing."
—Charles Bukowski

DUSTING BUKOWSKI's HEAD

Eight weeks since my husband bought the
head of Bukowski, a bronze life-size
masterpiece, and for weeks we had to
put up with all those puns and "head" jokes
the same sex joke in 1970 between Bukowski
and the sculptress that brought them
together for years, the original head they'd
fight over for custody like a love child.
Eight weeks since Bukowski's bronze head
came to live in our living room on the
coffeetable amongst our personal debris
and Bukowski books and you should see
how amazing it is how sunlight or candlelight
adheres to Bukowski's bronze head and makes
his hair glow as if perspiring alive or
pomaded with electricity and you should
listen to the cool quietude of this piece
of art-man and how it makes you imagine
you hear him ha-ha-ing among the trumpets,
eight weeks and I go to dust the bronze
head of Bukowski, the wooden base white
with dust but when I do there's not one
speck of dust on the dustcloth or the
bronze head of Bukowski. I swear.

"What we need is the line that allows
emotion . . .we probably need few other
things too . . ."
—C.B.

from

THE LIBERATED BILLIE AND THE OLD TROLL:

Tales of Linda King and Charles Bukowski

Linda King

Bukowski had a poetry reading at one of the colleges. He called me and said there was a party going on at his house.

"A gang of people followed me home from a poetry reading. Come on over. You like parties."

I had a closet full of fabulous outfits that I had bought shopping and strolling with my baby on Hollywood Boulevard. Also, I was avid thrift store shopper. My husband had lived not five blocks from Bukowski before moving to Burbank. I had wanted to a be an actress and I was ready, at least, with my wardrobe.

When I got to Bukowski's place on De Longpre, about an hour later, I looked great. The court was full and overflowing into the yard and street. Bukowski was being Bukowski, spouting original lines and insults as only he could do. There was no place to sit and hardly anyplace to stand. I got myself a beer and wandered about. Bukowski gave me a tiny kiss and went on talking. Bukowski, with a beer in hand, was a stand up comedian, raw and outrageous. He was a showman.

Bukowski was downing one beer after another. He wasn't talking to me. He didn't introduce me as sculptor or girlfriend. I got a beer and hung around listening. It was very crowded and smoky in his little place. I don't smoke, and decided to go outside for some fresh air. I slipped out the kitchen into the yard. I leaned against a car outside. A tall dark handsome man walked up and started talking to me.

In five or ten minutes I heard Bukowski screaming from the house.

"I WANT YOU ALL OUT OF HERE. DO YOU HEAR ME? I WANT YOU OUT OF MY HOUSE. WHAT DO YOU THINK I AM . . . A CIRCUS FREAK?" People came flying out the door. "AND YOU, I WANT YOU OUT OF HERE, FIRST." A man went flying into his front yard bushes. "GET OUT. ALL OF YOU! OUT!"

Bukowski went inside, locked the door and turned off the lights. I was shocked. What kind of madman had I got involved with? He had just asked me over just an hour ago. Two guys rolled together, throwing punches, in the yard.

I went to the house and knocked on the door. I was sure the police were going to arrive any minute.

"Bukowski," I yelled. "It's Linda. My purse is in there. I can't leave without the keys to my car."

There was no response.

At this time, I had not been around Bukowski much when he was drinking, as he had been tapering off. It did not enter my head that his behavior had anything to do with me. It didn't enter my head that he even noticed what I was doing.

"Bukowski," I yelled again. I knocked harder on the door. "Bukowski! I need my purse."

No response.

"BUKOWSKI! LET ME IN. GIVE ME MY PURSE!"

Suddenly I was furious. The sonofabitch, he had been writing all those bullshit love letters to me. Now, he was ordering me to get lost.

"YOU'RE GOING TO GIVE ME MY PURSE!" I screamed. This time I knocked on the glass. It shattered. I knocked on the second glass. "OPEN THIS DOOOR. YOU LYING SON-OF-A-BITCH! The third glass went. "YOU WILL OPEN THIS DOOR!" The fifth and sixth glass shattered. As the last glass broke, he opened the door. "You GIVE me my purse."

I kept my face to him circling the room, looking for my purse. All of the drunken insane nights my dad had put us through entered my head. My nerves were on overdrive alert. He moved toward me. "Don't you dare touch me," I said in a deadly cold voice. I circled him and spotted my purse behind a chair. I moved quickly. I was enraged. He reached for my arm and I pushed him away. As I went out the door, he tripped over the coffee table and fell drunkenly on the couch. I ran for my car as the police sirens and red lights moved into the street.

18

I woke the next morning with a noise at my front door. I went to the door and almost tripped on Bukowski's head. It was sitting between the screen and the door. Well, I thought, I guess this is the end of Charles Bukowski and Linda King. He didn't have much respect for my sculpture and all the time I had put into sculpturing it. Someone could have taken it right off my front porch. I thought about the party last night. I hadn't exactly been calm breaking his windows.

"How long have you been at my door, dear," I said to the head. "Have I kept you waiting long? Come on in." I picked it up and put it on the shelf over the fireplace.

I didn't hear from Bukowski for several days and then received a letter.

Dear Linda,
I am sitting here with his hole in my guy today. I can't even look at your photo. I have to hide it. I was going to drive over.
Then I thought, better not, better not.
It rains. It won't rain. It's dark. Jesus Christ.
love
Bukowski

His signature was shaky and slanted down. He sent a poem, part of which read.

and love died upside down
the chimes rang
hands tied backward

love dies again and again and again

like Indians like kikes like Jews like me like you
love dies again and again in little pieces
rather like cardboard slits (I can't quite explain it)
just, you know,—
you hit the punching bag again

your sleeves slide past the edge of the sky . . .
total elimination of the bliss of pain
like farting in church with a Sunday hangover while they
pass the plate.

a few points made along the
way. your eyes look upon a carnation then you
die.

. . . Bukowski

More days went by and the phone would ring, but no one would answer.

"Hello, Hello." I knew it was Bukowski.

When the phone rang again I said, "I know this is you, Bukowski." He finally answered in a slurred voice.

"Did you and 'Pretty Boy' get it on?" It was obvious he was very drunk.

"Pretty Boy?" I don't know what you are talking about."

"I saw you out there sitting with that pretty boy. Did you give him your phone number?"

"I truly don't know what you're talking about."

"You were leaning against him outside at the party."

"No Bukowski, I was not leaning against anyone or making any dates. I don't even think we exchanged names." I was shocked. I couldn't believe that his actions could have been triggered by jealousy.

"You seemed to be having a good time inside. You were acting as if you didn't even know me."

"There were a lot of GUYS there."

"It was *your* party."

"How come you didn't stay with me?"

"I don't smoke. I was getting out of that smoky house. You were on a roll. I thought you were enjoying yourself."

"I saw you leaning up to that 'Pretty Boy.' "

"Bukowski, you are out of your mind."

"I'M CHARLES BUKOWSKI. YOU DON'T KNOW WHO YOU'RE WITH." He hung up.

I called him back. "I happen to be LINDA KING, the sculptress . . . remember. I understand that you are the great writer, Charles Bukowski, who finds it easy to write a bunch of bullshit love letters he doesn't even mean."

"Who says I don't mean them?"

"You ordered me out of there, along with the rest of the world population, who was bothering the great Charles Bukowski. You sure as hell didn't act or sound much in love. Maybe you can only be in love on paper."

"I was drinking."

"That doesn't slice ice with me. Who is Bukowski? Is he the man I have been sculpturing or the madman I saw the other night. Is this what happens every time you get drunk? Maybe I should say drunk and jealous. I think you better get yourself another woman." I hang up.

He called back. "Is this the very sane and sensible woman who broke all my windows. It cost me good money to get those windows replaced. My landlady was ready to throw me out."

"Why didn't you open the door?"

"I thought you were one of them."

"Come on."

"I had been drinking since noon. Look, I'm sorry. I really do love you. I miss you. I want to see you. Can I come over."

"I'm going to the zoo with my kids."

"Did you get the head?"

"Someone could have taken it."

"I was watching it. I was down the street. I didn't leave until I saw you take it in the house."

"No!"

"Really."

"When will you be back from the zoo? I've been drinking and I feel like hell. I've got to see you. You don't know how much better you make me feel. I don't like to feel sick like this anymore."

"You scare me when you're so drunk. It's like I'm dealing with another person."

"Let me come over and just lay down next to you. I need to see you."

"I don't know."

"I love you. The letters are true. Let's just talk."

"Okay," I said hesitantly. "Come around nine tonight when the kids are in bed. What if my kids saw you like that?"

Drinking for a week had reversed his emerging Bogart looks and returned the red nose, red eyes, and swollen belly. He looked like hell, but he felt the same. All the vibes between us were the same and working. We curled up in bed together. He was so sick, he didn't really want to talk. We gently began to fall back inside each other.

* * *

The next night I went to his place to stay since he needed to work on some drawings. When I drove over, I took the head with me.

"Look who's back." I sat the head down on his desk. "You are suppose to show this and get me commissions from this head. More people will see it here."

"Look at that smile. I haven't smiled like that in years."

"You were smiling then. I don't know about now. Are the smiles over? Does this mean that true love can really last, only, about three months?"

"I am still sick, but feeling better. My stomach can't take drinking anymore. I was feeling so good."

When we lay down in his bed the lights started blinking off and on.

"Oh, oh," I said. "It's the spirits. They're trying to talk to us."

"Sure they are."

"This happens with my lights all the time."

"Of course."

"If you don't believe me, ask them some questions. This is the rules. The light will blink one time for 'yes' and two times for 'no.' "

"This is the great Charles Bukowski. Am I going to be famous?"

The light blinked once for Yes.

"Is *Post Office* going to be a best seller?"

The light blinked twice for "no."

We went on asking questions. My questions were answered as quickly as his. The light continued to blink with such consistency that we both got spooked.

Bukowski asked a nonsensical bizarre question and the light went off altogether and refused to go on.

"Let's get out of here. This place feels like death," he said.

"The spirits are too close."

"I could die in this place."

I had been getting messages for years in various ways. The light show tonight was extra long.

"They just want us to know they're around. My dreams are so accurate that I almost get a two-week preview of what is going to be happening in my life."

"I am suddenly feeling very hungry," Bukowski said. "I didn't eat much while we were separated. Let's go eat. Let's celebrate. Let's make love. We're back together."

The light suddenly flashed on. We both jumped.

"Let's sleep at your place." he said.

He went to the bathroom and I closed the bedroom door. On the back of the bedroom door was a huge knife taped to the back of the door.

I couldn't believe the knife. Who was he afraid of? Who did he intend to use that knife on? I was living alone with my kids and I never feared anything. I couldn't help wondering if he'd thought of using that knife the night I broke the windows at his party. I decided not to mention it.

54

Bukowski and I were both asked to read at the second annual Santa Cruz Poetry Festival to take place on November 25, 1974. It was a benefit for Americans in Mexican jails. There was money and a plane ticket for the reading. Bukowski never read anywhere free. I had read several places in and around Los Angeles, but this was going to be a huge audience. I'm not sure who drove us to Santa Cruz, it might have been Al Winans or Neeli Cherkovsky but I do remember that I was in the back seat with this bald-headed man. Before I knew who it was, I said, "I'm reading up here, but last night I dreamed that I was reading poetry at the Grand Old Opry in Nashville."

"That was me. I did that last week. I was the first one to ever just read poetry at the Grand Old Opry," he said.

"No, it wasn't you. It was me, anyway I want it to be me."

The driver turned and introduced us. "Linda King this is Shel Silverstein."

How did my dreams know that I was going to be riding in the back seat with Shel Silverstein.

"Okay now I know this dream is you, but I hope it is me, too, years from now. I love your songs and your poetry." I said to him.

I was reading that day with some heavyweights, Allen Ginsberg, James Dalessandro, Lawrence Ferlinghetti, Gary Snyder, Jerry Kamstra, Paul Mann, Larry Hosford. Diane Ramsey was one of few women . . . And of course Charles Bukowski. I was very nervous about the reading and especially when I found out I was going on second, I walked outside. I needed some oxygen. I would just have to give it my best. Bukowski read first, before he got too drunk, and I started my reading with *Love for a Mad Poet* and ended with my reading with my old crowd shocker and pleaser, *A Cock*.

The reading was reviewed in the *Berkeley Barb* (Dec. 6–12, 1974). I was surprised and pleased that they had used a photo of me reading in the paper. The review read . . .

> Linda King was just getting hot when she was aced off the stage.
> Jerry Kamstra took the full blame. "It was my fault. She was one of the best-received poets and I should have given her a half and hour."

On the cover of the *Berkley Barb* was a story "Partying with the Poets." The party after the reading had got front page news. William Johnson did a great cartoon likeness of all the poets. He had Bukowski saying to Gingberg:

> *People who go to poetry readings aren't interesting in poetry. They want to see what you look like, they want to see you vomit, they want to see you die. People who go to poetry readiness are peep freaks. They want to fuck the poet or tame him or read to him of their own inept works.*

Apparently, that night Bukowski was going to give the people what they wanted. When Allen Ginsberg came in he shouted, "Ladies and Gentlemen, We have Allen Ginsberg as guest of honor tonight. Can you believe it Allen Ginsberg. A man of genius, the first poet to cut through light and consciousness for two thousand years and these bastards don't even appreciate it. Have a drink, Allen."

He put a drink in Allen's hand and undid what he had just said by saying, "God, it's good to see you Allen, really. I don't care if you are a fake. Did you hear that folks? Washed up. Everybody knows that after *Howl* you never wrote anything worth a shit. How about that folks, a vote? Has Allen written anything worth a shit since *Howl* and *Kay . . . dish*?" He was slurring his words and acting like a drunken jackass. He had drank enough to sink one of those beautiful bay sailboats.

"COME ON YOU BASTARDS, LET'S PARTY." he shouted to the crowd. This party was the first time I remember consciously disconnecting myself from Bukowski. I was talking to myself. "He is Charles Bukowski. I am Linda King. What he does will not affect or touch me. I am me. I am not Charles Bukowski's girlfriend. I am Linda King."

He started dancing a wild dance. It was the first of many times after that that Bukowski did his dance. So, something more than his nympho girlfriend did get through to his brain at my Utah party. He added dancing to his Bukowski show. It was still a one man show. I doubt if he could ever perform as a couple. The crowd liked it. The only bad thing, he had spilled a lot of wine out of those little wine glasses and he suddenly slipped and fell flat on his back in the middle of the wine. Normally, I would have run over and helped him up, but I just disappeared in the crowd.

Someone who hadn't been to the reading asked me, "Who is that ass making such a fool of himself?"

"I don't know." I shrugged my shoulders. I looked back at him and he was laying flat on his back kicking his legs straight up in the air to the music and he was laughing.

I was in and out of crowd like quicksilver, sliding here and there talking to whomever looked interesting. I knew Bukowski was in one of his blackouts. He would never remember anything he did tomorrow. I knew that creepy, ugly, cockroach *slime* who inhabited Bukowski when he got too drunk. He wouldn't even know me because I'd just had my hair cut. I was right, he didn't see me all night.

Later on in the night some guy came in from the other room.

"Bukowski is getting his cock sucked in the bathroom," he said.

I didn't turn a hair. I just slid off and started talking to someone else. The people who didn't know I came up with Bukowski, would never know that *quicksilver* was his girlfriend. When we left together they probably just thought we were two poets from Los Angeles.

In the motel, *he* passed out in an ugly, heavy, black, unconscious, death-like sleep. I didn't lay myself down next to *slime.* I slept in the chair.

In the morning Bukowski was back, bleary eyed, stinking breath and red-faced. We got back together with our ride. They waited while Bukowski puked his guts out in the bathroom. I was puking in my soul. We had a cheery breakfast and coffee. Bukowski could only puke some more. We went to see Shel's place which was on an beautiful old polished hardwood boat in Sausalito. It looked like a heavenly place to live. *It would be nice to have a boyfriend like Shel, talented, funny, sober, full of witty remarks and he lives in a place like this . . . And he writes songs for the country western boys.*

We went to a party somewhere else in the Hay Area where there were more drinking and more drugs. I decided to try a line of cocaine at this party. It was my first and my last. The afternoon and evening become a fog of sights and sounds. Bukowski who couldn't play decided to play the piano and I who couldn't sing decided to sing. The real musicians who were at the party probably weren't amused.

They took us to the plane. We didn't speak all the way home. We were in separate blurs. The glacier between us didn't melt down for weeks. Bukowski, supposedly, didn't remember anything of the drunken party after the poetry reading. I didn't want to be his memory. *Slime* wasn't worth talking about.

A BUK ELEGY

Paul Trachtenberg

While he mowed the fucking St. Augustine lawn
boils emerged on his adolescent face.
His daddy whipped him like butter—do this, do that.
Finally, he withdrew accompanied by pocks and arias.

Dazzled by operas, he grew belovedly mean.
He composed beer bottles and rusty bobby pins.
He buried his daddy under St. Augustine grass.
His lyrics become saltier, spicier and wryier.

Bolting hard whiskey he womanized Linda and Lizzie.
He danced with scintillating sluts on red-lit corners.
Those sullied ladies waltzed into varied operettas.
In between Fifth and Main, Buk sired a lovely daughter.

He did heaps of horse playing—Beadle-bomb, a sure bet.
He wrangled for ripped tavern barstools from San Pedro
to Santa Anita horse tracks—winning á la bruises.
Only Maria Callas could've licked his purple wounds.

He rode his Mercedes to Cabrillo Beach bluffs,
then leaped-off with a high white blood cell count.
St. Augustine in skid-row drag pens fresh, risible,
longwinded and twisted sonnets with a celestial quill.

ELEGY FOR A GIANT

Fred Voss

First, I discovered Bukowski in the University library, and it was magic—nights up smoking cheap cigars and drinking cheap booze getting gloriously drunk and enlightened with Bukowski all night, reading everything, the *Erections, Ejaculations, Exhibitions and General TALES OF ORDINARY MADNESS*, the *Crucifix in a Deathhand*, all the poetry and prose and that picture of him hanging onto that boxcar ladder . . .

It was magic and it changed me and I was never the same and though I went to graduate school for a year I quickly dropped out and found myself filling up a boardinghouse room and then a dive apartment in Long Beach with the smell of chain smoking and beer drinking and on-the-edge-of-suicide survival working busboy and factory jobs and knowing it was worth it, knowing it was right as I read *Burning in Water Drowning in Flame* and *The Days Run Away Like Wild Horses Over the Hills*, and something he'd given me made me burn inside as I suffered and made it on not even knowing that I would be a writer, just that I was doing what I had to do and that it was right, days

and nights of steel dust and furnaces and a burned-up mattress and tears in my beer listening to Hank Williams and no woman for years like

Bukowski at the start of *Women* still I held on with nothing but his poems and some kind of crazy stubborn will to go on
  and I did go on
  Bukowski
  leading me though suicide madness and bikers
and women who threw me down into the hard asphalt of their rejection
  without my own poem, without my own voice, I had
  Bukowski
  somehow leading me out of the darkness and toward the light
  of finally finding my own voice and my own poetry
  which I owe to him
  as much as maybe my life
  and much more and so
  you see
  that for me a great great light has gone out of this world

  Yet
  I look at my bookshelf 30 Bukowski books wide and realize that
  light can only really get brighter
  and brighter
  and that I will have it
  always.

THE FUNERAL OF CHARLES BUKOWSKI

Gerald Locklin

I have spent the weekend writing a remembrance of him for the Los Angeles *Reader*. Many revisions in between jockeying my youngest children, fifteen and thirteen, to whale watching, coffee houses, and the houses of friends. On Sunday night I drop the finished copy in the English department mail slot for faxing first thing Monday morning. I check my voice mail once more for any word of funeral services, memorial services, whatever. Nothing. No one I've talked to has heard a thing and there's been no such information in any of the newspapers. I've received inquiries myself. I've also received a surprising number of expressions of sympathy for me on the death of my friend.

I've had his address for twenty-five years, and for a long time I had his phone number, but I never used it, not once, and I never dropped in on him uninvited, and, after his number was changed, I didn't ask for it. I don't make myself readily available to others—as one who puts in a lot of his work hours at home and who puts a high priority on the privacy and protection of his family. I always felt that one of a number of reasons why he and I got along so well over such a long period of time was that I didn't force myself upon him. We corresponded when there was a reason to, and if invited to a party or premiere, I showed up if possible. I did not, as so many did, show up on his doorstep, with two six-packs and the conviction that I was doing him a favor. He probably wouldn't have minded, in the years before his marriage, if I had brought along a couple of young female admirers, but I didn't do that either. An awful lot of people did themselves a big favor under the guise of doing one for him.

So I don't have a number at which to call his wife Linda, and I don't make any attempt to obtain one. I figure he might well have made it clear that he wanted no commemoration of his death.

Green Hills Memorial Park looks down upon San Pedro and the Los Angeles Harbor from the side of Palos Verdes peninsula. The uniformed old man in the guard booth waves me up a lane to the chapel, where my car is one of two in the parking lot. Three young men are chatting quietly in pews near the front of the chapel. I grew up used to Catholic churches, where the Host, the Transubstantiated body of Christ, was allegedly in residence in the Tabernacle; thus I've never entirely become accustomed to the more relaxed conditions of other places of worship such as this non-denominational one.

I recognize Sean Penn in spite of his formal attire. He is shorter than I would have imagined, but what movie star isn't? I slip into a pew a few rows back. One of his companions looks like the L.A. poet Steve Richmond, but younger. He catches me staring at him. "Steve?" I say. He says, "My name is Jack." "Sorry," I say, "you look a little like a guy I used to know who was a friend of Bukowski's also." I figure then that Jack and the other recruits are Penn's bodyguards or chauffeurs or both. Why not? There's no such thing as too much precaution in L.A. these days, and it doesn't really matter if you know how to use your fists. Unless, like Superman, you've learned how to snatch bullets from the air.

Soon the three of them arise and move towards the back. Probably I've made them uncomfortable. But it's bad for my circulation to sit too long, so I'm soon heading back up the aisle myself.

John Martin, the publisher of Black Sparrow Press and of the bulk of Bukowski's work for the last twenty-five years, is arriving with his wife. I've been in the same room with him at Bukowski's wedding reception, and we've corresponded frequently in response to my reviewing of Hank's books and my using of them in my classes, but this is the first time I've had the opportunity to shake his hand. He shows me the final poem Bukowski ever sent him, dated February 28 and faxed on Hank's first such machine. It's a gently humorous piece alluding to the fax-machine itself, an appropriately typical poem. Sean Penn is standing nearby so I introduce myself to him now also. He speaks his own name very quietly and I say, "Yes. I know."

Sean tells me that he last talked to Hank two weeks ago, at which time he invited him to come to this very cemetery for the filming of a scene in the movie Sean is now directing. But Hank declined. Probably his health was already relapsing and he didn't want anyone outside his family to know. He was only back in the hospital a week or so before his death.

People are filing into the church now. I embrace Carl Weissner, who translated my *Case of the Missing Blue Volkswagen* as well as most of Bukowski and who boarded the first flight he could arrange from Germany in order to be here in time for the funeral. Carl is a gentle, committed man who was personally responsible for launching the Bukowski phenomenon in Europe. He tells me that Bukowski's constant photographer, Michael Montfort, is devastated that he will not be able to be here because of a court appearance that cannot be postponed. I realize that for Carl and Michael, whose own work has been so intimately associated with Bukowski's, the death will create a personal void similar to that in the lives of his wife and daughter.

Ironically, John Martin has been transported from the airport by a former student of mine, Michael Cahill, who now owns a bookstore in Fountain Valley after for a few years operating a Chinese restaurant that I often patronized in Seal Beach.

The only writers from the old days besides myself that I recognize are the intellectual and physical giant John Thomas and his wife Philomene Long, although a couple of white-haired ladies seem to be writers or academics perhaps associated with Black Sparrow Press. I'm told that most of the mourners are non-literary friends that the Bukowskis knew and enjoyed from their neighborhood and from the local restaurants, shops, and coffeehouses. This privateness is a side of Bukowski that few of his readers were aware of, just as the Hemingway who was so often embattled with professors, critics, and fellow writers, had innumerable friends among the ordinary people of all the places in which he lived.

As the service begins I take a place near the back, so often the preference of writers. The pallbearers include Carl Weissner, John Martin, Sean Penn, a doctor Bukowski became good friends with in the hospital, "Red"—the owner of Baroque Books in Hollywood—and a young man whom I do not recognize. Sean Penn tells briefly from the pulpit what he has told me about the recent filming here. John Martin speaks of what he and Bukowski were able to accomplish in their literary partnership from that day so long ago when he recognized in Hank "a great writer and a great man." In his grief, Carl Weissner is virtually inaudible, which is the most eloquent of testimonials.

The religious rites are conducted by a trio of Buddhist monks, with a great deal of chanting and bowing. I figure this is Linda's preference, that Bukowski wouldn't have cared one way or the other, except that he would have wanted her to have things however she wanted them. Later, though, she will tell me that Bukowski actually became very interested in Buddhism near the end, even to the extent of receiving his own mantra and practicing meditation. Apparently the notion of purification held some appeal for him. I can believe that and understand it, having been not too far removed from my own death just six months before.

The monk in charge, a Sri Lankan, speaks in two languages from the pulpit, but is about equally difficult to understand in both. As far as I can make out, he is saying pretty much what any minister or priest or rabbi would, that at times such as these we realize that life is short. He doesn't seem to have known Bukowski very well, or at all, judging from the general nature of his remarks. To his credit those remarks are kept blessedly brief. We file from the chapel to the parking lot and proceed in a caravan of automobiles to the ridge of the hill on the side of which the grave awaits. John Thomas and I have little trouble descending the green slope, but climbing back up we both risk joining the ranks of the deceased. What a fine literary anecdote that would make, an exquisite piece of literary trivia: Name the two poets who simultaneously expired at the funeral of Charles Bukowski.

In a poem written that week by Philomene, she will mention that the casket almost got away from its handlers on its way down the hill and that one of the monks positioned himself for a photo opportunity at the grave. But I can't claim to have observed those occurrences. I was impressed by the subtle authority with which Sean Penn directed his limo to await him on a road beneath the gravesite. Quiet exercise of authority. I was getting to like the guy quite a bit. Later he would appear unannounced at a tribute reading for Bukowski at the Sacred Grounds coffeehouse in San Pedro, accompanied by Sinead O'Connor, who would sing *a capella* an ancient Irish ballad on the subject of death. It was no wonder that Bukowski was so fond of him, that they had had such good times at the track and elsewhere. You have to understand with what contempt most writers are treated by Hollywood people in order fully to appreciate those few who have an uncorrupted sense of literary and personal worth.

The ceremony at the grave was also brief; a few tapped the coffin in the gambler's gesture of "Good Luck," before turning back up the hill.

* * *

Having a three-hour class to teach back at the university, I can only stay an hour at the reception at what is now Linda's home on the quiet residential street in San Pedro. I have been here twice before, at a party for Hank's sixtieth birthday and after the wedding reception of Hank and Linda at a Thai restaurant in Ports-of-Call a couple of years later. The buffet today is Thai also. I find myself a Diet Coke and notice how many others are drinking non-alcoholic or low-alcoholic beverages as well. At most a bottle of Becks, perhaps, or a glass of white German wine. We are all getting old. None of the beer-chugging or shooters of the hard stuff of the parties circa 1970. But those had often ended badly, although there are some with little else to write about who are still invoking them. We have learned a few lessons from life, as Bukowski did also.

I peruse again the many bookcases stacked with the books and anthologies and periodicals of many languages containing Bukowski's works. Given the circumstances of his life, it is an incredible achievement. Linda has arranged a modest shrine to his memory, with flowers in front of an enlarged photograph. She speaks of making the home a private museum of his work and I wonder if she realizes the hordes of admirers that might besiege it. I advise her to make sure the collection is adequately insured. In a later phone conversation she will tell me what a practical and efficient person her husband truly was, at least in the years she knew him, paying all bills promptly, eschewing left turns in traffic, and putting everything in her name before he died. Another side seldom recognized by those who would prefer to use him as a model for getting drunk and staying drunk and collecting unemployment while writing pale imitations of his work.

"He used to say," Linda tells me, "they are all Little Bukowskis." The truth of this is highlighted at one subsequent Bukowski tribute reading in Orange County that reportedly degenerates into a drunken brawl.

On the patio, near the narrow pool and the gardens that Bukowski came to love, I hear a lot of talk of the prices rare editions of his work are bringing. John Martin tells how Bukowski was able to buy the lovely large old home and gardens before the soaring inflation of property values for a mortgage of a mere four hundred dollars a month, but that he worried constantly that he might not be able to pay it.

John Thomas (a pseudonym), and his wife solicit my advice on the disposition of their own literary papers, which include letters from the personal tapes of Bukowski. My own letters from him are in the Special Collections at Cal State University, Long Beach.

They ask what I thought of the Buddhists. I say, "I've always been a firm believer in *To Each His Own.*"

"Ah well," John says, "That's certainly non-committal."

That suits me. Bukowski made few demands of life and I don't either. A little time and space in which to write. Booze when we needed it. The women that we couldn't live with and couldn't live without and for whom we were not all that easy to live with either. Mostly, though, the writing that was the *sine qua non*, a term he would have abhorred, just as he would have *ars longa; vita brevis*, although it is probably the ultimate commentary on his death.

Red's wife introduces herself and asks if we haven't met. When her husband tells her that I write, she goes out of her way to make me feel comfortable. Red himself has a reputation of being a curmudgeon but he is also gracious to me and tells me of the Hemingway collection he sold cheap rather than move it to California. I don't collect literary things myself. I give them to the university library where my wife won't be able to incinerate them along with my carcass.

Bukowski's daughter, Marina, is finally unoccupied. I only met her once, at the premiere and reception for *Barfly*, but we hit it off at once and she and her husband and I had a good time, bubbling like the free-flowing champagne and totally out of our element among the Hollywood people. Bukowski protected her as best he could from his notoriety, and watched out for her as best he could as she was growing up. She was the joy of his life, but, again, this was one more side of his life that few ever saw. She attended the university I teach at, but we never met there. A lot of people say they will miss Bukowski but she is one of the few who really will because she is one of the few who ever really knew him, and I tell her this. For millions the Bukowski they know is an image created less by him than by themselves, as was certainly true of Hemingway as well.

Marina has traveled widely, but is thinking now of returning to Southern California. I think her father would like that. She is not a "tough" person in any coarse or external sense—she is a bright and charming young lady—but he would be proud of her inherited resiliency.

I tell Linda that I have to leave. I will call her because I know there will be low points in the next few weeks. Across the room a little girl has tears in her eyes. I ask if she is a relative. "No," Linda tells me, "she lives across the street. Hank loved her and she adored him. She may be taking his death the hardest of any of us."

* * *

Two weeks later, through circuitous routes, a quip of Sean Penn's is related to me. As the pigtailed, teal-veiled monks are chanting around the casket, he whispers to the pall-bearer next to him, "Don't they know this is America? Why aren't they speaking Spanish?"

Bukowski would have laughed. Maybe, in fact, he did. He deserved to have the last laugh.

TOUGH GUYS WRITE POETRY

CHARLES BUKOWSKI

An Interview by Sean Penn

On Bars:

Don't do too much bar stuff anymore. Got that out of my system. Now when I walk into a bar, I almost gag. I've seen so many of them, it's just too fuckin' much—that stuff's for when you're younger, you know, and you like to duke it with a guy, you know you play that macho shit—try to pick up broads—at my age. I don't need all that. Nowadays, I just go into bars to piss. Too many years in the bar. It just got so bad, that I'd walk into a bar, I'd walk through the door and I'd start to puke.

On Alcohol:

Alcohol is probably one of the greatest things to arrive upon the earth—alongside of me. Yes . . . these are two of the greatest arrivals upon the surface of the earth. So . . . we get along. It is ultimately destructive to most people. I'm just one apart from that. I do all of my creative work while I'm intoxicated. Even with women, you know, I've always been reticent in the love-making act, so alcohol has allowed me, sexually, to be more free. It's a release, because basically I am a shy, withdrawn person, and alcohol allows me to be this hero, striding through space and time, doing all these daring things . . . So I like it . . . yeah.

On Smoking:

I like to smoke. Smoke and alcohol counterbalance each other. I used to wake up from drinking, you know, and you smoke so much, both your hands are yellow, see, like you've got gloves on . . . almost brown . . . and yousay. "Oh, shit . . . what do my lungs look like? Oh Jesus!"

On Fighting:

The best feeling is when you whip a guy you're not supposed to whip, I got into it with a guy one time, he was giving me a lot of lip. I said, "Okay. Let's go." He was no problem at all—I whipped him easy. He was laying there on the ground. He's got a bloody nose, the whole works. He says, "Jesus, you move slow, man. I thought you'd be easy—the goddamn fight started—I couldn't see your hands anymore, you were so fucking fast. What happened?" I said, "I don't know, man. That's just the way it goes." You save it. You save it for the moment.

My cat, Beeker, is a fighter. He gets mauled up a bit sometimes, but he's always the winner. I taught him it all, you know . . . lead with the left, set up the right.

On Cats:

Having a bunch of cats around is good. If you're feeling bad, you just look at the cats, you'll feel better, because they know that everything is, just as it is. There's nothing to get excited about. They just know. They're saviors. The more cats you have, the longer you live. If you have a hundred cats, you'll live ten times longer than if you have ten. Someday this will be discovered, and people will have a thousand cats and live forever. It's truly ridiculous.

On Women and Sex:

I call 'em complaining machines. Things are never right with a guy to them. And man, when you throw that hysteria in there . . . forget it. I gotta get out, get in the car, and *go*. Anywhere. Get a cup of coffee somewhere. Anywhere. Anything but another woman. I guess they're just built different, right?

[*He's on a roll now.*]

The hysteria starts . . . they're gone. You go to leave, they don't understand.

[*In a high woman's screech:*]

"WHERE ARE YOU GOING?"

"I'm getting the hell out of here, baby!" They think I'm a woman hater, but I'm not. A lot of it is word of mouth. They just hear "Bukowski's a male-chauvinist pig," but they don't check the source. Sure I make women look bad sometimes, but I make men look bad too. I make *myself* look bad. If I really think it's bad, I say it's bad—man, woman, child, dog. The women are so touchy, they think they're being singled out. That's their problem.

The First One:

Fuckin' first one was the strangest—I didn't know—she taught me how to eat pussy and all these fucking things. I didn't know anything. She said, "You know, Hank, you're a great writer, but you don't know a damn thing about women!"

"What do you mean? I've fucked a lot of women."

"No, you don't know. Let me teach you some things."

I said, "Okay."

She said. "You're a good student, man. You catch on right away."

That's all—

[*He got a little embarrassed. Not by the specifics, but rather by the sentimentality of the reminiscence.*]

But all that eatin' pussy shit can get kinda subservient. I like to please them, but . . .

It's all overrated, man. Sex is only a great thing if you're not getting any.

On Sex Before AIDS (And His Marriage):

I just used to pop in and out of those sheets. I don't know, it was kind of a trance, a fuck trance. I'd just kinda fuck, and fuck [*laughs*] . . . I did! [*laughs*]

And the women, you know, you'd say a few words, and you just grab 'em by the wrist, "Come on, baby." Lead 'em in the bedroom and fuck 'em. And they'd go with it, man. Once you get in that rhythm, man, you'd just go. There are a lot of lonely women out there, man. They look good, they just don't connect. They're sitting there all alone, going to work, coming home . . . it's a big thing for 'em to have some guy pop 'em. And if he sits around, drinks and talks, you know, it's entertainment. It was all right . . . and I was lucky.

Modern women . . . they don't sew your pockets . . . forget that.

On Writing:

I wrote a short story from the viewpoint of a rapist who raped a little girl. So people accused me. I was interviewed. They'd say, "You like to rape little girls?" I said, "Of course not. I'm photographing life." I've gotten in trouble *with a* lot of my shit. On the other hand, *trouble* sells some books. But, bottom line, when I write, it's for me.

[*He draws a deep drag off his cigarette.*]

It's like this. The "drag" is for me, the ash is for the tray . . . that's publication.

I never write in the daytime. It's like running through the shopping mall with your clothes off. Everybody can see you. At night . . . that's when you pull the tricks . . . magic.

On Poetry:

I always remember the schoolyards in grammar school, when the word "poet" or "poetry" came up, all the little guys would laugh and mock it. I can see why, because it's a fake product. It's been fake and snobbish and inbred for centuries. It's over-delicate. It's over-precious. It's a bunch of trash. Poetry for the centuries is almost total trash. It's a con, a fake.

There have been a very few good poets, don't mistake me. There's a Chinese poet called Li Po. He could put more feeling, realism, and passion in four or five simple lines than most poets can in the twelve or fourteen pages of their shit. And he drank wine too. He used to set his poems on fire, sail down the river, and drink wine. The emperors loved him, because they could understand what he was saying . . . but, of course, he only burned his bad poems. [*laughs*]

What *I've* tried to do, if you'll pardon me, is bring in the factory-workers aspect of life . . . the screaming wife when he comes home from work. The basic realities of the everyman existence . . . something seldom mentioned in the poetry of the centuries. Just put me down as saying that the poetry of the centuries is shit. It's shameful.

On Celine:

The first time I read Céline, I went to bed with a big box of Ritz crackers. I started reading him and eating these Ritz crackers, and laughing, and eating the Ritz crackers. I read the whole novel straight through. And the box of Ritz was empty, man. And I got up and drank water, man. You should've seen me. I couldn't move. That's what a good writer will do to you. He'll damn near kill you . . . a bad writer will too.

On Shakespeare:

He's unreadable and overrated. But people don't want to hear that. You see, you cannot attack shrines. Shakespeare is embedded through the centuries. You can say "So-and-so is a lousy actor!" But you can't say Shakespeare is shit. The longer something is around, snobs begin to attach themselves to it, like suckerfish. When snobs feel something is safe . . . they attach. The moment you tell them the truth, they go wild. They can't handle it. It's attacking their own thought process. They disgust me.

On His Favorite Reading Material:

I read in *The National Enquirer*, "Is your husband homosexual?" Linda had said to me, "You have a voice like a fag!" I said, "Oh, yeah. I always wondered." [*laughs*] This article says, "Does he pull his eyebrows out?" I thought, shit! I do that all the time. Now I know what I am. I pull my eyebrows out . . . I'm a fag! Okay. It's nice for *The National Enquirer* to tell me what I am.

On Humor and Death:

There's very little. About the last best humorist was a guy called James Thurber. But his humor was so great, they had to overlook it. Now, this guy was what you call a psychologist/psychiatrist of the ages. He had the man/woman thing—you know, people seeing things. He was a cure-all. His humor was so real, you almost have to scream out your laughter in a frantic release. Outside of Thurber, I can't think of anybody . . . I've got a little touch of it . . . but not like he did. What I've got I don't really call humor. I'd call it . . . "a comic edge." I'm almost hooked on the comic edge. No matter what happens . . . it's ludicrous. Almost everything, is ludicrous. You know, we shit every day. That's ludicrous. Don't you think? We have to keep pissing, putting food in our mouths, wax comes in our ears, hair? We have to scratch ourselves. Really ugly and dumb, you know? Tits are useless, unless . . .

You know, we're monstrosities. If we could really see this, we could love ourselves . . . realize how ridiculous we are, with our intestines wound around, shit slowly running through as we look each other in the eyes and say "I love you," our stuff is carbonizing, turning into shit, and we never fart near each other. It all has a comic edge . . .

And then we die. But, death has not earned us. It hasn't shown any credentials—we've shown all the credentials.

With birth, have we earned life? Not really, but we're sure caught with the fucker . . . I resent it, I resent death. I resent life. I resent being caught between the two. You know how many times I've tried suicide?

[*Linda asks, "Tried?"*]

Give me time, I'm only sixty-six years old. Still working at it.

* * *

When you have a suicide complex, nothing bothers you . . . except losing at the track. Somehow that bothers you. Why is that? . . . Because you're using your mind [at the track] not your heart.

I never rode a horse.

I'm not so interested in the horse, as in the process of being right and wrong . . . selectively.

On the Track:

I tried to make my living at the track for a while. It's painful. It's exhilarating. Everything is on the line—the rent—everything. But, you tend to be too cautious . . . it's not the same.

One time I was sitting way down at the curve. There were twelve horses in the race and they all got bunched together. It looked like a big charge. All I saw were these big horses' asses going up and down. They looked wild. I looked at those horse asses and I thought, "This is madness, this is total madness!" But then you have other days where you win four or five hundred dollars, you've won eight or nine races in a row, you feel like God, you know everything. It all fits together.

[*Then to me.*]

CB: All your days aren't good, are they?
SP: *No.*
CB: Some of them good?
SP: *Yeah.*
CB: Many of them?
SP: *Yeah.*
[*After a pause, the laughter of surprise*]
CB: I thought you were going to say "Just a few . . ." How disappointing!

On People:

I don't look too much at people. It's disturbing. They say if you look too much at someone, you start to look like them. Poor Linda.

* * *

People, mostly, I can do without. They don't fill me, they empty me. I respect no man. I have a problem that way . . . I'm lying, but believe me, it's true.

The valet at the track is okay. Sometimes I'm leaving the track and he'll say, "Well, how you doing, man?" I'll say, "Shit, I'm ready to go for the jugular . . . throw up the white flag, man. I've had it." He'll say "Oh no! Come on, man! I'll tell you what. Let's go out tonight, get drunk. We'll kick some ass, and suck pussy." I'll say "Frank, let me consider that." He'll say "You know, the worse it gets, the wiser you get." I'll say, "You must be a pretty wise man, Frank." He'll say, "You know it's a good thing you and I didn't meet when we were younger." I'll say, "Yeah, I know what you're going to say, Frank We'd both be in San Quentin." "Right!" he says.

On Being Recognized At The Track:

The other day I'm sitting there and I see them staring at me. I know what's coming so I get up to move, you know? And he says, "Excuse me?" And I say, "Yes, what is it?" He says, "Are you Bukowski? I say, "No!" He says, "I guess people ask you that all the time, don't they?" And I say, "Yes!" and I walked away. You know we've discussed this before. There's nothing like privacy. You know, I like people. It's nice that they might like my books and all that . . . but I'm not the book. I'm the guy who wrote it, but I don't want them to come up and throw roses on me or anything. I want them to *let me breathe*. They wanna hang out with me. They think I'll bring some whores, wild music, that I'm gonna slug somebody . . . you know. They read the stories! Shit, these things happened twenty to thirty years ago, baby!

On Fame:

It's a destructor. It's the whore. Fame is really terrible. . . . It is a measuring scale of the common denominator. It is working on a low level. It's worthless. A select audience is much better.

On Loneliness

I've never been lonely. I've been in a room—I've felt suicidal. I've been depressed. I've felt awful—awful beyond all—but never felt that one *other person* could enter that room and cure what was bothering me . . . or that any *number* of people could enter that room. In other words, loneliness is something I've never been bothered with because I've always had this terrible itch for solitude. It's being at a party, or at a stadium full of people cheering for something, that I might feel loneliness. I'll quote Ibsen, "The strongest men are the most alone." I've never thought, "Well, some beautiful blond will come in here and give me a fuck-job, rub my balls, and I'll feel good." No, that won't help. You know the typical crowd, "Wow, it's Friday night, what are you going to do? Just sit there?" Well, yeah. Because there's nothing out there. It's stupidity. Stupid people mingling with stupid people. Let them stupidify themselves. I've never been bothered with the need to rush out into the night. I hid in bars, because I didn't want to hide in factories. That's all. Sorry for all the millions, but I've never been lonely. I like myself. I'm the best form of entertainment I have. Let's drink more wine!

On Leisure:

This is very important—to take leisure time. Pace is the essence. Without *stopping* entirely and doing nothing at all for great periods, you're gonna lose everything. Whether you're an actor, anything, a housewife . . . there has to be great pauses between highs, where you do nothing at all. You just lay on a bed and stare at the ceiling. This is very, very important . . . just to do nothing at all, very, very important. And how many people do this in modern society? Very few. That's why they're all totally mad, frustrated, angry and hateful.

In the old days, before I was married, or knew a lot of women, I would just pull down all the shades and go to bed for three or four days. I'd get up to shit. I'd eat a can of beans, go back to bed, just stay there for three or four days. Then I'd put on my clothes and I'd walk outside, and the sunlight was brilliant, and the sounds were great. I felt powerful, like a recharged battery. But you know the first bring-down? The first human face I saw on the sidewalk, I lost half my charge right there. This monstrous, blank, dumb, unfeeling face, charged up with capitalism—the "grind." And you went "Oooh! That took half away." But it was still worth it, I had half left. So, yeah, leisure. And I don't mean having profound thoughts. I mean having *no* thoughts at all. Without thoughts of progress, without any self-thoughts of trying to further yourself. Just . . . like a slug. It's beautiful.

On Beauty:

There is no such thing as beauty, especially in the human face . . . what we call the physiognomy. It's all a mathematical and imagined alignment of features. Like, if the nose doesn't stick out too much, the sides are in fashion, if the earlobes aren't too large, if the hair is long . . . It's kind of a mirage of generalization. People think of certain faces as beautiful, but, truly, in the final measure, they are not. It's a mathematical equation of zero. "True beauty" comes, of course, of character. Not through how the eyebrows are shaped. So many women that I'm told are beautiful . . . hell, it's like looking into a soup bowl.

On Ugliness:

There's no such thing as ugliness. There is a thing called deformity, but *outward* "ugliness" does not exist . . . I have spoken.

Once Upon a Time:

It was wintertime. I was starving to death trying to be a writer in New York. I hadn't eaten for three or four days. So, I finally said, "I'm gonna have a big bag of popcorn." And God, I hadn't tasted food for so long, it was so good. Each kernel, you know, each one was like a steak! I chewed and it would just drop into my poor stomach. My stomach would say. "THANK YOU THANK YOU THANK YOU!" I was in heaven, just walking along, and two guys happened by, and one said to the other, "Jesus Christ!" The other one said, "What was it?" "Did you see that guy eating popcorn? God, it was awful!" And so I couldn't enjoy the rest of the popcorn. I thought, what do you mean, "it was awful?" I'm in heaven here. I guess I was kinda dirty. They can always tell a fucked-up guy.

On the Press:

I kind of like being attacked. "Bukowski's disgusting!" That makes me smile, you know, I like it. "Oh, he's a horrible writer!" I smile some more. I kind of feed on that. It's when a guy tells me, "Hey, you know, they're teaching you at such and such a university," my mouth drops. I don't know . . . to be too much accepted is terrifying You feel you've done something wrong.

I enjoy the bad things that are said about me. It enhances [book] sales and makes me feel evil. I don't like to feel good 'cause I am good. But evil? Yes. It gives me another dimension.

[*Bringing up the pinky finger of his left hand* . . .]

Did you ever see this finger?

[*The finger seems paralyzed in a downward "L" configuration.*]

I broke it, drunk one night. Don't know how, but . . . I guess it just didn't set right. But, it works just fine for the "a" key [*on his typewriter*] and . . . what the hell . . . it adds to my character. See, now I've got character and dimension. [*He laughs.*]

On Bravery:

Most so-called brave people lack imagination. As though they can't conceive of what would happen if something went wrong. The *truly* brave overcome their imagination and do what they have to do.

On Fear:

I don't know a thing about it. [*He laughs.*]

On Violence:

I think violence is often misinterpreted. Certain violence is needed. There is, in all of us, an energy that demands an outlet. I think that if the energy is constrained, we go mad. The ultimate peacefulness we all desire is not a desirable area. Somehow in our construction, it is not meant to be. This is why I like to see boxing matches, and why, in my younger days, I'd like to duke it in back alleys. "Expulsion of energy with honor," is sometimes called violence. There is "interesting madness" and "disgusting madness." There are good and bad forms of violence. So, in fact . . . it's a loose term. Let it not be too much at the expense of others, and it's okay.

On Physical Pain:

When I was a kid, they used to drill me. I had these big boils. You toughen up to physical pain. When I was in General Hospital they were drilling away, and a guy walked in, and he said, "I never saw anyone go under the needle that cool." That's not bravery—if you get enough physical pain, you relent—it's a process, an adjustment.

Mental pain can't be adjusted to. Keep me away from it.

On Psychiatry:

What do psychiatric patients get? They get a bill.

I think the problem between the psychiatrist and the patient is that the psychiatrist *goes by the book*, while the patient arrives because of what life has done to him or her. And even though the book may have certain insights, the pages are always the same in the book, and each patient is a little bit different. There are many more individual problems than pages. Get it? There are too many mad people to do it by saying, "dollars per hour, when this bell rings, you're finished." That alone will drive any near-mad person to madness. They've just started to open up and feel good, when the shrink says, "Nurse, make the next appointment," and they've lost track of the price, which is also abnormal. It's all too stinking *worldly*. The guy is out to take your ass. He's not out to cure you. He wants his money. When the bell rings, bring in the next "nut." Now the sensitive "nut" will realize when that bell rings, he's being fucked. There's no time limit to curing madness, and there's no bills for it either. Most psychiatrists I've seen look a little close to the edge themselves. But they're too comfortable . . . I think they're all too comfortable. I think a patient wants to see a little madness, not too much. Ahhhh! *[bored]* PSYCHIATRISTS ARE TOTALLY USELESS! Next question?

On Faith:

Faith is all right for those who have it. Just don't load it on me.

I have more faith in my plumber than I do in the eternal being. Plumbers do a good job. They keep the shit flowing.

On Cynicism:

I've always been accused of being a cynic. I think cynicism is sour grapes. I think cynicism is a weakness. It's saying "everything is wrong! EVERYTHING IS WRONG!" You know? "This is not right! That is not right!" Cynicism is the weakness that keeps one from being able to adjust to what is occurring at the moment. Yes, cynicism is definitely a weakness, just as optimism is. "The sun is shining, the birds are singing—so smile." That's bullshit too. The truth lies somewhere in between. What is, just is. So you're not ready to handle it . . . too bad.

On Conventional Morality:

There may not be a hell, but those who judge may create one. I think people are over-taught. They are over-taught everything. You have to find out by what happens to you, how you will react. I'll have to use a strange term here . . . "good." I don't know where it comes from, but I feel that there's an ultimate strain of goodness born in each of us. I don't believe in God, but I believe in this "goodness" like a tube running through our bodies. It can be nurtured. It's always magic, when on a freeway packed with traffic, a stranger makes room for you to change lanes . . . it gives you hope.

On Being Interviewed:

It's almost like being caught in the corner. It's embarrassing. So, I don't always tell the total truth. I like to play around and jest a bit, so I do give out some misinformation just for the sake of entertainment and bullshit. So if you want to know about me never read an interview. Ignore this one.

BUKOWSKI IS DEAD BUKOWSKI IS DEAD

Steve Abee

Bukowski is Dead
Bukowski is Dead

The blue brained bottle lipped lover of WHAT?
the world is, demons and all, is dead
like he he knew he would be and wondered why
it hadn't happened before.

He was good.
Better than the world he lived in,
more in love than his world deserved to be.
His hands laid out the all night
sharp lined fangs of the buried life,
the spit whispered pulse of the hearts tragic ferns,
the scarred blood of love emptied
onto the impossible prostitute streets—blood
that flowed the cracks to the curb
to the severed neck storm drain shit whiskey
crab sewer belly boiled sore desert stung blind
and robbed back broken suicide

door of this sphere's unknown roll,
blood spilt for the face of the ass of the soul
of all these fingers, rings and toilet bowls,
all these severe sperm wanting folds of bone and need,
blood making his ink pornographically clear.

The man had good punchlines, roped lines, love lines
and did not lie but told the mistaken truth
that wasn't supposed to be, smoked
cigars in the cum stained nude,
made poems that had been too fucked up
the night before and still made it to the clock,
words from the floor of mean love's teeth
laughing like a boil raging in the sun,
like the scars on his deep psycho flowered face,
killing the contradictions of this stone seared in mud.
This is a good year to turn your marrow over
to the worm fingered hand's of the dust,
now you drink but not for thirst but to salute
the wounds you could not heal.

What creature is this world?

Not the warriors, not the winos, nor the working,
nor the worked, not the killers, not the Saints
or the nurses or the driver's of old trains,
Nobody but the dead know
how love calls home, how the seed drips from the bone,

Yes, fuckers, Yes, mothers, only the still bones know
"The What" Beethoven heard in his tattered strings
and now you, soft handed drunk, now you Sir, know
how these orbits sing.

THE BUKOWSKI READING: LONG BEACH, 1972

John Kay

Locklin drove to Los Angeles to pick up Bukowski the morning of the poetry readings, historically known as "Three Evenings of Poetry." It wasn't more than a thirty mile drive from Long Beach, but in Locklin's car (and to my knowledge, he has never had a dependable car), on the L.A. freeways, the prospects of the readings actually materializing were in jeopardy. And if that alone wasn't enough, it was certain that he had loaded the back seat of the faded, red and white Edsel with vodka and Coors. It wasn't that he expected to be sociable on the return trip; he was just taking the necessary, usual "precautions," as he might have put it.

While he was on the road, I was busy tidying up the details: making sure the lectern arrived at the hall and that it was placed solidly on the stage, making sure the audio system had enough power, making the dinner reservations. That kind of thing. There isn't much to preparing for a poetry reading beyond dealing with the poet and the publicity, but this one demanded special attention. This was the big one. Bukowski. The name alone sounded ominous. There were other poets on other days during the week: Lyn Lifshin and Brother Antoninus (William Everson), but the largest crowd would be coming to *see* and hear Charles Bukowski, local oddity and celebrity of the underground press. He was scheduled to give two readings: one at noon and another at eight the same evening. I wasn't only concerned with how the readings themselves would go, but I was also a little worried about the time between them. He would have seven long hours to mull over the first reading, recharge, and forget the morning if it failed. It was my job to keep him sober and on time.

I picked up his check from the activities chairman, folded it into thirds and tucked it in my shirt pocket behind a pack of Winstons. $300. Was he worth it? Was he worth more? In retrospect, I'm a little ashamed that I didn't offer him more. There was more in the coffer, but I was doing what most young entrepreneurial types do: spending the minimum. It wasn't even my money. If it had been, I would probably have started the bidding at $150 or $175, and he probably would have accepted. Nevertheless, I made him the offer about six weeks prior to the readings at a party at his apartment in Los Angeles. It was a "coming out" party, a bar mitzvah of sorts, for a freshly issued collection called *Anthology of L.A. Poets*—a thin book with deep, chocolate-brown covers that made the printing hard to read. Probably a collector's item now. It was published by Red Hill Press, and even though Locklin was not an official L.A. poet, but a Long Beach poet, he figured prominently in it. He had the spirit of an L.A. poet, I suppose. He asked me if I'd like to go to the party, so I did, thinking that I would make the proposal for the readings to Bukowski sometime during the evening.

Bukowski lived in a small, one bedroom, courtyard apartment that needed paint ten years ago. Most of his furniture was broken or ripped but functional. The bed slumped heavily to one side, and across from it were three, six foot wide shelves of what looked to be most of the small press books and magazines that had published him. At one point during the evening he was showing them to me and he said, "All of 'em, $500 bucks. First editions included." He cuffed the air with the back of his hand and acted as if they meant nothing to him—an easy gesture, considering he knew I didn't have that kind of money. I was broke. I couldn't even buy a copy of the anthology.

The party took place in the living room, which was far too small and tight; people leaned against the walls or sat on the floor, positioning themselves so that they could watch Bukowski as if he were a television. He sat in a cushioned rocker in a far corner. His hair was greased back in long gray and black strands that turned up in matted patches at his neckline. He spoke in a soft but gravelly manner, his narrow eyes bouncing, darting, glancing around the room incessantly. There were other good poets in the room, most of them published in the new anthology, but Bukowski was definitely the center of attention. That is, no one was really interested in hearing anyone else say anything. He was on stage—he knew it, and he loved it. At one point he allowed, even encouraged somebody's spaniel to hump his leg. He said, "Am I the only one willing to make the fool of himself?" as the little dog straddled and worked his outstretched leg. He chuckled to himself as the dog gradually discovered the futility of its endeavor. Later, the dog tried again, and Bukowski let him. No one else could have gotten away with it a second time; they would have lacked his keen sense of timing, and would have just looked stupid.

Locklin and I were propped against the wall next to the door. At regular intervals he would take my empty can, drop it into a paper bag next to him, and then reach down and pull out a fresh one and hand it to me. As a rule, Bukowski doesn't like academics, but Locklin is an exception. Locklin seemed able to deal with Bukowski eye to eye. Locklin was his friend, an honor bestowed upon few.

If you, dear reader, have only just casually happened upon Bukowski, your initial fascination may not be broad enough to include the idea that Bukowski could like anyone or anything other than the whore's hip he holds in one hand and the beer he holds in the other, but that would be far from the truth. You have only seen the mask. When you arrive at the poems about visiting his daughter who lives with one of his ex-wives or the story "The Most Beautiful Woman in Town," you will discover his great capacity for loving, caring, laughing, and friendship. I doubt that he would ever admit to this, but I also doubt that any of us would have bothered with such an apparent asshole if that weren't the case. Beneath his battered surface a war between love and hate raged incessantly and it was easier to allow the hate to surface than the love. There was too much feeling in Bukowski, and it couldn't be all bad, though I suppose the possibility of that made him all the more interesting.

Half-way through the party, there was a tapping at one of the windows in the door. It wasn't another poet, but a neighbor from a few doors down, who, according to Bukowski, had just taken out his dried and brown Christmas tree and that was the reason for the tinsel on the lawn and walkway. It was then March, and the whole scene seemed so typical, so much like something you might have read in one of his poems, it was hard to believe that it wasn't staged. The neighbor, obviously drunk, stepped over the outstretched bodies with great difficulty and sat down on the arm of the couch opposite Bukowski.

"I saw all the cars. What's the occasion? Birthday?"

"No. This is a gathering of most of the great literary minds in Los Angeles. Mostly writers."

"Bullshit."

"See that typer, I earn my living with it. And all those letters in all those boxes are from editors. I took the boxes with me when I quit the post office. I haven't worked in two years."

"You're on welfare."

"Beer?"

And just as the word was coming out, someone bumped an empty beer bottle of the window sill and it landed on the stereo sitting on the floor behind Bukowski. The needle bounced and bit into the already noticeably worn record. It could have been Brahms, it could have been Mingus; my memory does not serve me. The needle raged across the record and the conversation came to an abrupt end along with the music. He reached back blithely and turned the machine off. It was one of those cheap $79 component systems encased in green vinyl. He said, "Fuck," and someone else said, "Sorry," and it was over.

The neighbor said "Beer?" He didn't talk much when he talked.

Bukowski got up and walked into the kitchen, which was brilliantly lit. Entering it from the living room was like exiting a theater in the middle of the afternoon. He got out two beers, one for his friend, and the other for himself. I had followed them in. I stuck out my hand and said, "John Kay, from Long Beach." A rather feminine, thin hand reached out and shook my hand loosely. His eyes narrowed as he looked me over, and he cacodemonized, "Kaaaaaaaaay!" stretching the *a* like a pair of shrunken pants to get them back in shape. He knew me from my magazine.

"Would you like to do a reading in Long Beach, at the college?" I asked. There was a long pause as he stood there in his black stockinged feet, taking a hit off his Coors. He looked over at his neighbor and smiled, softly. Not a salesman by nature, I blurted out, "300 dollars!" I think he asked "When?" and we went on to make the arrangements as best we could. For a poet he was doing well, but a poet doing well just from his writing isn't usually doing very well. The reading would help.

Bukowski was the king. He could do no wrong. He was an inspiration in a time when there were few others. And around him there grew up a handful of poets who took up his banner, though he would spit on them as he did on everything else that got too close. A style of writing was spawned in Los Angeles that has never had an exact name. Locklin once called it the poetry of "assault," and, for the time, that will have to do.

This assault, and it was a genuine barrage, was on the academic world. Bukowski led this attack, and anyone familiar with his poems can recall more than one account of the airplane trip back to L.A. from some small college in the midwest where they frowned upon drinking and all the professors that ushered him about were a little embarrassed about this curiosity who tended to be rude. He was supposed to be the hottest thing in actually like the person in the poems. Beneath the surface an e. e. cummings-like character lurked, they suspected, and maybe they were right, but when you met him you knew that you would probably never see that side of him. The only person home was the king. He had a responsibility, and we all expected him to live up to the reputation, and he wasn't about to let us down, not on paper, and certainly not at his party.

"Sure, Kay," he said. "Poetry. Long Beach. Sure." And with that said he had his hand on my shoulder like a father or a car salesman, I'm not sure which, and he took me into the bedroom to try and sell me his archives. At that point I ducked back into the party, and a young thin black woman with masculine cheeks began to strum her guitar, and mumble. I didn't pay much attention because I was too high from the beer and the fact that I had made the deal with Bukowski.

Locklin wasn't too thrilled with the Myriam Makeba look-alike and sing-alike either, so he suggested that we return to Long Beach and have a few beers at the 49er. I was in agreement; I had gotten what I had come for, and I feared that if I drank any more, I'd probably wind up hanging out the window of the car, praying and puking, and making all sorts of silly commitments that I'd never keep. The party was over.

Six weeks later Locklin pulled into the 49er again but with a different cargo: Bukowski and his girlfriend, Linda King. She seemed the quiet type and polite to a degree that contrasted dramatically with Bukowski. At least that's how she presented herself that morning. Stories rumored that she was quite capable of doing battle with Bukowski and that she had on occasion. It was about 11:30 A.M. when Locklin called me at the University Activity Center to let me know that they had arrived safely, and that they were having a few beers to calm the nerves.

The reading started at noon and everything went as planned. Bukowski read many of his best early poems to an overwhelmingly apologetic audience. The first leg of the reading came off without a hitch. He has been known to puke into grand pianos that might be standing near him on the stage, so I was relieved. Locklin suggested that we all return to the 49er for lunch and a few beers—again, to calm the nerves. After about an hour it looked as if Bukowski was beginning to get drunk.

Locklin came over to me and said, "Maybe we ought to get him outta here." Everything was still under control, but you never knew how long that might last. The long afternoon lull between readings was upon us. Keeping Bukowski out of trouble when he was under so much pressure was like juggling hot coals. You knew that somewhere down the line you wouldn't be quick enough and that you were going to get burned.

Linda King helped us get him into the car, and in a few minutes we were pulling into the driveway of the house where I lived. It was a huge two-story house in one of the older sections of Long Beach. I was living with two inner city ministers who spent every waking hour trying to save down-and outers, blacks, the trodden-upon, and the simple poor. Todd was the wayward son of a rich industrialist from back east. He ran a Christian coffee house with his father's money. Ron and Margie had two kids just old enough to understand what was going on. Ron and Margie were well-meaning farm kids who had come to the city to minister to a flock of drunks, wife beaters, and prostitutes. After a couple of years they were back in one of the Dakotas. Another story. I only mention these friends, because they were all there drinking coffee when I came in with Bukowski and Linda King. They knew who he was, and we didn't come unexpected. I didn't have a plan for the afternoon stretch, so I made them all aware that I might be bringing him home. The initial surprise on their faces, then, I think, was that he was so ugly. The kids just stood next to the table, their little hands gripping the top, and stared.

Everyone stared, and I said, "This is Charles Bukowski and his friend Linda King." I introduced everyone around the table and we sat down. We all had coffee, and Margie, the only other person in the house to have read Bukowski's poems, asked him some intelligent and, fortunately, not foolish questions, which he answered agreeably. Margie understood people.

The situation was under control, even though Beth, one of the kids, had worked her way up onto his lap. They were carrying on an inaudible conversation, and as usual, Bukowski was the center of attention. I wondered whether he tired of the attention. I wondered whether he only put up with it for the money. I wondered whether he would have been happier just sorting mail. Bukowski makes you wonder. When you're around him for any period, you can't help but want to know why such a creature as Bukowski exists. He is bigger, he is sicker, he is uglier, he is meaner, he is smarter, and he is usually drunker than anyone else; and as a result he is surely a very difficult man to live with, and that may be why we all rather admired Linda King. Her nerve was as big as his. Beth seemed to have no problem with Bukowski either. It may be that women and kids are the only people privy to the side of Bukowski that is weaker, that is kinder, that is gentler.

Whatever the case may be, in a few minutes he said that he was tired and that he would like to lie down. He and Linda King found the living room couch where they began to tangle in each other's arms, and within minutes they were dry-humping in God's house. He was also cruder than most. He was easily fifty years old and he was acting as if he was at the drive-in theater finger-fucking in the back seat of a Chevy. I thought it was funny, and silently I climbed the stairs, feeling lucky that he was here, in this house, with these people. He didn't let me down.

They apparently fell asleep with no further disturbance. It was about 3:00 P.M. and Locklin was on the phone. "Lyn Lifshin is here." He was at the 49er. "A friend of hers brought her down from the airport, and we're here having a few beers to calm the nerves."

"I could use one myself," I said.

"Any problems?"

"No. He's sleeping."

"Good."

"Yeah," I said. "We'll be by the 'Niner at about 5:00 to pick you and Lyn up. Bobby coming?"

"Yeah."

"Mexican place at the harbor still sound good?"

"Always."

Lyn Lifshin was scheduled to read twice on Friday, so she came early to hear and meet Bukowski. In many ways, at that time in the small press scene, she was very much Bukowski's female counterpart. She was as prolific, as street wise, as anti-academic, and as likely to show up in any magazine as he was. They shared a hard-earned emotional toughness, but she was a gem, a ruby in a slightly worn gold brooch. Rumor has it that Locklin swept her away one afternoon to the cliffs south of Laguna Beach where he sought to pleasure her. But I don't know that. What I do know is that she gave an outstanding reading two days later. I believe that her reading in Long Beach was the first time that she had been paid substantially in addition to air fare from New York. When I called her initially, she thought it was a crank call.

It was customary to wine and dine guest speakers, so I had a budget for dinner which allowed for a few guests. I invited Locklin, his girlfriend, Bobby, and Lyn Lifshin. I got Bukowski ready and out the door at about 5:00. I remember that we were late, speeding up Pacific Coast Highway in my Mustang when he jerked suddenly like a dog waking from a dream and reached into the back seat. We were approaching the top of the hill where P.C.H. intersects Bellflower Boulevard. He found his empty thermos rolled in his jacket and with a look of terror on his face, he said, "Pull in that liquor store," which was on the right. He bought a pint of vodka and some orange juice, and poured both in the thermos without spilling a drop as we entered the 49er parking lot. We were late and I didn't want to blow the reservation at the restaurant, so I left the motor running, ran into the bar and got Locklin and Lyn. Roaring down the hill towards Seal Beach, we all stared into the California sunset: black clouds splattered against a deep red sky. Locklin gave me a hit off his Bud, and everything was okay. A few oil rigs. A black ocean, huge and inaudible. Bukowski smiling.

Bobby was waiting in the lobby of the restaurant when we arrived. It was almost dark. The squat, blue-globed candles were lit, and all the Mexican waiters wore tuxedos. The maitre d', clutching a handful of tall menus with leather covers, led us to a table in the middle of the room where we sat in deep red chairs, drinking cocktails. Bukowski cleared his throat and peered out at the yachts lolling in the canal beyond the darkly tinted plate-glass window. He scanned the dinning room and saw high society in diamonds, and he cleared his throat again and spoke back toward our table.

"I should jump through that window."

Sipping on his scotch and water, he refused to look at the menu, demanding that his girlfriend order for him.

"I'm so screwed up, I don't know how to live with people." He said it more to himself than to us, as if he were thinking out loud. Turning back toward the plate glass, he continued, "I would like to learn, I really would—but I think I'm too old now."

Chiles Rellenos and tacos arrived on hot plates. He kept looking at the big window and repeated, "I should jump through that window." Fearing that he might actually do it, I said, "Look man, if you jump and don't make it—just bounce off—you'll look foolish. The glass is thick and it's difficult to get down to blood and tendons."

He didn't say another word about the window, just ate his Chiles Rellenos and had a few more scotches. I ate very little, thinking about the poetry reading he would give. One down and one to go, and if he didn't get too soaked, the second part of Poetry Week would be out of the way. The Mariachis roamed about the restaurant and the general atmosphere was festive for a Wednesday evening. There was very little conversation while we ate, and after the plates were cleared, Bukowski—probably feeling a little anxious about the silence and the evening's prospects—decided to make some small talk.

"You know the bust Linda did of me, not bad, eh? She wants to do one of my scrotum next. I just want to make sure she gets it right. I want to make sure history doesn't get any wrong ideas." Who was going to say anything? Again, I wanted to laugh but didn't. To this day, I don't know whether she ever worked on the piece. Needless to say, she was embarrassed by the statement and left the table with a deep, resolute frown that meant business. As usual, Bukowski had made the moment meaningful and memorable. He knew intuitively that to jump through the window was a good metaphor but not good enough for the occasion; the idea of his scrotum in marble or terra cotta or plaster of paris hanging on the wall of a museum pleased him tremendously. He had risen to the level of metonymy. People would pass it and say, "That's Bukowski," and in time the world would forget his ugly face, and he would be no different than anyone else. That is, unless he was exceptionally hung, which is probably not the case. (I should probably strike this section. Bukowski would derive too much pleasure from the knowledge that the young poets of the world are now speculating about his pecker.) There are people out there who would pay thousands for such a sculpture, but in the hands of the unappreciative, it would probably end up in a box in a closet, having no more status than a plastic skull that glows in the dark.

I paid the bill, left a tip, folded the receipt.

The long, unpredictable stretch of time between the readings had been filled with a handful of innocent but characteristic events. All my friendships were still intact, I had Bukowski at the outer edge of campus in my Mustang, and his second reading was going to take place. I found a parking spot at the top of the hill. Bukowski was already drunk, but he seemed okay, he was under control. And Linda King was still mad. While Bukowski tucked in his wrinkled pin-striped, Italian-cut, silk shirt and combed his hair, she leaned up against the rear of the car, her back to us, whistling. He called me over and he said, "When they whistle, they're mad. Remember that. It's a sure sign." Then he turned to her and said, "I'm sorry, c'mon."

It was past eight already. The thermos of vodka and orange juice tucked snugly under his arm and his girlfriend braced beneath the other, we three ambled down a long flight of steps toward the crowded dining room for his poetry reading. He said to her, "Someday you'll give readings and you won't need booze. This is my courage. You were born with it."

After a few more steps he continued, "They want to drain every immortal drop of my blood, and I've got to give it to them. I'll let them ask questions after each poem." We arrived at the room and I led him to the stage where he immediately sat down and poured himself a drink. I folded my arms and listened to the master of wordsmen and toughness as he tried to give away some of his spoiled blood. His $300 check was folded in my pocket.

Someone asked him to sing "Melancholy Baby," so he sang it. Then someone brought up the *Free Press* and he said, "The *Free Press* is shit, and people only buy it to read me." He went on pouring from his thermos, and thirty-five minutes from word one he was mumbling inaudibly and nearly fell from the stage.

I looked over at Chuck Stetler, a professor friend of Locklin's, who had been laughing all evening, then I looked back to the face of one of the ugliest men alive and wondered: is there some sort of sacrifice going on here? Knowing that in the end there would be no forgetting his scarred face and his performance. What he had been in his books was the real McCoy.

It's at this point that my memory begins to fade, the images blur into a mass and time no longer moves forward. It stops and envelopes the rest of the evening like a large hand, and only little snippets of clear memory fall from its grasp. Bukowski was reeling by the time he abbreviated the reading, and when I tried to give him the check, he asked Linda—who was then holding him up—to look after it. We all wound up at the 49er, where I found a spot against the wall at the end of a bench and drank a beer, to calm my nerves. I had another. I don't know how many I had. A few.

BUKOWSKI MEETS SHUNRYU SUZUKI

John Bennett

A Letter from John Bennett to Len Fulton

Dear Len,

Finances are a little too tight for me to fork up the 25 smackeroos for Gerald Locklin's tome on Bukowski, but if the book (apparently a collection of essays) in any way points out the much-overlooked compassion of the man, then I'm glad it's out there for those who can afford it. But I suspect, judging from David Newman's lighter-than-air review in the Dec/97 issue of *SPR*, that the main thrust of *A Sure Bet* is to shrink Buk (not Buke) to a size head and shoulders below his genius.

The most disturbing thing about the review, other than the fact that it tells the reader almost nothing substantial about the book, is Newman's declaration that there has been a "changing of the guard," and it is Locklin who is now marching into the future carrying the Bukowski standard. My God. The one indisputable attribute of a personality and talent as complex as Bukowski is uniqueness, and uniqueness is not transferable. I'd imagine Newman's declaring Locklin Bukowski's successor has caused Locklin no small amount of embarrassment.

Newman further credits Locklin with perceiving Bukowski to be at his worst when he's off on a surreal tangent (personally, I think that's when he's at his best), and he asserts that Bukowski continued writing about his hard-drinking poverty-struck days long after those days were gone, and that the writing suffered; maybe so, but so what? Well, Locklin's *The Firebird Poems*, that's so what, poems that have, according to Newman, ". . . moved into places Bukowski could never touch." At this point I began to wonder if I was reading a review or a public-relations release.

Having made it clear that the Bukowski vacuum has been filled by Locklin, Newman gives us a little inside scope—Bukowski was human. He worried about the mortgage on his house. He liked to putter in his garden. And he liked little children. And as if that isn't enough, Newman informs us that it is possible that Bukowski aspired to be a Buddhist! In this connection, I'm sending along a piece I wrote some time ago titled "Bukowski meets Shunryu Suzuki." Maybe you can tag it on the end of this letter if space allows.

I don't think Bukowski aspired to anything. He absorbed and evolved, and even in his "waning years" he spoke to an amazingly wide and diverse audience. There was something in the *substance* of the man that reached people where they live and defies analysis. To this day, when life has me in a particularly tight corner and darkness is closing in all around, I can pick up Bukowski, *any* Bukowski, and inexplicably gain solace, something I seriously doubt the author of the toad poems, good man that he is, will ever be able to do for me.

Sincerely,
John Bennett

Nothing extra, admonishes Shunryu Suzuki. A dull thing done with style is worth more than a bird in the bush, says Bukowski.

Someone laid these video tapes on me. A series of mini Bukowski interviews, ranging from one to three minutes in length. Over fifty of them, like a string of battered haiku. Sometimes Bukowski is drunk, other times he seems quite sober. Either way, he says the same old Bukowski stuff.

When just a child, Bukowski climbed into a ring so small that there was no room left for anyone else. He commenced shadow boxing. Years later, someone turned on the camera, and the geek show began. THIS IS YOUR LIFE, CHARLES BUKOWSKI!

In a geek show, the spectators are the geeks.

* * *

These interviews were done by a crew of young Belgians in the early '80s, after Bukowski had finally made it and moved into his consolation prize, his mansion on the hill. They're simple in format: the camera is focused on Bukowski, a plaintive piano begins playing the same refrain over and over, and Bukowski starts in biting the heads off of chickens. For the most part, the interviews are conducted in Bukowski's spacious backyard with a backdrop of crickets and chirping birds, or on the couch in the living room. For the most part, Bukowski is dressed like a tourist in Bermuda shorts and a polyester shirt. On the couch with him are Linda, his wife, and someone else, possibly another woman. You can't be sure. The camera stayed trained almost exclusively on Bukowski. Only once, when Bukowski turned on Linda, calling her a bitch, a whore, a cunt, telling her she was out of there, he was going to see his lawyer about it, who the fuck did she think she was, staying out every night, until midnight, until two in the morning, until *five* in the morning—only then did the camera pan to Linda while she offered her protest. It wasn't like it seemed! She wasn't up to the things Bukowski insinuated!

Somewhere in the middle of Linda's protest, we get a glimpse of a leg, the leg of the third person on the couch. Maybe there wasn't a third person, maybe it was just a leg, something left over from the previous woman.

Bukowski, thinking about what Linda must have been up to in the wee hours of the morning, finally gets *really* pissed, hoists his massive legs, and begins pummelling her with his feet.

"Uh-oh," someone off-camera says, and that's the end of *that* interview.

Nothing extra in a world of chaos. This is the truth, and the truth shall set you free. Ready, camera, ACTION!

Truth sucks, Bukowski said in one interview. Fuck truth. Style is more important—how you do each and every little thing.

"Well, that's right," says Shunryu Suzuki, rising up out of his ashes. "Where were you when I was conducting all those dreary workshops for the well-to-do up in Palo Alto? I had a cushion reserved for you. A black cushion to sit on and let your mind wander."

"Fuck that!" says Bukowski. "Fuck your cushion and the horse you rode in on, Chinaman!"

Shunryu smiles. Bukowski says this, he says that, and that's that.

"How about a beer?" Shunryu asks.

"Why not?" says Bukowski.

Shunryu floats up off his cushion. Glides over to the refrigerator. Brings out two bottles of Japanese beer. He's Japanese, not Chinese, but who cares? Not Shunryu, that's for sure. He has bigger fish to fry. He twists the caps off the beer and places them neatly on the counter top. Settles in on his cushion again, his robes floating in place around him. Holds out a beer to Bukowski, who is sitting slouched in a big recliner, looking down at Shunryu.

Bukowski looks at Shunryu thru hooded eyes. Shunryu smiles a just-right smile. The way he fetched the beer, the way he's holding this particular beer out to Bukowski, the smile on his face—it's all *just right.* Bukowski knows what just right is. It's a secret he and Shunryu share.

"Elizabeth Taylor is *ugly*, man!" a drunk Bukowski is saying to the camera. I mean *really* ugly. Women aren't beautiful. *This* is beautiful. The camera pans to where Bukowski gestures. Red and yellow tulips in a clear vase, centered on the top of the white lawn table.

"You're okay," Bukowski says, and takes the beer from Shunryu. They both take a hit and settle into smiling at each other. Time swirls around them like dust devils over parched earth.

The Belgians have Bukowski driving around in the back of a red convertible. Thru the old neighborhood. "Pimps and hookers," Bukowski says. "Murderers and thieves. People with style."

I remember visiting Bukowski for the first time back in the late '60s with some on-the-road crazies. We'd been up for three days drinking like there was no tomorrow and eating Black Beauties by the handful. We'd just driven straight thru from New Orleans to L.A. After a few hours sitting around Bukowski's living room on De Longpre, we had to make a beer run. Bukowski tiptoed out the door and tiptoed back in again. He was terrified outside his one-man ring. He didn't breathe easy until he was back on his ratty couch. Then he began throwing bottles against the wall and challenging people to go outside and fight.

"Six-foot poets," Bukowski said as we were leaving. "You guys are six-foot poets. I like that."

Riding around in the convertible, they passed a motel.

"Ah," Bukowski said. "I stayed there once. When Linda (another

Linda) threw me out. We were having some problems. There was a pool back then—yes!"

The car glides past the motel and the camera catches a glimpse of the pool.

"There were some fat wise guys in the pool. I had to take care of them . . ."

When was that? 1972? '73? I was there. Sandra and I and Gentleman Jim and Minski and Minski's wife Sal had flown down from San Francisco for the Party to End All Parties. It went on for two or three days, depending on when you arrived, and it got pretty strange. Toward the end, Sandra, Bukowski, and I wound up in this motel room. It wasn't what you might be thinking. Bukowski had been thrown out, like he said in the interview. We just crashed and slept the sleep of the dead.

The next morning Bukowski and I each opened a beer and got sick. I puked in the toilet bowl and Bukowski got hold of a trash basket. We felt better. Opened two more beers and kept them down. I stepped out onto the landing and leaned over the railing. We were on the second floor. Below, these fat guys were jumping off the diving board, sending great geysers of water high into the air. I started flipping them shit.

"You want us to come up there and clean your clock for you?" they said.

"Don't do it, Bushmills," Bukowski said from inside the motel room door. "Don't make them come up here . . ."

Bukowski embraced himself and shut out the world. What got thru to the bluebird in his heart he reduced to shadow.

"No one can to this day explain to my satisfaction how Bukowski took off like he did," Carl Weissner, Bukowski's German translator, said in a *Gargoyle* magazine interview.

Bukowski took off in Germany, and then he spread like wild fire throughout Europe and most of the known world. At one time he had two books on Brazil's best-seller list—*simultaneously*.

Bukowski and Shunryu, drinking beer and nodding from time to time.

It is better to walk alone than walk with fools, the Buddha said.

What's love got to do with it?, said Tina Turner.

What goes around comes around, don't you know. If it feels good—do it. If it feels good, you're already doing it.

Clever men and grocers, they weigh everything, said Zorba.

Signs and symbols.

The scales of justice. The blindfold stands for what? Impartiality? A lady on the take? Kinky sex?

Bukowski came and went without being detected, and if you think that's a koan, you've got some serious problems. When you're done, you still have not Donne. That sort of thing.

THE OLD MAN'S WAITING

Todd Moore

There are a handful of writers I wish I'd have known. It's a fairly short list. I've tried to keep it simple. Let's start with Rimbaud. He probably would've been dangerous to know at any time in his life, but what the hell. It would've been better to go to the edge with him than hang out with some chickenshit poet who never takes chances. The most dangerous time of all to be around Rimbaud might've been during Scorpio when anything can happen. Try to picture Rimbaud and William S. Burroughs shooting bottles off each other's heads. And later, stoned playing russian roulette.

And Hemingway. Knowing Hemingway at any time in his life would sure as hell have been a ride. Hemingway in Paris. Hemingway in Africa. Hemingway on the Pilar. Hemingway under fire. Hemingway with the most beautiful woman in the world. Hemingway in Montana. Hemingway bellying up to any bar in the world and making it his own. And, Hemingway anywhere with a gun in his hand.

And Dashiell Hammett. The idea of hanging out with Hammett in Butte, Montana, in 1917 when the copper kings tried to hire him to kill some union guy. Hammett shadowing a fugitive for the Pinkertons down a dark 'Frisco street. Hammett gloriously drunk in Hollywood for years and years. Hammett in the Aleutians during World War Two and Hammett telling the House Un-American Activities Committee to fuck themselves in hell.

Last of all Bukowski. In 1970 I was just starting out as a poet. I was thirty-three years old, a college grad, stupid as hell, and had bounced out of public school teaching and then back into it. This time I'd made up my mind to write poetry. It was a do or die thing. A jump into a bonfire, a throw of the dice, an all out run to the edge. Sounds like the same old story with a slightly different twist. And, I'd been reading poetry by the carloads, the truckloads, the boatloads, the trainloads, whole libraries of poetry just to catch up. Or, at least I thought that's what you had to do if you wanted to slap the words on the paper. I didn't realize all it took was opening a door to the blood.

Strangely enough it wasn't Bukowski who pointed the way. *Life Studies*, Robert Lowell's book, somehow got me digging into my own background and origins. And, I started to write about my alcoholic father and the whorehouse hotel I'd lived in with my parents, my two brothers and sister. We were holed up in two rooms, it was more like a cockroach infested cave. Still, we had our own toilet which was one of the perks.

For at least half of the fifties I lived the life of a con artist and small-time thief. Some of my best friends would graduate to burglary, arson, stickups, and murder. The only thing that saved me was an abiding idea that I was going to be a writer. Somehow, some way I was going to be a writer.

And, when I finally was able to put it all together at thirty-three, I started mining the memories of what I had seen and what I had been. And that's when I began to read Charles Bukowski. Not in big gulps at first, because I still wanted to hold onto my own voice, my own staked out piece of authenticity and I wasn't going to compromise that for one second. But, I still read Bukowski in quick outlaw snatches. I stuck mostly to the poetry, though I did end up reading some of his novels.

This was sometime in the late seventies when I finally knew who I was as a poet. By this time, I was writing *Dillinger* and had a few chapbooks out and finally felt I had the world by the ass. Which was an illusion.

The one thing that I began to realize was that Bukowski and I were appearing regularly in some of the same little magazines. I'd known for some time that I had a writing style all my own. The short line, the quick stroke of in your face violence was my little noir invention. And, now here I was being published in the same magazines with Charles Bukowski. That, alone, gave me the added illusion that we were competing, going at it, head to head, toe to toe, mano a mano. It was an illusion that would carry me along for ten years. Maybe as many as fifteen tops.

The thing is I was competing with him but he probably had no more idea of who I was than he had of the hookers who passed him on the street. Still, it gave me something to go on. It was the gas I poured into the engine of poetry.

That whole time it seemed as though Bukowski was indestructible. I suppose it was part of his tough guy persona. Every time I think of Bukowski, I see him as a slim fortysomething show off sitting on a park bench smoking a cigarette. Just the way he holds himself there in that photo reminded me of so many guys I used to know who did the same damned thing. Or that shot of him chugging a bottle of beer as he walks along some city street. He's oblivious to everything except the beer and maybe the way it's washing down his throat. Or that snapshot of him bent over a book during a reading, half smirking into it, maybe in the act of heckling a heckler. Or maybe just telling the world to get fucked.

Bukowski always came across as the Bogart of poetry. The Bogie who went straight from *Dead End Kids* to *The Treasure of Sierra Madre*, without so much as *The Maltese Falcon* or *Casablanca* to soften the image. His face was craggier than Bogart's. His head was oversized and almost too big for his body. The same was true of Lorca but Lorca was handsome and Bukowski was simply straight out homely. And, yet, despite his pocked looks, Bukowski had a peculiar kind of charisma. Or call it whatever you want to. Still, he gave off something like an energy charge that got your attention. It probably didn't matter if you were watching him on video or there with him in person. The camera should have hated him, but instead it fell in love with his face. With that large beaten, totalled out wreckage of a face.

And, suddenly, he was just simply a celebrity. He'd been talking about being famous for years and then it happened. And, I have a sneaking hunch it scared the shit out of him. Otherwise, why did he move out of L.A. to that little out of the way tree-lined street in San Pedro? I'll always wonder about that.

Also, somewhere in the late eighties or early nineties the toughness went out of him. You can catch glimpses of a certain fragility in some of his later poems. The way he became obsessed with death and the way he looked in his late snapshots. Like someone or something had sucked the life right out of him.

I wasn't surprised by the news of his death but I was shocked. Shocked in the way that I was shocked by the news of my own father's death even though I knew he was dying of cancer. Shocked because both Bukowski and my father had been such vital and alive men.

And, for a long time, it seemed as though there was a gaping hole in that part of American poetry where Bukowski had been such a large force. And the illusion of competition had passed away along with Bukowski. And, there were no more lies I could tell myself. Now, there was only the void to write against. Maybe that was the way it had been all along. And, I'm sure Bukowski had known that.

If anyone possessed an authentic voice in twentieth-century American poetry, it was Charles Bukowski. There was none of that mincing academic pretentiousness that you see in so many of our official poets. No attempt to be nice, obliging, or politically correct. He belonged in the company of giants, writers like Ernest Hemingway, Jack Kerouac, William Carlos Williams, Thomas McGrath, Allen Ginsberg. He was an original. Which is to say he had that certain something that makes you want to say, yeah, I'd know that voice anywhere.

Bukowski wasn't as sophisticated as Hemingway, though neither one had a college education. Bukowski was strictly L.A. and Hemingway was the man of the world. Yet, what Bukowski lacked in sophistication he more than made up in energy, drive, the balls-out way that he lived, and his unerring honesty about the way things are out on the street.

Even now, years after his death, his work is still as strong as ever and it's not going to go away. Not long ago a slam poet came up to me at a reading and said, "You know that Charles Bukowski. Shit, I'm gonna kick his ass." I just smiled and said, "The old man's waiting."

SELECTED BIBLIOGRAPHY OF CHARLES BUKOWSKI

Novels

Post Office (Black Sparrow Press, 1971)
Factotum (Black Sparrow Press, 1975)
Women (Black Sparrow Press, 1978)
Ham on Rye (Black Sparrow Press, 1982)
Hollywood (Black Sparrow Press, 1989)
Pulp (Black Sparrow Press, 1994)

Poetry Collections

Flower, Fist and Bestial Wail (Hearse Press, 1960)
Longshot Pomes for Broke Players (7 Poets Press, 1962)
Run with the Hunted (Midwest Press, 1962)
It Catches My Heart in Its Hands (Loujon Press, 1963)
Crucifix in a Deathhand (Loujon Press, 1965)
Cold Dogs in the Courtyard (Literary Times-Cyfoeth, 1965)
The Genius of the Crowd (7 Flowers Press, 1966)
2 Poems (Black Sparrow Press, 1967)

The Curtains are Waving and People Walk Through/The Afternoon/Here and in Berlin and in New York City and in Mexico (Black Sparrow Press, 1967)
At Terror Street and Agony Way (Black Sparrow Press, 1968)
Poems Written Before Jumping out of an 8-Storey Window (Poetry X/Change, 1968)
The Days Run Away Like Wild Horses Over the Hills (Black Sparrow Press, 1969)
Penguin Modern Poets 13: Charles Bukowski/Philip Lamantia/Harold Norse (Penguin Books London, 1969)
If We Take (Black Sparrow Press, 1970)
Fire Station (Capricorn Press, 1970)
Me and You Sometimes Love Poems (Kisskill Press, 1972)
Mockingbird Wish Me Luck (Black Sparrow Press, 1972)
Burning in Water, Drowning in Flame: Poems 1955–1973 (Black Sparrow Press, 1974)
Tough Company (Black Sparrow Press, 1976)
Scarlet (Black Sparrow Press, 1976)
Art (Black Sparrow Press, 1977)
Love is a Dog from Hell: Poems 1974–1977 (Black Sparrow Press, 1977)
A Love Poem (Black Sparrow Press, 1979)
Play the Piano Drunk/Like a Percussion Instrument/Until the Fingers Begin to Bleed a Bit (Black Sparrow Press, 1979)
Dangling in the Tournefortia (Black Sparrow Press, 1981)
War All the Time: Poems 1981–1984 (Black Sparrow Press, 1984)
The Last Generation (Black Sparrow Press, 1982)
Sparks (Black Sparrow Press, 1983)
You Get So Alone at Times That it Just Makes Sense (Black Sparrow Press, 1986)
The Roominghouse Madrigals: Early Selected Poems 1946–1966 (Black Sparrow Press, 1988)
In the Shadow of the Rose (Black Sparrow Press, 1991)
Three by Bukowski (Black Sparrow Press, 1992)
The Last Night of the Earth Poems (Black Sparrow Press, 1992)
Those Marvelous Lunches (Black Sparrow Press, 1993)
Heat Wave (Black Sparrow Graphic Arts, 1995)
A New War (Black Sparrow Press, 1997)
Bone Palace Ballet: New Poems (Black Sparrow Press, 1997)
What Matters Most is How Well You Walk Through Fire (Black Sparrow Press, 1999)

Short Stories

Confessions of a Man Insane Enough to Live with Beasts (Mimeo Press, 1965)
All the Assholes in the World and Mine (Open Skull Press, 1966)
Notes of a Dirty Old Man (City Lights Books, 1969)
A Bukowski Sampler (Quixote Press, 1969)
Erections, Ejaculations, Exhibitions and General Tales of Ordinary Madness (City Lights Books, 1972)
South of No North (Black Sparrow Press, 1973)
Tales of Ordinary Madness (City Lights Books, 1983)
The Most Beautiful Woman in Town (City Lights Books, 1983)
Bring Me Your Love (Black Sparrow Press, 1983)
Hot Water Music (Black Sparrow Press, 1983)
Scarlet (Black Sparrow Press, 1976)
Art (Black Sparrow Press, 1977)
Love is a Dog from Hell: Poems 1974–1977 (Black Sparrow Press, 1977)
A Love Poem (Black Sparrow Press, 1979)
Play the Piano Drunk/Like a Percussion Instrument/Until the Fingers Begin to Bleed a Bit (Black Sparrow Press, 1979)
Dangling in the Tournefortia (Black Sparrow Press, 1981)
War All the Time: Poems 1981–1984 (Black Sparrow Press, 1984)
The Last Generation (Black Sparrow Press, 1982)
Sparks (Black Sparrow Press, 1983)
You Get So Alone at Times That it Just Makes Sense (Black Sparrow Press, 1986)
The Roominghouse Madrigals: Early Selected Poems 1946–1966 (Black Sparrow Press, 1988)
In the Shadow of the Rose (Black Sparrow Press, 1991)
Three by Bukowski (Black Sparrow Press, 1992)
The Last Night of the Earth Poems (Black Sparrow Press, 1992)
Those Marvelous Lunches (Black Sparrow Press, 1993)
Heat Wave (Black Sparrow Graphic Arts, 1995)
A New War (Black Sparrow Press, 1997)
Bone Palace Ballet: New Poems (Black Sparrow Press, 1997)
What Matters Most is How Well You Walk Through Fire (Black Sparrow Press, 1999)

Short Stories

Confessions of a Man Insane Enough to Live with Beasts (Mimeo Press, 1965)
All the Assholes in the World and Mine (Open Skull Press, 1966)
Notes of a Dirty Old Man (City Lights Books, 1969)
A Bukowski Sampler (Quixote Press, 1969)
Erections, Ejaculations, Exhibitions and General Tales of Ordinary Madness (City Lights Books, 1972)
South of No North (Black Sparrow Press, 1973)
Tales of Ordinary Madness (City Lights Books, 1983)
The Most Beautiful Woman in Town (City Lights Books, 1983)
Bring Me Your Love (Black Sparrow Press, 1983)
Hot Water Music (Black Sparrow Press, 1983)
There's No Business (Black Sparrow Press, 1984)
Confessions of a Coward (Black Sparrow Press, 1995)

Miscellaneous

The Bukowski/Purdy Letters 1964–1974 (Paget Press, 1983)
The Movie: *Barfly* (Black Sparrow Press, 1987)
Septaugenarian Stew: Stories and Poems (Black Sparrow Press, 1990)
Run with the Hunted: A Charles Bukowski Reader (HarperCollins, 1993)
Screams from the Balcony: Selected Letters 1960–1970 (Black Sparrow Press, 1993)
Living on Luck: Selected Letters 1960s–1970s (Black Sparrow Press, 1995)
Shakespeare Never Did This (Black Sparrow Press, 1995)
Betting on the Muse: Poems and Stories (Black Sparrow Press, 1996)
The Captain is Out to Lunch and the Sailors Have Taken Over the Ship (Black Sparrow Graphic Arts, 1997)

Recordings

Bukowski/Poems and Insults! (City Lights Books, 1972)
Hostage (Rhino Records, 1994)
Bukowski Reads His Poetry (Black Sparrow Graphic Arts, 1995)

PERMISSIONS AND ACKNOWLEDGMENTS

"How to Get Along with Charles Bukowski" and "The Funeral of Charles Bukowski" © 1996 by Gerald Locklin. Used with permission of Water Row Press.

"An Evening at Buk's Place" by Jean-François Duval originally published in *Buk et les Beats* as Un Soir chez Buk, Paris: Michalon, 1998. From *Bukowski and the Beats*, forthcoming from Sun Dog Press, Northville, Michigan. With thanks to Al Berlinski.

"The Death of Charles Bukowski" © 1994 by John Bryan. Reprinted with permission of the author.

"his woman his party his price" from *African Sleeping Sickness*, Black Sparrow Press, Santa Rosa, California; © 1979, 1990 by Wanda Coleman; reprinted with permission of the author.

"Confessions of a Bukowski Collector" © 1999 by Al Fogel. Reprinted with permission of the author.

"every time i" and "The Old Man's Waiting" © 1999 by Todd Moore. Reprinted with permission of the author.

"What Did Bukowski Smell Like?" and "Did Bukowski Ever Use Your Bathtub?" from Bukowski in the Bathtub © 1997 by Philomene Long and John Thomas. Reprinted with permission of Water Row Press.

"You Don't Know What Love Is" © 1983, 1984 by the Estate of Raymond Carver. Used with permission of Vintage Books, a division of Random House, Inc.

"This Thing Upon Me" © 1992 by Jack Grapes. Used with permission of the author.

"When Bukowski Met Colin the Jock" © 2000 by Ray Clark Dickson. Used with permission of the author.

"Charles Bukowski Spit In My Face" © 1982, 1984 by David Barker. This work was first published in a private edition by the author.

"Sleeping With the Bard" by Jill Young, from *Das ist Alles: Charles Bukowski Recollected*, edited by Joan Jobe Smith © 1995. Used with permission of Joan Jobe Smith.

"Subj: Bukowski Book" © 2000 by Pamela Miller Brandes. Used with permission of the author

"Laughter in Hell" from the preface to the forthcoming correspondence between Charles Bukowski and Harold Norse *Fly Like a Bat Out of Hell* © 2000 by Harold Norse.

"I'm Producing Steel, Man" © 2000 by Harvey Kubernik. Used with permission of the author.

Spinning Off Bukowski © 1996 by Steve Richmond. Reprinted with permission of Sun Dog Press, Northville, Michigan.

"An Affair to Remember" © 2000 by Karen Finley. Used with permission of the author.

"The Poem Will Save You" © 1999 by RD Armstrong. Used with permission of the author.

"Notes On A Dirty Old Man" from *Whitman's Wild Children: Portraits of Twelve Poets* © 1988, 1999 by Neeli Cherkovski. Reprinted by permission of Steerforth Press, South Royalton, Vermont.

"Just Browsing," "To Drink Driven," "Christ I feel shitty," "Outsider," "Still the Outsider," "P.S." from *Das ist Alles: Charles Bukowski Recollected*, edited by Joan Jobe Smith © 1995. Used with permission of FrancEyE.

"The Outsiders" © 1999 by Julia Kamyz Lane. Used with permission of the author.

"I Met Hank in 1968" © 1999 by Michael C. Ford. Used with permission of the author.

"Bukowski on the Mic" © 1999 by Barry Miles. Used with permission of the author.

The Holy Grail: My Friendship with Charles Bukowski from a work in progress © 2000 by A.D. Winans. Used with permission of the author.

"Bukowski Boulevard," "Life's One Big Rotten Tooth" "Notes of a Dirty Old Man," "Eggs Overeasy," "Dusting Bukowski's Head" from *Bukowski Boulevard* © 1999 by Joan Jobe Smith. Used with permission of the author.

"The Liberated Billie and the Old Troll: The Tales of Linda King and Charles Bukowski" from a work in progress © 1999 by Linda King. Used with the permission of the author.

"A Buk Elegy" from *Das ist Alles: Charles Bukowski Recollected*, edited by Joan Jobe Smith © 1995. Used with permission of the author.

"Elegy for a Giant" from *Das ist Alles: Charles Bukowski Recollected*, edited by Joan Jobe Smith © 1995. Used with permission of the author.

"Tough Guys Write Poetry" © 1987. Interview Magazine. All rights reserved. Reprinted with permission of Interview Magazine.

"Bukowski is Dead" © 1999 by Steve Abee. Used with permission of the author.

"The Bukowski Reading: Long Beach, 1972" © 1979 by John Kay. Used with permission of the author.

"Bukowski Meets Shunryu Suzuki" © 1997 by John Bennett. Used with permission of the author.